Cliques, Hicks, and Ugly Sticks:

Confessions of April Grace

Other Confessions of April Grace:

In Front of God and Everybody

Cliques, Hicks, and Ugly Sticks:

Confessions of April Grace

by K.D. McCRITE

Tommy® NELSON
A Division of Thomas Nelson Publishers
NASHVILLE DALLAS MEXICO CITY RIO DE JANEIRO

I dedicate this book to Robinson (Dot) Barnwell, who wrote my all-time favorite book, Head Into the Wind. From reading that book so often, I learned to create pacing and presence in my own stories.

Published in Nashville, Tennessee, by Tommy Nelson. Tommy Nelson is a registered trademark of Thomas Nelson, Inc.

Represented by Jeanie Pantelakis of Sullivan Maxx Literary Agency.

Cover design by JuiceBox Design.

Cover photo by Scott Thomas.

Tommy Nelson® titles may be purchased in bulk for educational, business, fund-raising, or sales promotional use. For information, please e-mail SpecialMarkets@ThomasNelson.com.

All Scripture quotations are taken from the King James Version of the Bible.

Library of Congress Cataloging-in-Publication Data

McCrite, K. D. (Kathaleen Deiser)
Cliques, hicks, and ugly sticks / by KD McCrite.
p. cm. — (Confessions of April Grace ; bk. 2)
Summary: Autumn of 1986 in the Ozarks finds eleven-year-old April Grace adjusting to middle school, coping with her mother's difficult pregnancy, helping Isabel with the church play, and trying to figure out why the new boy at school will not leave her alone.
ISBN 978-1-4003-1826-1 (pbk. : alk. paper)
[1. Family life—Arkansas—Fiction. 2. Farm life—Arkansas—Fiction. 3. Middle schools—Fiction. 4. Schools—Fiction. 5. Theater—Fiction. 6. Christian life—Fiction. 7. Arkansas—History—20th century—Fiction.]
I. Title.
PZ7.M4784146Cli 2011
[Fic]—dc22 2011027541

Printed in the United States of America

11 12 13 14 15 QG 6 5 4 3 2 1

Mfr: Quad Graphics / Fairfield, PA / November 2011 / PPO # 125602

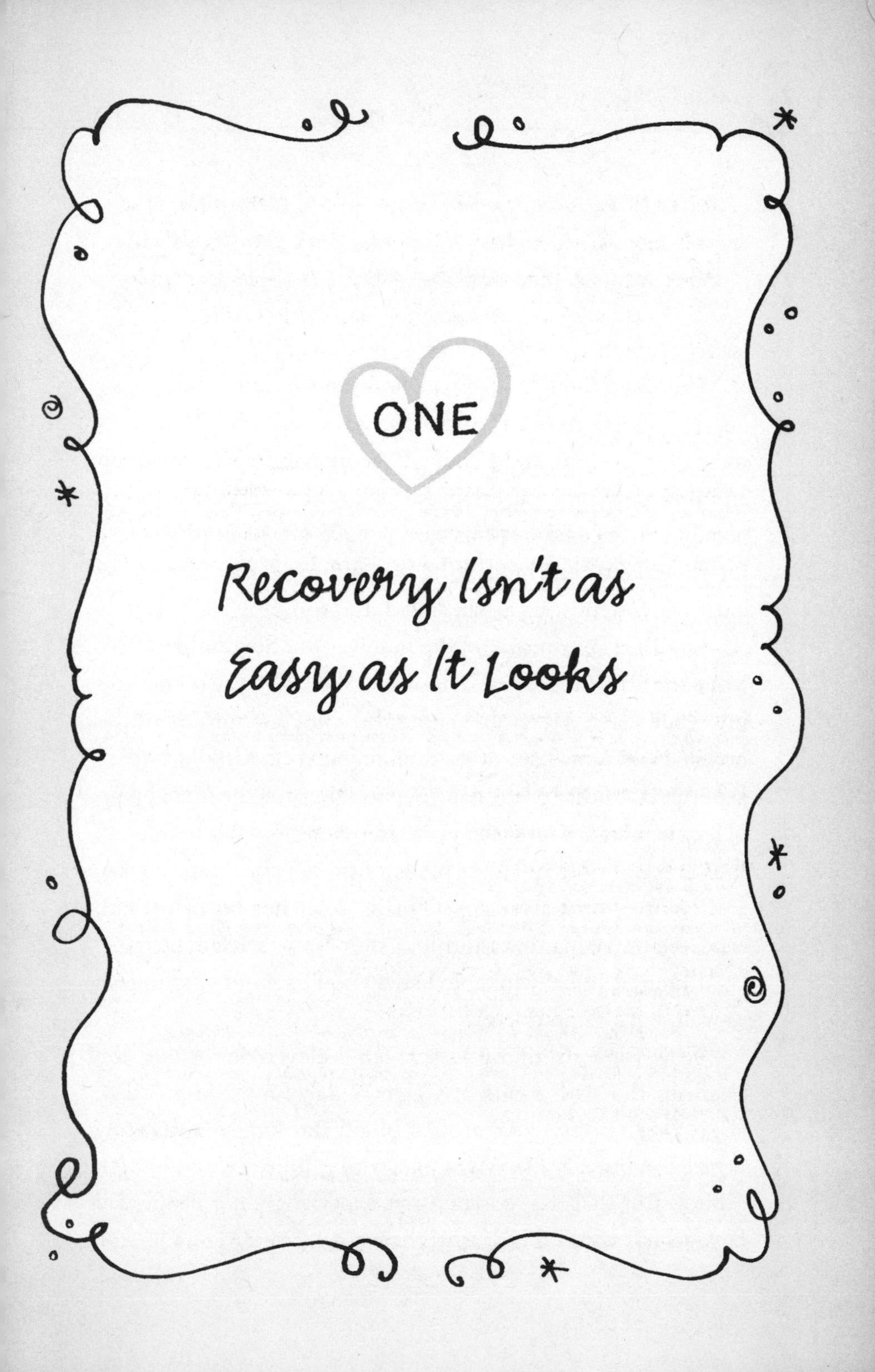

ONE

Recovery Isn't as Easy as It Looks

♡

Autumn 1986

Isabel St. James is a recovering hypochondriac.

She once thought she had hoof-and-mouth disease just because she skittered through the barnyard while the cows were there waiting to be milked. Another time she swore up and down and sideways that the air in the Ozarks was full of poison and begged her husband to take her back to the city for the sake of her lungs. She was puffing on a cigarette as hard as a freight train when she said it, too. Boy, oh boy.

On Tuesday afternoon, the first week of September 1986, right after the first day of school, I walked with my mama and my older sister, Myra Sue, along the shiny gray floors of the hospital corridor. I seriously doubted anything in ole Isabel's experience to that point had prepared her for the actual pain of a concussion, two black eyes, a broken nose, a broken leg, four cracked ribs, and a purple knot on her forehead the size and color of an Easter egg. This is what her husband, Ian, reported to Mama that morning, after Isabel's accident.

I figured Isabel probably had a good case of the whiplash as well, but I'm no doctor.

Now, for a girl of my age (which is eleven) and education (I am in the sixth grade at Cedar Ridge Junior High), I've always been pretty good around blood and scrapes and runny noses. I'm no sissy like Myra Sue, who is fourteen and in high school. But that day was my first experience in a hospital. I have to tell you, I felt downright woozy. Even Mama looked queasy. Maybe it was because of all the busyness and the noise: phones ringing and people talking and nurses scurrying up and down the hallway with clipboards. I guess it made us both want to lose our lunches, but if Mama could buck up and face it down, so could I. We redheads are pretty tough.

Those nurses didn't bother to make eye contact with anyone. I wondered if they ever looked at the people they took care of, or if all they did was scribble on those clipboards and read what other people wrote.

In one room we passed, the door stood wide open and a blond-haired lady was barfing right over the edge of her bed and onto the floor. And in the hallway, a gray-faced old man was lying on a hospital bed right out in the open so everyone had to step around him. He kept raising one thin, white hand every time a nurse passed. None of them bothered to say to him, "Good afternoon" or "Excuse me" or "Are you having a heart attack?"

I smiled at him, hoping to make him feel less invisible, but he just looked at me as if he was on his way out of this world. He'd probably be dead a week and a half before anyone from that hospital noticed.

I looked around and saw a chubby nurse with short, frizzy brown hair and great big pink-framed glasses. She was just standing there staring at nothing on the wall.

I walked away from Mama and went right up to that nurse. "That old man over there needs some help," I said. "I think he's dying."

She looked at me over the top of those glasses.

"I hardly think you qualify as an expert."

"But—"

"Children have no business on this floor." She moved away from me, and her pale blue-green scrub pants made *shish-shish* noises as she walked toward the desk where two nurses were sipping coffee.

"Charlene," she said to one of them, "I keep telling 'em that kids don't need to be up here; they're always underfoot. Has the office changed the minimum age?"

Well, as I said, I'm just a little bit under the age of twelve, which is the minimum age to be a visitor on the floor, so I hurried to catch up with Mama and my sister before I could be thrown out for trying to save that old man's life.

I felt downright sorry for ole Isabel if she needed anything because I don't believe anyone in those aqua outfits had time or interest enough to actually take care of the sick and injured.

Right then I promised myself to never, in a million years, go to the hospital in Blue Reed, Arkansas, unless I was in a big hurry to be ushered out of this world and into the next.

"There's Isabel's room," Mama said as quietly as if we were in church. "Room 316."

"I hope she isn't asleep," Myra Sue whispered, her eyes big and scared. She dearly loved and adored Isabel St. James.

Somebody, somewhere, dropped something loud and metallic, and it clattered a good ten seconds before it finally collapsed.

"How could she sleep in all this racket?" I asked in a perfectly reasonable volume given all that was going on around us.

"Shh," Mama cautioned. "We're in the hospital."

"Yes, you dork," Myra Sue added. "Speak appropriately."

I hardly saw the point, especially when about ten feet behind us that frizzy-haired nurse yelled for Kelly, who hollered back at her from the far end of the corridor. Apparently Nurse Frizzy had wanted Sugar Free Dr Pepper, *not* Diet Coke, and in case you're wondering, the vending machine on the third floor of that hospital has never, *ever* sold Fanta Orange, and probably never will. Kelly said so. In fact, she yelled it right down that big, shiny hall so all of us could hear.

Mama tapped on the door, which, unlike most of the doors we'd passed, was half closed.

"*Entrez-vous*," came the unmistakably miserable and somewhat nasally voice of Isabel St. James, who is *not* French, just in case you're wondering.

With her shiny blond curls flying, Myra Sue left us in the dust as she rushed into the room.

"Isabel!" she shrieked woefully in the most un-hospital-appropriate and unladylike manner you can imagine.

"Dearest girl!" Isabel did not shriek, but her whimper was not exactly genteel, either.

Boy, oh boy, ole Isabel looked like she'd been beat with a shovel and poked in the face with an ugly stick. She lay black and blue and purple against the white pillow and sheets. Both eyes were black. Her nose was all bandaged, and her lips were twice their normal size. Her right leg was all bundled up like a package, and I don't think Isabel or any of the busy nurses had bothered to comb her short, dark hair since her car wreck, and it stood out all over her head. I have to say, I've seen ole Isabel St. James look much better, and that's saying something, because believe me, even on her very best day, she's no prize in the looks department.

For a minute, you would have thought Myra Sue was going to jump right up on the bed with Isabel, but she stopped herself and tenderly hugged the woman. Isabel attempted to kiss her cheek with those big, swole-up ole lips, then looked past her at Mama and me. She reached out her bruised right hand.

"Lily! April!" she said with a little more spirit than you might have thought. "Oh, it's so good to see you both. I thought I might never see another living soul."

We hugged her as gently as possible. She moaned but she didn't scream, for which I was grateful. Isabel can put on the dog pretty good when it comes to High Drama, that's the truth.

She looked past us. "Didn't Grace come with you?"

Grace is my grandma, after whom my sister and I are named. Grandma's full name is Myra Grace Reilly.

"No," Mama said. "She has come down with a cold, and she won't leave her house until she's sure she's no longer contagious. You know Mama Grace."

Isabel shook her head. "And she won't see a doctor, will she?"

"You know Grandma," Myra Sue said, sounding like she thought she was as wise as Mama.

"Stubborn to the very core," said Mama.

"And then some," I added. "I just hope she don't get the pneumonia."

"When I called to tell her about your accident, she said

to tell you she's praying for your quick recovery," Mama told Isabel.

Isabel lay back against the pillows and sighed. "That's kind of her. But after everything I've been through in the last eight hours . . ."

Her voice trailed into nothing as Ian came into the room. He looked worse for wear, let me tell you—all wrinkled and droopy, with bags under his pale blue eyes and his shirt half untucked. Ian usually looks well-groomed, even in work clothes. Right then his wispy blond hair was wispier than ever, and he had mud on his shoes. He saw us and smiled a little bit. Ian's not so bad once you get used to him.

"Afternoon," he said wearily. I have to say, we three Reilly females greeted him with a lot more enthusiasm than his wife did.

"Is that my coffee?" Isabel said to him without so much as a howdy-do. Have I told you yet that she can be rude? R-u-d-e, rude.

"Yes. I had them brew it fresh for you at Gourmet Coffee, just like you told me." He peeled back the little tab on the lid. Steam came out, and the smell of coffee temporarily overcame the icky stink of medicine and sick people.

"There's a coffee vending machine at the end of the hall," I told him. "Right next to the machine that sells potato chips and gum and Oreos."

He gave me a tight smile. "She didn't want that."

"Oh." Enough said.

"And where are my cigarettes?" Isabel took the Styrofoam cup from him.

Ole Isabel says she's going to quit smoking, but your guess is as good as mine as to when that will be.

Ian hesitated. "Your doctor said you must not smoke until he's sure you're all right," he said finally. "You might have injured your lungs in that accident, lambkins."

She glared at him from her black-and-blue eyes.

"Have a little pity, can't you? I am in deadly pain, I've totally lost the use of my leg, and I haven't had a cigarette since . . . since . . ." Her look of outrage fled as panic replaced it. "Oh! *Oh!* I can't remember the last time I had a cigarette."

She leaned toward Ian in desperation. "I might have brain damage, darling! Oh! Oh, please don't leave me, darling!"

See what I mean about High Drama? Good grief.

"Oh, *Isabel*!" hollered Myra Sue, as if someone were taking out her own personal appendix without her permission.

"You're recovering from a wreck, Isabel, so it's only natural to have a little memory lapse or two," Mama said soothingly, a complete Voice of Reason.

"Yes, lamb," Ian murmured, all sweet and kind. "The doctor said your concussion was mild."

He tried to smooth her messy hair, but she jerked her head away. "A lot you care. Or know. And I can remember just fine what happened right up until I . . . until I . . ."

It was obvious the way she visibly grasped for memories that she couldn't remember right up until Whatever. I tried to help.

"Why don't you just tell us what you remember? Then maybe all the rest of it will come back to you."

She dragged her pitiful, bruised gaze from her mister and

looked at me. When her swollen lips parted in a smile, I saw that her two front teeth were chipped. I wondered if she knew about that. I bet she didn't, because if she did, she would already be screeching for a Beverly Hills plastic surgeon to give her a mouth transplant.

"You always have the *best* ideas, April," she said.

"Well, I try," I said modestly, but boy, oh boy, had her tune changed! Used to be, she couldn't stand the sight of me. And I always thought she hated my ideas. Especially the good ones.

She attempted to sip her hot coffee, squealing a bit when she burned her fat lips. She blinked a bunch of times, a habit I find highly annoying. It's a trait my silly sister has adopted when she's feeling put-upon or uppity—which is most of the time.

"I'll blow on it for you, dear," Ian said, "and you tell the Reillys about your accident."

"Thank you, darling." Was that soft, gooey voice Isabel's? Yep, I guess so, because she gave him a dopey-eyed look as he took the cup from her bandaged hand and walked to the window. He gazed outside while he blew across Isabel's coffee to cool it. She launched into an account of what happened that morning after Myra Sue and I had climbed onto the school bus and Mama had gone to Ava, a town near us, real early on some errand she had refused to tell us about.

"I was running late for school," Isabel began, "and I had not had my morning coffee because it never got made." She slung a meaningful look at her mister, who gave every appearance of not having heard the remark. But I bet he heard every syllable of it.

"Oh, Isabel, I'm so sorry," Mama said. "I was in such a rush this morning—"

Isabel held up one hand.

"I don't expect you to wait on me hand and foot," she sniffed.

"Yes, that's *my* job," Ian said. I think he would've rolled his eyes, except Isabel was glaring at him, and you could see she was getting ready to throw something at his head—if she could find anything heavy enough—if he said another word.

Ian and Isabel had been staying with us for a while now, and used to be, she expected my mama to cook special things and clean up after her and do her laundry and everything, but Mama finally set her straight. It takes a lot to get on Lily Reilly's last nerve, but ole Isabel had done it.

You see, when Ian and Isabel first showed up on Rough Creek Road this past summer, they had just left California because of money problems, and they didn't have hardly anything except a bunch of clothes. The house they bought down the road from us was purely a rat haven, so Daddy made a deal with Ian that he would help fix the St. Jameses' house up if Ian would help on the farm the rest of the summer. Then Mama invited them to move in with us until their house was ready.

Well, let me tell you something: I thought none of us would survive that. But the St. Jameses finally learned that they weren't better than everybody in Arkansas, and I learned they were pretty good folks once I bothered to get to know them. It was an eye-opening experience all around, but not exactly a pleasant one.

They are still in our house, but only for a couple more months. Some of the other men in the neighborhood have promised to help Daddy and Ian do all the repairs once the summer farming season wraps up. In the meantime, the Cedar Ridge school hired ole Isabel to teach a few dance and drama classes. She's a professional dancer and has quite a bit of acting experience, so it seemed logical to hire her. The thing I had to ask myself, though, was how in the world was that woman gonna teach dance if she had a broken leg? I had a feeling ole Isabel's teaching career was over before it started. That was not a good thing for a lot of reasons, but mainly because she had been looking forward to it so much that she'd often forget to be a pain in everybody's neck.

"About the time I got to the highway," she was saying right then, "I realized that, in my haste, I had forgotten the video of *As You Like It* at home. I had to go back and get it because I wanted to show it to the senior drama club on their first day." She looked a little concerned. "I do hope those children do not think good acting starts and stops with *Dallas* or *The Dukes of Hazzard*." She thought about that a minute, shuddered, then continued, "Well, anyway. Lily, girls, you *know* what Rough Creek Road is like since that deluge last week."

You better believe we all knew what she was talking about. Our old country road is a mess, and will be for the next seven or eight million years unless I miss my guess.

"It took me a good fifteen minutes just to get to the highway, dodging those loathsome rocks and holes," Isabel said. "And, of course, it took another fifteen to get back home. I was not pleased."

No one would ever argue that. Isabel St. James was often disgruntled because so many things displeased her.

"When I got back to the house," she went on, "I saw that Ian had made the coffee *after* I left." She huffed loudly. "Why he couldn't have made it earlier is beyond me. Especially since he knows *I need my morning coffee*!"

Ole Ian just stood there, cooling her coffee while she stabbed him with fiery darts from her eyes. He continued to look out the window as if his wife weren't even in the room.

"I would have made it for you, dearest Isabel, if you'd asked me to," Myra Sue said, her eyes all shiny.

"Oh, darling, I know you would have." Isabel gave Myra Sue the best smile she could muster from those busted-up lips. "You are such a precious child."

Oh brother! I looked around for barf bags because those two were making me sick. I thought they were making Mama sick, too, because right then she was so pale that her freckles stood out, but she was smiling. I could not do that. Instead, I sighed.

"So I poured myself a cup to drink on the drive to school," Isabel continued. "Of course it sloshed everywhere as soon as I got out on that wretched road, so I got only a mere sip. Well, it was all just too much! That dreadful road, no coffee, an inconsiderate husband, *and* being late." She and Myra Sue sighed in unison. "The school board will not allow anyone to smoke in the school, so I knew if I was going to have a cigarette that day, it would have to be on my way into town. I got one out of my purse, then pressed the lighter on that *horrid* little car Ian bought. Wouldn't you know, the foul thing did not work. It's all Ian's fault, of course, for buying such a *dreadful* automobile."

Ian looked over his shoulder at her. "Want your coffee now, lambkins? It has cooled off some."

She stared at him a minute like she had totally forgotten that she had demanded someone brew it fresh for her Spoiled Majesty at the coffee place.

"Yes! Oh yes, thank you, Ian, my darling."

Good gravy, but those two have a weird relationship.

She delicately sipped between her bruised lips with her eyes closed. "Ahhhh," she murmured.

"So what happened?" I prodded. "The lighter in your car didn't work, and . . . ?"

One eye opened and stared at me. Then she opened the other one and said, "I fished the lighter out of my purse, of course. But just as I was about to use it, I hit an enormous pothole and dropped the wretched thing. It fell right on the floor of the passenger side. I slowed the Tercel to a crawl, reached over to retrieve it, and . . . woke up here."

"With the car nose-first and totaled out in that low-water culvert at the foot of Howard's Hill," Ian added.

We all stared at Isabel, who calmly sipped her coffee and blinked a bunch of times.

"Yikes, Isabel," I said, shuddering. "Johnny Fields was killed running off that culvert three years ago."

She choked. Coffee dribbled out of her mouth.

"What? I could have been killed?" She threw a wild gaze to her husband. "Did you hear, darling? *I could have been killed, Ian! Killed!*"

Well, I guess I should have kept my big mouth shut about that, because I'll tell you something: when Isabel St. James gets going, there's no telling where she'll stop. Thank goodness she got interrupted right then.

"Yoo-hoo!" Temple Freebird called as she walked through the doorway. Right behind came Forest, her other half.

They are two old hippies who live on the property next door to the St. Jameses' place. That afternoon, their combined body odors chased out the smell of medicine, antiseptic, clean sheets, sick people, and coffee in about three seconds.

I coughed. Myra Sue shuddered. Ian took a step backward. It looked like Isabel tried to shrink into that hospital mattress. As usual, Mama smiled warmly at them, but I noticed she looked paler than ever.

"Mama," I said, looking up at her. "You okay?"

She smiled weakly. "Yes, honey. Fine."

She still had one hand on my shoulder, and I patted it. I noticed it was puffy and soft—not at all like her usual strong, slim hands. And guess what? Her face was kinda puffy, too. That just was not normal. I decided to say something to my daddy about all this, because Mama had not been herself the last several days, and I was pretty sure she was getting sick, no matter what she said.

"Hello," Isabel said to Forest and Temple. She gave them a quick, thin smile that never reached her eyes.

She had stopped calling her hippie next-door neighbors "those vile creatures," but she barely tolerated their presence, especially when they avoided bathing for a while—which, let me tell you, was more often than not. Today, the pair looked freshly washed. Their gray ponytails were clean, and so were Temple's faded prairie skirt and tank top and Forest's frazzled overalls and T-shirt. Even his bald head above the ponytail shone all clean and bright.

Also, I noticed Forest wore those funny paper hospital slippers over his bare feet. I reckon kids under twelve and bare feet are both forbidden on the third floor of Blue Reed General Hospital.

"Oh, Isabel!" Temple cried. She rushed right to the woman's bedside with almost as much enthusiasm as Myra Sue. "How are you feeling?"

She touched the other woman's purple-blotched forehead—which resulted in a sharp, hissing intake of Isabel's breath.

Isabel's eyes darted back and forth between her two newest visitors. Then she yanked the thin bedcovers up to her chin, clutching them with her bony fingers. "I've had some miserable experiences since we left California, but this has been the absolute worst."

I would give my last Kraft Caramel if ole Isabel could prove that her day was any worse than mine, except for that wreck, of course. Let me tell you what happened.

TWO

Junior High Stinks in More Ways Than One

❀

I had looked forward to that first day of junior high for many reasons. Number one: I wouldn't have to spend the entire day with Myra Sue or Isabel St. James. Number two: I could see my best friend, Melissa Kay Carlyle, and number three: I like school.

So, after riding good ole bus number 9 for nearly an hour and finally being let off at the front of Cedar Ridge Junior High, I was all set to have a memorable experience. In fact, I expected it would be great. But guess what? I thought wrong.

Melissa Kay Carlyle met me at the front door of that building, which probably was built twenty years before Columbus discovered America. It stunk like his sailing crew had left their gym socks in the old, beat-up gray lockers that lined the hallway. The smell was so bad, you could almost taste it.

"I'm glad you're here!" Melissa said, grabbing my forearm so hard I nearly dropped my brand-new red-and-blue Trapper Keeper.

During summer break, Melissa's mom always sent her to summer camp, so I hadn't seen her most of the summer vacation. We had a lot to catch up on.

That day, Melissa's light brown hair hung in a shiny bob just below her earlobes, and her pale hazel eyes sparkled, as always, like clear creek water. Melissa has a tiny little nose and rosy mouth that look more like they belong to a baby doll than a girl of eleven, but my mama says that when she grows up, those round features will keep her young-looking.

That morning, she looked wide-eyed and pretty scared.

"What's wrong?" I said, feeling some alarm.

"We don't belong here, that's what's wrong!" she said. "I am telling you, April Grace, sixth graders have no business being in the same building as seventh and eighth graders."

I frowned at her.

"What d'you mean? Of course we belong here. We are—" Someone shoved me right into Melissa, who bumped into someone who pushed her back into me.

"Out of the way, worms," said the boy who pushed Melissa. He had a pink, pimply face and a turned-up nose.

"Yeah, worms," said the boy who pushed me. "Don't you realize that sixth graders are the worms of junior high?"

"I'd rather be a worm than a doofus like you," I said. I started to shove him back, but Melissa grabbed my arm again.

"Sorry," she said to the boys as she pulled me over to the wall and out of their way. They sneered and swaggered away.

"Melissa Kay Carlyle, do *not* tell them 'sorry' when they—"

"Listen, April Grace. We aren't in elementary school anymore, and we don't fit in here. Take a look around."

I glared good and hard at her because I saw no reason to be all apologetic to those nasty boys who had shoved us and called us names. Then I noticed my friend's frightened face.

"Look around!" she said again.

So I looked. Here's what I saw: Except for some of us sixth graders, most of the girls looked like *Jem and the Holograms* cartoon rock stars, complete with leggings, slouch socks, and oversized sweaters with big shoulders. They wore their big hair pulled into banana clips or on the side in ponytails. Their makeup jobs consisted of bright blue gunk on their eyes, spots of red blush on their cheeks, and vivid pink lipstick.

The boys came in all sizes. Most of them looked like their hands and legs had grown too big for the rest of their bodies. They wore their hair all poufed up, too. They swaggered when they walked. Oh brother.

Most of us sixth graders wore the kind of clothes we wore last year. For instance, I wore red shorts and a white T-shirt. Melissa's own blue-and-red shorts outfit was new. We looked like we always did as far as I could tell. Some of the girls wore their hair in regular ponytails or had new, short haircuts. Those older kids were looking at us all like we were weird.

I'll tell you something: the Cedar Ridge sixth graders might have stuck out like a pimple on Myra Sue's face, but as far as I was concerned, we were not the weird ones in that noisy, stinky hallway.

"So we don't exactly fit in," I said to my friend. "So what? There's no way I'd ever wear my hair fixed like that." I pointed to one particular awful-looking hairdo. "Her bangs look like a rooster comb. I like my braid." I grasped that thick, red braid and pulled it over my shoulder, waving the end of it at Melissa. "And wearing makeup is about as dumb a thing as anyone can do. Who wants to look like a clown?"

"But don't you want to be fashionable?" Melissa said as if she could hardly believe what I'd just said.

"Fashion is a big fat pain!" I declared. "That's my motto."

"April Grace, you have a lot of mottoes."

We stood there eyeballing that milling herd while the odor of perfume, aftershave lotion (what boys need *that*, I'd like to know?), armpits, mildew, and floor wax nearly gave me a lung disease from the foulness of it all. I liked grade school, where the air smelled like books and chalk dust.

"Wait until you see Lottie Fuhrman," Melissa muttered.

"Why? Is something wrong with her?"

"You know how she spent an entire month this summer in Little Rock? With her cousin Cassie?"

I nodded.

"You know how her mom and new stepdaddy went on their honeymoon and then moved into their new house? Did you know it's over there in that fancy new neighborhood, Acacia Heights?"

I nodded again.

"Well, oh brother, has *she* changed!"

"Changed?" I asked. "Changed how? What do you mean?"

Lottie had been friends with me and Melissa since we were little. She wasn't a best friend, like Melissa, but we did all go to the same church, and we'd had sleepovers and birthday parties and stuff. She had always been prissier than me or Melissa, but we always had fun and got along just fine. I couldn't imagine her being any different than usual.

"Right there," Melissa said. "Look!"

My gaze followed her pointing finger.

That first day of school, in that hot, narrow, smelly hallway full of scared sixth graders, loud seventh graders, and swaggering eighth graders, one thing stood out more than anything else. A group of five girls stood together, and it was as if an invisible cone around them kept everyone else away. Let me tell you, they looked like a clump of vividly identical, blond-haired, overdressed, red-lipped, clown-cheeked Barbie dolls.

Mystified, I said to Melissa, "What is that?"

She sniffed. "*That* is 'the Lotties.'"

"*The Lotties?* What in the world are the Lotties?"

Melissa shrugged and wrinkled her small nose. "That bunch of girls."

I looked again and saw Brittany Johnson, Aimee Dillard, Heather Franks, and Ashley Cummings. I didn't know them very well because they had always been kinda standoffish.

"You are not allowed to speak to them unless they say you can," Melissa said.

"*What?* How do you know?"

"Because when I said hi to them a bit ago, Lottie said in a snotty voice, 'You cannot speak to us unless we tell you that you may do so. It's a rule, and don't forget it!'"

"That's the dumbest thing I've ever heard."

She shrugged. "That's the way it is, April Grace."

I squinted hard at that silly group of girls.

"Well, I'm fixin' to find out what this is all about," I told Melissa.

"Oh, April, I don't think—"

But I wasn't going to let her stop me from speaking this time. I waved off her warning, shook her hand from my arm, and marched right over into the awfullest cloud of perfume you can imagine.

"Hey, Lottie," I said, friendly as all get-out and trying not to sneeze. "Did you have a good time with your cousins and grandparents? How's your mama and her new husband?"

That girl slid her mascaraed gaze over me, then started whispering to that goofy Aimee Dillard, who has always thought she was the hottest thing since fried potatoes because her daddy owned the only hardware store in Cedar Ridge.

"Lottie? Aren't you going to say hi?" I was still just as warm and friendly as a piece of apple pie.

"Lottie," said Aimee, "I'm not sure everyone understands our rules. Especially certain bus riders. Especially riders of *bus 9*."

"What are you talking about, Aimee?" I said. "You ride the school bus."

Ole Aimee looked at Lottie and said, "Isn't it funny, Lots, how some people think that riders of bus 7, who live on the west end of town, are like riders of *bus 9*, who live on Rough Creek Road?"

"As if anyone from the west end of town would ever in our lives hang out with *hicks* from Rough Creek Road. Gross me out!" Brittany added, rolling her eyes.

All those girls laughed way too loudly.

"Maybe we should post our rules on the bulletin board," Aimee said, "so everyone will know them."

"That's an excellent idea, Aims," Lottie said with all the snootiness you can imagine. "That is your assignment tonight. Make a list of our rules and post them in the morning. In the meantime, those who are not a Lottie should mind their own beeswax."

"Have you lost your ever-lovin' mind, Lottie Fuhrman? We're friends."

"I just hate that annoying buzz in the air," she said, swishing her hand back and forth as if she were waving away a bad smell. Those girls giggled and waved their hands, too.

"It might be the smell of the *barnyard*," Aimee said.

"It might be the smell of those red shorts," said Heather.

All of them giggled even more, then they turned as a single unit and walked down the hallway. Students moved to the side for them, half on one side and half on the other, and the hall looked like the Red Sea parting for Moses and the children of Israel.

"See what I mean?" Melissa said behind me.

"That's the craziest thing I've ever seen in my life!" I declared just as the bell rang.

The sad thing is, that might have been the high point of my day because the rest of it went downhill from there.

We all clomped over to the gym for First Day Assembly, in which square-built, gray-haired, flat-footed Mrs. Patsy Farber, the principal, lectured us about the rules of junior high. All that mess went on and on until I thought my ears would bleed.

From the gym we went to our homeroom. Our school was so small, there was only one homeroom class for each grade—and wouldn't you know, I had to sit next to that obnoxious ole J.H. Henry. For some reason, J.H. decided he was too cool or something. He like to have driven me nuts winking and calling me "baby" and "hot stuff." Where in the world did he come up with *that*? Since I have made a decision to be a nicer person, I didn't hit him with my history book or tell him to go jump up a stump or anything, but I figured if he kept up that nonsense, he'd be winking out of two black eyes sooner or later.

Even if I hadn't been feeling completely yucky by lunchtime, the gross food smell of the cafeteria and my one bite each of the rubber macaroni and cheese, cold, greasy green beans, and too-sweet applesauce would have put me over the edge. I took my tray right up to one of the lunch ladies and handed it over. She looked at my full tray, then she looked at me.

"Aren't you hungry?" she asked.

"I am starving out of my mind, but I guess I'll survive." I sighed and trudged back the way I came.

The one bright spot in that day was Mrs. Scrivner, the English teacher, who told us we'd be reading literature and writing stories. Now, I figured that right there might make junior high worth the trouble. I nearly stood up and cheered.

But, even with that bit of good news, I was glad to get home from that first day.

I walked up the lane to the house beside my sister after the bus dropped me and Myra Sue off. The junior high shares buses with the high school, so there was no peace from Myra Sue at the end of my school days. My empty stomach growled like eighteen grizzly bears who were eyeballing a solitary Snickers bar. All I wanted to do was eat until I exploded. And with all that school nonsense and Lottie stuff and J.H. Henry irritations, the only thing my brain wanted was to read my book until my eyes crossed. But it didn't happen that way.

Instead Mama met us at the door with her car keys in her hand.

"Put your books on the table, girls, then pile in the car. Isabel's in the hospital."

THREE

Meanwhile, Back on the Farm

When we finally got home from visiting Isabel in the hospital, I shucked off my school clothes and put on jeans and my favorite green T-shirt and sneakers. Then I headed down the slope behind the house to the barn. The sun made the western sky all golden and orange as it edged down toward the horizon.

Before you get to the milk barn, you pass the original barn that my great-grandfather built about a million years ago. The wood is all gray and weather-beaten, and you don't see many like it these days. Up in that barn is the loft where Daddy stores the hay for winter, and down below is where he keeps the tractor and the baler and other equipment. I like to hang out in there sometimes, but that day I needed to see my father.

The dairy barn is large, built of concrete blocks, and painted a pure white. The corrugated metal roof is gray, and whirling air ventilators on top keep dampness from building up inside. Plus there are plenty of windows on the south side to let in the sunlight and air.

As I approached the barn, I could hear the *whoosh-whoosh* of the automatic milkers and the sound of my daddy talking with our hired man, Mr. Brett. The men spoke softly because loud noises bother the cows. If I were to yell a "howdy" to the men, one of them dumb cows would like as not kick or jump or make a poopy mess right there on the barn floor, and that would agitate the others, and they'd all do the same, and guess who'd get to help clean it up? Yours Very Truly, that's who.

I went through the washroom and entered the milking parlor, warm from the cows' body heat. Big black-and-white Holstein cows stood with their necks locked loosely in stanchions and happily munched the feed Daddy had put in the trough in front of them. Daddy and Mr. Brett stood well away from the backsides of the cows. Nobody wants to get kicked, you know.

Mr. Brett—who is very nice-looking with dark eyes, black hair, and a short black beard—saw me immediately. He gave me a grin and held up one hand in greeting. Daddy turned and saw me.

My daddy is Mike Reilly. He is the handsomest man in all of Zachary County. He has dark brown hair and blue, blue eyes. I know nothing bad will ever get me when my daddy is around.

"Hey, punkin," he said as I approached him. "You just get home?"

"Yep. Hi, Daddy. Hiya, Mr. Brett."

"How's Miss Isabel?" Daddy asked.

"She's got a broke leg. I mean, she has a *broken* leg, and she's all black and blue and purple, and she purely looks like a mess. I bet she hurts pretty good, too."

"I'm sure she does," Daddy agreed.

"Ian said she drove right off the road there at the culvert on Howard's Hill," Mr. Brett said. "Worst place on this entire road."

Daddy and I agreed with him, then I said, "Daddy, I need to talk to you."

He turned to Mr. Brett and said, "Would you check

Flossie? She's more restless than usual. Maybe give her a little more grain; that'll calm her a bit." He looked at me. "What is it, honey? We're a little busy here."

"I know, but it's important."

"Well then, you better tell me."

"Daddy, remember when I told you a few weeks ago that something was wrong with ole Myra Sue?"

He nodded. "Sure. And there *was* something wrong. Thanks to you we got her some help, and now she's eating like a normal girl again."

My sister had decided she wanted to be super skinny like Isabel, so she stopped eating for a little while. Thank goodness that's all over with.

"I'm glad you remember that because, Daddy, now I'm worried about Mama."

"You are?"

"She's all pale. I can practically count her freckles."

"Oh?"

I nodded. "And she looks tired. And her hands are puffy."

He just looked at me for a minute.

"Okay, April. Thanks for telling me. I'll check on her when I get finished here."

This puzzled me. I would have thought he'd forget about those dumb cows and run up to the house right then.

"But, Daddy . . ."

He took in a deep breath and let it out. "I'm sure she's okay, April Grace. I know she's not been feeling too good, but I can pretty much promise you she's all right."

I folded my arms across my chest. "*Daddy*."

He put his hand on my head and smiled into my eyes. "I *promise*. Okay?"

I knew he loved Mama as much as I did and that he would not let anything bad happen to her, either. I trusted him.

"Okay then," I said. "But you won't forget to check on her as soon as you get to the house, will you?"

"I'll check on her. I promise."

And he did. In fact, he talked to her for a long time in the upstairs bedroom they had been sharing ever since the St. Jameses had been living with us. It was Myra Sue's bedroom, and she was staying in my room with me. I hung around outside the closed bedroom door, hoping to find out what was what, and I was still hanging around there when Daddy opened the door unexpectedly.

"So!" he said, frowning. "Eavesdropping?"

I tried to smile. Then I shrugged. "Well, Daddy."

"Well, what? You know you're not supposed to snoop."

"I wasn't snooping. Not exactly. I just wanted to know if Mama is all right."

Mama called out to me, and Daddy stepped aside. Mama was sitting on the edge of the bed, but she stood up the minute I walked in. She gave me a big smile.

"Honey, I don't want you to worry. I'm fine. Just feeling a little under the weather lately."

I narrowed my eyes. "Are you sure?"

She kept smiling, but I saw her tiredness anyway. "I'm sure."

"Well, okay," I told her after a little pause. But I was not convinced.

That night, Ian stayed at Blue Reed General with his little woman. At home we had hot dogs and potato chips and store-bought cookies for supper.

As soon as Mama finished eating, she looked at us girls.

"I apologize for this meal."

"That's okay, Mama," I said. "Hot dogs are fun, and we hardly ever have them."

She smiled at me, all tired in her eyes.

"Thanks, honey." She pushed back her chair and got up. Then she added, "I'm going to bed now."

"Mama?" I said in considerable alarm.

She stroked my head, smiling. "I'm tired, honey, but I'm *fine*."

No matter how many times she said it, I still found it hard to believe. She gave us each a little kiss on our foreheads and went off to bed.

"Daddy?" I said, looking at him and feeling scared.

"Punkin, she's okay."

"But—"

"It would be a big help if you'll just be a good girl, you and your sister both. Now, go do your homework, and I'll clean the kitchen."

"But, Daddy—"

"Trust me on this, April Grace," he said gently. "I will take care of your mama. I promise."

The night was quiet and spooky without Mama, and I crept around the house like it was haunted. Seeing Daddy do kitchen duty instead of Mama, which is something she always does, gave me a fluttery feeling, too. But I finished my homework at the kitchen table, and at bedtime I went up to my bedroom, wishing Grandma was well enough that I could go see her and talk about all this. Myra Sue sat dejectedly in her pink pajamas on the edge of the bed, kinda slumped, staring down intently at her hands.

Sharing my room has not been a joy, let me tell you. And there are a lot of reasons for that. Number one: My sister is not the neatest person in our family. Well, neither am I, but I like to have my things where I can see them or get to them easily. Myra Sue would rather spend her time staring at her silly self in the mirror. Number two: She's so bossy you'd think it was her room. Number three: She never turns off that stupid radio she got for her birthday last year and sometimes sings along with it. And number four: She hogs the bed. You cannot imagine how awful it is to have her in my room, but it is just a burden I have to bear until Ian and Isabel move into their own place.

"What are you doing?" I asked her.

"I need a manicure. I have a hangnail."

Oh brother.

She sighed deeply. "Poor Isabel."

"Isabel will be just fine," I said. "Good grief. Just because she's in the hospital, the world is *not* coming to an end."

She looked up. Her bright blue eyes swam with tears. Her lips started to pooch out in a pout, and the blush on her cheeks got deeper. She ran the fingers of one hand through her blond curls.

"Instead of worrying about ole Isabel," I told her, "why don't you worry about Mama?"

"Daddy said she's okay."

I shrugged. "That's what he said, but she looks funny to me."

"Funny ha-ha or funny weird?"

"Not like Mama."

"Oh," she said, like she understood. But I doubt she did, especially as her mind seemed brimming over with Isabel.

A few days later, on Friday afternoon, Myra Sue and I hadn't been home from school very long when Ian brought Isabel home from the hospital. Let me tell you, that man carried her and her crutches every step of the way from the car to the bed. Myra Sue and I followed them into the bedroom. Mama had the bedcovers pulled back, and he laid her down in it like she was a helpless little baby. He fluffed her pillow. Then he adjusted the top sheet a little. Then he patted her on the head until she snapped at him in the most unrefined way you can imagine. In fact, I thought she was gonna bite his hand.

Ole Ian took a few steps back, sat down in the little wicker chair, and closed his eyes. As Grandma would say, that poor man looked like he'd been sent for and couldn't go—meaning he was plumb wore out. He let out a long, long breath. Poor ole Ian.

Isabel looked at Mama and said, "You will not believe what happened. That wretched school board president called me at the hospital this morning and told me that due to my injuries, they were going to postpone my classes until next semester."

"Oh, Isabel, I'm so sorry," Mama said. "I know how you were looking forward to that."

Isabel sighed. "Yes. Oh yes. And now what will I do? You know I love to stay busy."

Oh brother. Isabel's busyness usually involved exercising on the front porch, and it hardly ever involved any actual work.

"Maybe you could learn to knit," I volunteered, and received a dirty look for my suggestion.

"I just don't know what I'll do with myself, lying here a complete invalid."

"Don't worry, Isabel dearest," my goofy sister said. "I'll keep you company."

Isabel smiled at her. "Thank you, darling. You're a treasure."

Oh, gag me.

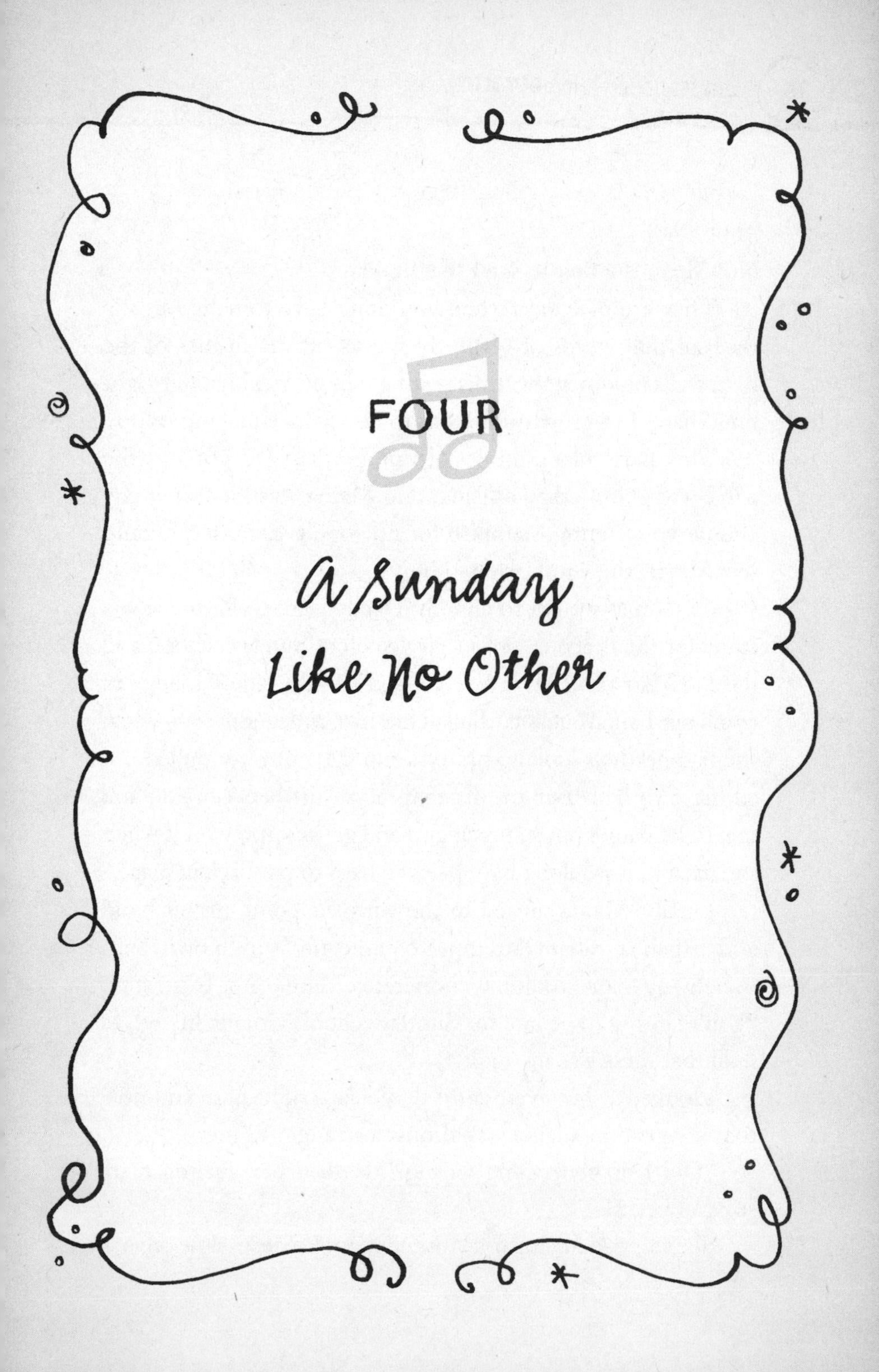

FOUR

A Sunday Like No Other

♫

Now, I am the first to say I like Sundays.

They are nice days when you don't have to hang out the wash or pull weeds or scrub fly specks off the insides of the barn walls or any of those disgusting jobs every kid in her right mind hates but grown-ups seem to dearly love making us do.

This particular Sunday morning when we got up, the wind was going crazy outside, and Mama was kinda twitchy and nervous-acting, snappish for no good reason that I could see. Maybe the wind irritated her.

As soon as we got to church, Daddy went to Pastor Ross's study for the deacons' prayer circle before Sunday school, and me and Mama and Myra Sue stepped into the ladies' lounge to comb our hair. Mama scowled at her own reflection, even when she had her hair looking pretty again. Myra nearly pulled out all her own hair trying to fix that mess. Just between you and me, if she hadn't put so much goo and gel and spray on it when she fixed it, it wouldn't have been so hard to put back in place.

Finally, Mama turned to me with the comb in her hand and began a valiant attempt to tame my windblown hair. When my hair wouldn't cooperate, Mama got frustrated. "You're going to be late for Sunday school!" Mama hissed, as if all that mess was my fault.

I looked at her eyes, and I do declare right here and now that my grumpy mama was almost a stranger to me.

"Did I do something wrong?" I asked her, feeling tears sting my eyes.

She stopped fussing for a moment, took a deep, slow breath,

and said, "No, April Grace. I have a little headache, that's all. I'm sorry for snapping at you."

"It's okay. I hope you feel better soon."

She smiled at me.

"I'm sure I will, honey."

I just kept staring at her while she checked her hair one last time, blew out a breath at her own reflection, and sighed again.

"Come on, girls," she said, even though Myra Sue was still poking around with her own hair. "*Now*, Myra Sue!"

"I can't believe you're making me go out in public when I look absolutely hideous!" Myra Sue growled. Boy, oh boy, if she'd been paying any attention at all to Mama's sour mood, she would not have said that. But Mama just nudged her out the door and said nothing.

We had no more than stepped into the corridor when Pastor Ross approached us.

"Good morning!" he said, cheerful as always. He must not have been out in that wind 'cause it probably would've blown the good nature right out of him like it did my mama.

I have heard some of the teenage girls at church say Reverend Will Ross looks like Don Johnson on that cop show *Miami Vice*. Once I heard that little tidbit, I watched the show, and sure enough, he does, but I think the way he dresses has a lot to do with it. If you were to see him during the week, he'd be wearing his hair kinda scruffy, and he'd look like he forgot to shave for a day or two. He'd wear T-shirts with his suits and have his jacket sleeves pushed up to his elbows when he'd call on shut-ins, or when you'd see him at the store. Myra Sue called him "hunky," which I think is Totally Inappropriate when you're talking about your very own preacher, even if he is an available bachelor.

On Sunday mornings, though, he looked like most ministers, all shaved and combed, and wearing socks with his shoes and everything.

"Lily, I'm so glad I ran into you before church," he said. "I found a great play for our Christmas program this year. Now, I know it's a little early, but I think you never err if you get started earlier rather than later. If you could come to my office for a minute, I'd like you to take a look at it."

For a minute Mama looked like she'd never heard of such a thing as a Christmas play in her whole entire life, even though she directs the one at church every year. Then her face cleared, and she gave Pastor Ross her special warm smile.

"My goodness, Pastor, time does fly, doesn't it? Yes, the sooner we get started, the better we'll do."

They moved toward the back of the church where his office was, but she paused, looking over her shoulder at us.

"Run on to your classes. Scoot."

I scooted, but Myra Sue trudged. I'm sure she thought a dead toad in the middle of the highway looked better than she did right then.

I couldn't help but think that Lily Reilly, in her current state of health and moodiness, had no business directing a Christmas play, but I knew saying so right out loud was a bad idea.

I entered my classroom as silently as possible because Mama had worked on our hair for so long that class had already started.

I could hardly believe my very own eyes when I saw Melissa

sitting next to Lottie Fuhrman in the back of the room, especially after the way ole Lottie had changed and acted this past week at school. Well, there was no way I was going to sit near Lottie my own personal self, so I sat down in the first empty seat I saw, which was, of course, in the very front row where no one else wanted to sit, right smack-dab in front of our teacher, Miss Chrissy Chestnut.

I should tell you that Miss Chestnut is an elderly spinster who takes her Sunday school teaching very seriously. She looks like a prune that's been sucking on a lemon, but if you give her a chance, she's actually pretty nice. I believe she used to teach history at the high school, back in the olden days when Mama and Daddy were teenagers. Miss Chestnut expects her church pupils to sit still and pay attention, just like she's a real teacher. This was my second year in her middle-grade class, which is fifth and sixth graders. I figure she's gonna give us a pop quiz on the entire Bible someday.

Ole Lottie Fuhrman was in Sunday school for the first time in several weeks, and not a moment too soon, in my opinion. That girl could do with a good dose of church.

Now, you should know that Lottie has never liked Miss Chestnut, but up to that point, she'd always kept her dislike hidden from everyone but me and Melissa. That Sunday, though, she made snide remarks under her breath all through class. When poor Miss Chestnut would raise her head from her teacher's quarterly to see who was talking, Lottie looked all innocent and sweet. I glanced back there, and Melissa was all big-eyed like she wished she was sitting somewhere else.

I reckon Miss Chestnut thought the Tinker twins were

talking during class, because she frowned at them right hard. Those two boys are ornerier than all get-out, but not actually *mean*. I guess she thought they were the ones talking and cutting up, but if Ricky and Micky Tinker are going to say something, they say it right out loud. If they throw spit wads, they are happy to take credit for it. The third time Lottie went, "Blah, blah, blah," Miss Chestnut pulled her skinny self up to her full 5'1" and glared at the Tinker twins.

"Ricky and Micky Tinker. You go right to the pastor's study this minute."

In Miss Chestnut's world, the pastor's study was the same as the principal's office. I sincerely doubted Pastor Ross appreciated this belief.

The Tinker twins looked at each other, then at Miss Chestnut.

"But we didn't—" Ricky and Micky said together.

"No arguments! Go!"

The boys shrugged and left Sunday school. I gave ole Lottie a narrow look. She looked right at me and patted her big, poufy, permed blond curls, offering a snarky little smirk in return for my glare. Melissa Kay Carlyle squirmed like a fish on a hook, but she never said a word to that bratty Lottie.

Later, in church, I sat with my parents instead of that Melissa just to show her what I thought of her siding with rotten ole Lottie. Sometimes I liked to sit with Mama and Daddy instead of kids, anyway. It's nice to hear Mama sing, 'cause she has a pretty voice.

After a couple of congregational songs, Pastor Ross made the announcements. "I know Christmas is still a ways off," he said, "but it's never too early to think about our Christmas program. Lily Reilly and I talked this morning, and we have decided it would be nice for our fine youth group to present this year's play."

Hmm.

Now, here's the thing. I did *not* want to be on that platform, speaking lines in a play. Ever since I recited a poem to a bunch of snooty-snoots back when I was a little kid and they all laughed at me, I have never wanted to recite anything. Not a poem, not a speech, not a Bible verse. Nothing. Period.

I eyeballed Mama to see if this was her big idea, but she just smiled at me. Then I glanced behind me, where my sister sat with her friends in the teen group, and I saw that the idea of starring in the Christmas play made ole Myra Sue glow like a new lamp. Oh brother.

Up there behind his pulpit, Pastor Ross was still talking.

"Young people, I hope y'all will be willing to serve your church by cooperating when you're called on. Please be in prayerful consideration if you are asked to help with this. Cedar Ridge Community Church is known for offering a fine pageant for our community, and I trust this year will be no different."

I saw no earthly reason why adults shouldn't do that play instead of us young people, but there is no understanding the grown-up mind. I'll tell you something right now: I sorta dread growing up, because then I probably won't understand myself, and somebody surely needs to.

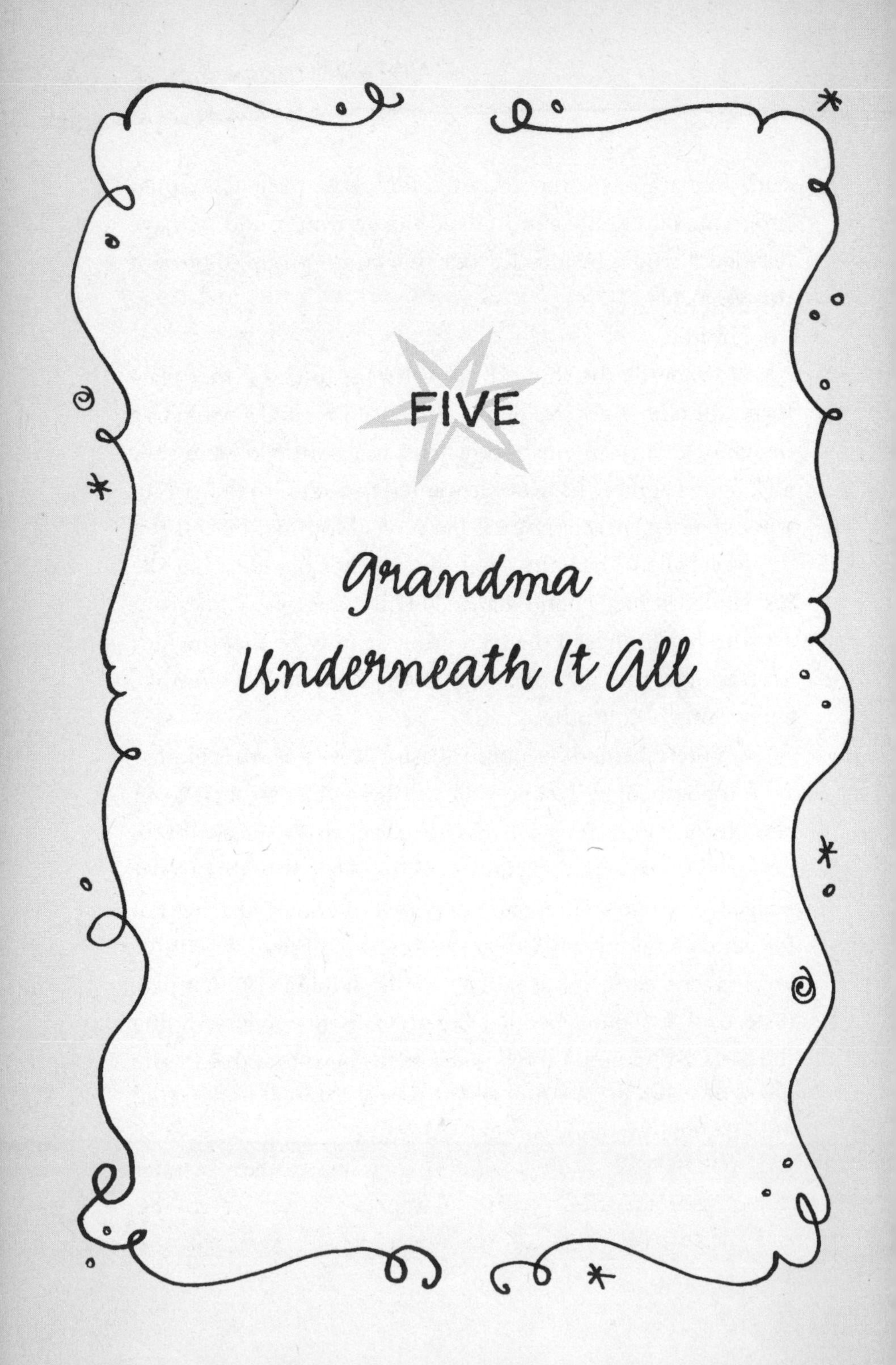

FIVE

Grandma Underneath It All

✲

When we got home from church that afternoon, there sat a pie on the counter, with golden peaks of meringue a mile high.

"Lemon pie!" I yelled with joy to anyone in my family who cared to listen. Mama and Daddy were still out by the back door of the service porch, smooching right out there in the open on a bright, sunny Sunday, if you can believe that, and my sister had trailed into the kitchen right behind me.

I touched the side of the pie pan. "It's warm. Grandma must have just been here."

Someone sneezed in the living room.

"She's still here!" I grinned real big.

"She brought us a germ-infested pie," Myra Sue said, glowering at the wonderful dessert, "and poor Isabel is still recovering just down the hall in the bedroom."

"Now, Myra Sue, be nice," Mama said, frowning at her as she came into the kitchen. Daddy went upstairs to change out of his church clothes, but not before he gave that pie a great big grin.

"You're a dipstick, Myra," I said. "A *dip*stick, heavy on the *dip*. You know Grandma always washes her hands when she cooks. Besides, she hasn't been around any of us since Monday night because she didn't want to spread her germs."

"I don't care," said my sister, all uppity. "I am *not* going to—"

I left that goofy girl grumbling in the kitchen while I dashed into the front room. Grandma was sitting in the small, faded rocker she always uses when she visits, and she held a blue box of Kleenex on her lap. She had missed her beauty parlor appointment that week, and her colored-from-a-bottle hair was not as fluffy as she'd been wearing it lately. Her face and her blue eyes were makeup-free, and she wore a pair of dark blue slacks and a lavender sweatshirt with a white cat painted on it. That day, she looked more like a grandma than she had since Isabel St. James made her over back in the summer.

I had about half expected ole Isabel to be in there, too, but I reckon she was still in bed, nursing all her wounds. Probably if she'd tried to come into the living room, Grandma would've made her go right back to bed. According to my grandma, bed rest and lots of food will heal you faster than a doctor's medicine.

I hugged Grandma and laid my hand against her forehead. Her skin was cool and soft and a little moist. It seemed like a year had passed instead of a few days since I last saw her.

"How's your cold?" I asked, kneeling on the floor by her chair.

"I'm still blowing a bit, but I'm finally drying up." Her voice was kinda gravelly and nasal. "And Rob said I'm not contagious. He oughta know; he used to be a pharmacist." I did not want to talk about Rob Estes, whom Grandma had dated a time or two or three. I preferred Ernie Beason from the Grocerteria. He had a stocky build with kinda messy gray-and-brown hair and a gray mustache. To me, he looks like a grandpa, and what's more, he has liked my grandma for many years. Ole Rob, though—his gray-and-black hair was always styled and neat. He wore nifty glasses that seemed to have no rims, and behind them his eyes were as brown as chocolate. I liked him well enough, but I'll tell you something: he looked more like a teacher than a grandpa. Besides that, I didn't think Grandma had any business whatsoever having two boyfriends. One was *more* than enough. Sheesh.

"You made a lemon pie," I said.

"Yep. Well, I had to do something. I was purely bored, and you know I like to keep busy."

"I've missed you, Grandma." I reached up and kissed her cheek. "You've never been away so long in my whole entire life!"

"I didn't want none of you to catch my cold."

"You've had colds before and never stayed home," I reminded her.

"Well, this time was different, with your mama feeling poorly."

I frowned. "So you've noticed that Mama hasn't been herself lately, too?"

She shrugged. "I know she's been under the weather."

I pulled a face, but I don't think Grandma noticed, since she was busy blowing her nose.

"Tell me about school. You learning a lot?"

I had not wanted to bother Mama or Daddy with school problems, so I was plenty glad to tell Grandma.

"They are teaching those of us who made really good grades last year an entire section on basic algebra this semester. I hate it." Then I brightened. "But I like literature. We have this cool teacher, Mrs. Scrivner. She is going to let us write stories next semester."

"Well, you oughta be good at that. You got an imagination that don't quit."

I beamed at her. "I know."

"What else is going on?"

"The food in the junior high cafeteria will make you barf up your socks."

"Mercy! That bad, is it?"

"I'd rather eat roadkill."

Grandma tsk-tsked.

"I am purely starving," I added fervently.

"Didn't you have breakfast this morning?"

"Yep, but I have to make up for all those days of rotten school lunches."

She nodded. "I see. Well, I'll go help your mama make lunch in just a minute. Think you can make it till then?"

I sighed. "I guess I can try. Grandma, do you know Lottie Fuhrman?"

"Of course I know Lottie. What about her, and why are you making that awful face? April Grace, stop that before your eyes stick that way. I thought you liked Lottie."

I made a gagging sound. Grandma raised her eyebrows.

"I *used* to. We used to be good friends, but she has become a Major Drip."

Grandma's frown deepened so much, you could probably measure her wrinkles with a ruler.

"Now, why would you say that?"

"She became someone else over the summer."

"Ah." As if she fully understood, but I know she didn't. At

least not yet, 'cause I had not told her anything. "She's growing up, is she?" Grandma said. "Well, so are you."

"I don't mean that. I mean, she used to be fun. Last spring her and me and Melissa built a playhouse in the hayloft and swore we'd always be friends. And she always comes to my birthday parties and my sleepovers, and I'd go to hers. Now, all of a sudden, she won't even speak to me."

"That doesn't sound like Lottie," Grandma said.

"That's what I mean! She has turned into the awfullest snoot you can imagine since she went to visit her cousin Cassie in Little Rock all summer. According to Melissa, who hears a lot of stuff because she lives in town, ole Lottie has decided she wants to be in a clique like the one Cassie belongs to in her school. But since there isn't one in our class, she has created it herself. There are four other girls in her little group and they call themselves the Lotties. Melissa and I call them the Snotties. They even made up a list of Lottie Laws and posted them on the sixth-grade homeroom bulletin board. But I think the teacher took them down."

"Laws?"

"Yeah, rules like, 'You can't speak to a Lottie unless spoken to,' or 'No one but a Lottie can wear pink hair clips on Tuesdays.' Stupid, dumb stuff like that."

"Well, I'll swan," Grandma said, using a Grandma phrase. "I can't hardly believe little Lottie Fuhrman would act like that."

"Believe it, Grandma, 'cause it's true."

She sighed. "I take it you won't never be a part of the Lotties, April Grace."

"No! They've been making fun of Jimmy Joe Pitts and the Wilkeses."

"I see."

Jimmy Joe Pitts has a hearing aid, and he wears thick glasses. The Wilkeses have eight kids, and they are probably the poorest family in all of Zachary County.

"She calls Portia Wilkes 'Poor as Dirt Wilkes,' and on Friday, when Eldon Marcus had an asthma attack, all the Lotties laughed like it was the funniest thing ever. The rest of the day, they kept gasping and wheezing. It was purely awful!"

"Well, April," Grandma said, dabbing at her nose with a Kleenex, "just see to it that you stay the same sweet girl you are."

Me? Sweet? "I'll try," I promised.

Mama came into the room right then. She smiled at Grandma.

"Hi, Mama Grace," she said. "I just looked in on Isabel. Ian said she'd taken a painkiller about thirty minutes ago, so she was sound asleep. I believe he could do with a good rest himself."

"I'm sure of it!" I offered. "She probably makes him sleep in that chair in the room like she did at the hospital."

She did not respond to that. Instead she looked at Grandma and asked, "How are you feeling today?"

"Much better. The question is, what about *you*?"

"I'm fine," Mama replied dismissively. "Now, don't you go pushing yourself, Mama Grace. You don't want—"

"I'm all right, Lily," Grandma said, "but I gotta say, you look a mite green around the gills."

"I think so, too, Grandma," I chimed in. "In fact, I think she ought to see a doctor, 'cause anyone with half an eyeball can see she's not feeling right."

"That's enough, April Grace," Mama said firmly, sounding irritated. "I said I'm fine and I am, so I don't want to hear another word about it."

I looked at Grandma, who just kept looking at Mama, who looked right back at her.

"How's Rob?" Mama asked after a short time, as if she wasn't irritated at all. In fact, you could see she was trying hard not to giggle when she asked that. Irritated one minute, teasing the next. See what I mean? It was so confusing.

Grandma's face turned pink. "He got over his cold a few days ago."

"But not before he gave it to you," Mama teased. "You better be careful around Ernie. We don't want him to get sick, too."

"Why, Lily!" said Grandma.

I did *not* want to hear that mess! "I hope you two aren't gonna talk about kissing and smooching because I heard more than enough of that stuff when old man Rance was here."

Mr. Rance was a rotten ole horse rancher who tried to hoodwink my grandma out of everything she owned by being all lovey-dovey with her. He almost succeeded, too, except yours very truly did a little investigation and found out what a noxious old goofball he was.

Mama laughed.

"You're living right on the edge, aren't you, Mama Grace?"

she said as she left the room, still giggling. Grandma scowled at the empty doorway.

I chose not to talk about Grandma's two boyfriends. It's bad enough that, thanks to Isabel's makeover skills, Grandma now dolls herself up and gets her hair dyed and wears makeup and trendy clothes like she's gonna guest-star on that dumb TV show *Dynasty*. At least she's still Grandma underneath all that hair spray and eyeliner.

"Grandma, you think Mama's sick, too, don't you?" I asked real quiet so Mama wouldn't hear.

"Child, your mama just said she don't want any talk about it, so I'm not talking about it."

She got up and went into the kitchen to help get dinner ready.

And that was that.

SIX

A Kid Knows When Something Is Wrong

❀

Now, here's something I can't figure out. Why don't the grown-ups in this house ever think I have a lick of sense? Why do I always have to prove things to them? I reckoned if I had a Polaroid camera, I could've taken pictures and showed them how my mama changed as the days passed. I wondered where I could get one.

The telephone rang and interrupted all my grand thought processes. If you'd lived on the moon, you still could've heard ole Myra's thundering steps as she ran to the hallway to answer it. She acted like she thought someone important was going to call her and tell her how wonderful she was. Well, I coulda told her that wasn't going to happen.

"April Grace!" she yelled from the other room. "Telephone." You could hear the disgust in her voice, and I like to have split my face grinning to know someone had called *me*, not her.

"Hey, whatcha doin'?" Melissa Kay Carlyle said the minute I answered the phone.

To which I said nothing. Because I wasn't sure if I was still mad at her, but sure as the world, my best friend had confused me by sitting next to that silly girl who had taken it into her head to be rude, crude, and snooty to us both.

With my fingertip, I traced the pattern of the floral wallpaper on the wall behind our telephone table.

"April Grace, I know you're mad at me," said Melissa, "but *I* did not sit by Lottie. She came into Sunday school after I did, and *she* plunked herself right down next to *me*."

I had not thought of that, and I felt the tightness in my

belly loosen just a fraction. After all, Melissa has been my best friend ever since we were little kids back in the third grade, and I did not like being mad at her. One thing about our friendship: we can tell each other anything. Kids used to tease us about our freckles and still do sometimes. That right there forged our friendship at first. No one understands freckles like someone who has them. And then we discovered we had a lot of other things in common, too. Such as reading books and liking dogs and certain foods. One thing we did not have in common was family. It's just Melissa and her mother. No daddy, no grandma, and lucky for her, no sister. Boy, oh boy, can you imagine that? I think it would be great, but she thinks I'm lucky to have a sister, even if it is Myra Sue. Let me tell you something. That girl does not know how lucky *she* is not to be related to Myra Sue Reilly, the Prissy Pants of the Universe.

"You could have moved away from Lottie," I told her, kinda sulky. I tried to poke a fingernail right through a little pink wallpaper rose.

"No, I could not have! Miss Chestnut was praying the opening prayer. You think I'm gonna get up and change seats in the middle of Miss Chestnut's prayer? No, thank you!"

"Well . . . ," I said, drawing out the moment. I felt bad about being mad at her, but I still think she could have sneaked under the radar of Miss Chestnut's prayer and sat somewhere else. But my world was all whopperjawed anyway, and I saw no reason to make it even more so by being mad. "All right, then. It's okay. But, Melissa, I felt sorry for poor old Miss Chestnut. Couldn't you have stopped ole Lottie from upsetting her?"

There was dead silence on the phone for a minute. I eyeballed the ivy that trailed through all those little roses and daisies and pansies on our wall.

"Well, April Grace," she said, kinda huffy, "what was I supposed to do? Hit her in the head with my Bible? I didn't notice *you* doing anything to help."

She had a point. I reckon I was as upset at Melissa as I was at myself.

"Let's not fight about it," I said, finally turning from the wall. "Did ole Lottie talk to you?"

"No. She just looked at me as if I smelled bad. I don't know why she sat next to me. Lottie Fuhrman is strange."

"Yep. She's always been a little different—you know, kinda sensitive and always getting her feelings hurt, thinking people are talking about her or making fun of her and stuff. But this stuck-up business is brand new."

"Yeah, I know," Melissa said. "I think something happened this summer."

"Like what?"

"Who knows? While she was in Little Rock, her mom married that ole guy."

I scooted my back down the wall until I was sitting on the floor. I could smell food cooking, and I was hoping we'd eat soon.

"You mean Carter Lee Ritter?"

"Yeah. Him. He's a lawyer or something. And guess what else? He's the new president of the school board."

"Huh!" I said. "That's probably why she's so rotten at school this year."

"Yeah. Maybe now that she's his daughter, she thinks she's hot stuff or something."

"Yeah, maybe so," I agreed. But I didn't want to waste time talking about Lottie. "Hey, listen, Melissa, did you notice anything different about my mama at church today?"

"Your mom? No. Why?"

"To tell you the honest truth, I'm downright worried about her."

I heard disgusting lip-smacking, crunching sounds, and then my best friend—who *knows* it drives me right up a tree to hear someone talk with their mouth full—said, with her mouth obviously full to overflowing, "Blag blakkim?"

I was especially put out by her eating noises right then when I was already tense. "Will you *please* not eat potato chips while I'm trying to pour out my heart to you?" I begged.

Crunch, crunch, smack. Rattle of the chip bag loud as anything right in the phone. A slosh and gurgle. A belch. I reckoned she was washing down those chips with some Mountain Dew, her favorite drink of all time.

"Sorry," she said finally. "I've been about to starve and thirst to death. Mom served liver and spinach salad for lunch."

"Eww."

"Yeah. Eww big-time."

Mrs. Carlyle is a rotten cook, but she likes to experiment. Sometimes she will serve something junky but try to salvage the nutrition by adding something that's supposed to be good for you. One time she added crushed peppermint candy to peas. This is probably one of the reasons Mrs. Carlyle is no longer a married lady.

I did not tell poor Melissa that we were having meat loaf and mashed potatoes and green beans and pickled beets (which Melissa dearly loves, but which I hate to the point it makes the little hairs on my arms stand up) and sliced tomatoes (which *I* dearly love).

"Well, I hope you can control your starvation long enough to talk to me."

"I'll try." She heaved a loud breath. "So tell me what's up with your mom."

"There is something severely wrong with her."

"What do you mean?" I heard true concern in her voice.

"I don't know what I mean! She has looked bad for a while, and she's kinda cranky."

There was a silence on her end of the phone.

"Well?" I prodded. "Are you still there?"

"That doesn't mean anything is wrong with your mother. *My* mom is cranky most of the time," she said.

"But *my* mama isn't."

"Well, April, at this point, I have to ask: What did you do?" She sounded just like a headshrinker on some TV show.

"Do?" As if I'd never heard the word before.

"Yes, April. If your mom is in a bad mood, you must've done something to upset her because she's always nice."

I pondered a moment, then announced with confidence, "I did not do a blessed thing to upset her."

"Well, then maybe your sister did something."

Now, *that* was a thought worth thinking.

"What about the St. Jameses?" she asked. "Did one of 'em say something dumb to your mom?"

"I don't think so. Ole Isabel is gonna be a great big pain while she recovers, though. She like to have worn her husband clear down to a nub having him do this and do that all the time."

"Maybe your mom is worried that ole Isabel is gonna wear her down to a nub, too," Melissa said with all the logic in the world.

"Yeah. She might be."

Right about then, Grandma called me to go change out of my church clothes because dinner was almost on the table. Melissa and I promised to talk later, said good-bye, and hung up.

❀

Let me say this: Ian St. James sat at the table and ate like there was no tomorrow. And then he had seconds of every blessed thing there. His little missus was sound asleep, but he sat on the edge of his seat, and you could tell he was listening for her to call him any second.

"I have missed your good food, Lily," he told Mama. "The hospital cuisine leaves a lot to be desired."

"That whole hospital leaves a lot to be desired!" I declared, but no one backed me up or said "Amen!" or anything.

Mama looked up and smiled like she was half asleep. "Thank you, Ian. It's good to have you and Isabel back home."

Trust Mama to say something sweet like that. I wondered if she'd still be saying it once ole Isabel's medication ran out and she commenced to hollering for help instead of snoring away in the bed.

"We got us a big crop of tomatoes out in the garden and will have 'em for a long spell yet," Grandma said as she passed the platter of thick red slices. "Here, Ian, get you some more."

Ian swallowed the last bite on his plate, pushed back his chair, and stood.

"Thanks, but I'm full." He patted his stomach. "I'd better get back to Isabel now. If she wakes up and I'm not there . . ." Who knows what he was gonna say, because his voice trailed off and so did he.

"Shall we let all the tomatoes ripen and then can 'em, Lily?" Grandma asked. "Or shall we pick 'em green and put up green tomato relish?"

Mama poked at her meat loaf with her fork. As far as I could tell, she had not eaten a single, solitary bite of it.

"If you want to, Mama Grace," she said quietly and all tired-sounding. She looked at the rest of us and said, "I declare. I feel like someone has pulled a plug on my energy today. If y'all will excuse me, I'm going to go lie down."

Now, let me tell you something. Going to bed early and a midday nap—that was not like Lily Reilly *at all*.

"Lily?" Daddy said. His concern was so obvious, you could nearly smell it.

"I'm all right, honey," she said.

"You still have your headache from this morning, Mama?" I asked.

"Yes, a bit. And I'm a little tired. You girls will clean the kitchen for me, won't you?"

"Yes'm," we chimed together quietly, watching her leave the room.

Grandma got up from her own half-eaten meal and followed Mama right up the stairs.

Daddy just sat there, looking worried and about half sick his own personal self. He stared out the window, but you could tell he wasn't looking at anything.

"Daddy?" I said. He did not reply, so I spoke again, louder the second time. "Daddy."

He blinked, threw off that somber stare, and looked at me.

"Finish your dinner, sweetheart. You, too, Myra. Then be good girls and keep quiet so your mama can get some rest."

"Daddy," I said firmly, "*what is wrong with my mama*?"

His smile looked forced. "You heard her, April. She's just tired. Not a thing for you to worry about. She'll be better by and by."

"Daddy, I ain't trying to argue with you, but I don't think she's just tired. She doesn't look right. She's all pale. And puffy. And she don't hardly eat anything. Look at her plate." All three of us looked at the full plate Mama had left on the table.

Daddy pushed back his chair. "I'll go up and check on her." He reached out and stroked my head, then chucked Myra Sue under the chin like she was a cute little baby. "You girls stop worrying. Your mama will be just fine."

He left the room before we could say another word.

"Sissy, what d'you think is wrong with her?" Myra Sue whispered to me, her eyes big and blue and worried.

"I don't know, Myra, but I'm scared," I said.

"Me, too. First Isabel and now Mama. This family is falling apart."

I didn't think it was the time to announce that Isabel St.

James was *not* a part of our family. In fact, right then I didn't have the heart to be sassy, even to my sister.

We forced ourselves to finish eating because we did not want to worry the others, and with great cooperation, we cleared the table, stored the leftovers, washed, rinsed, dried, and put away the dishes, and even swept the floor.

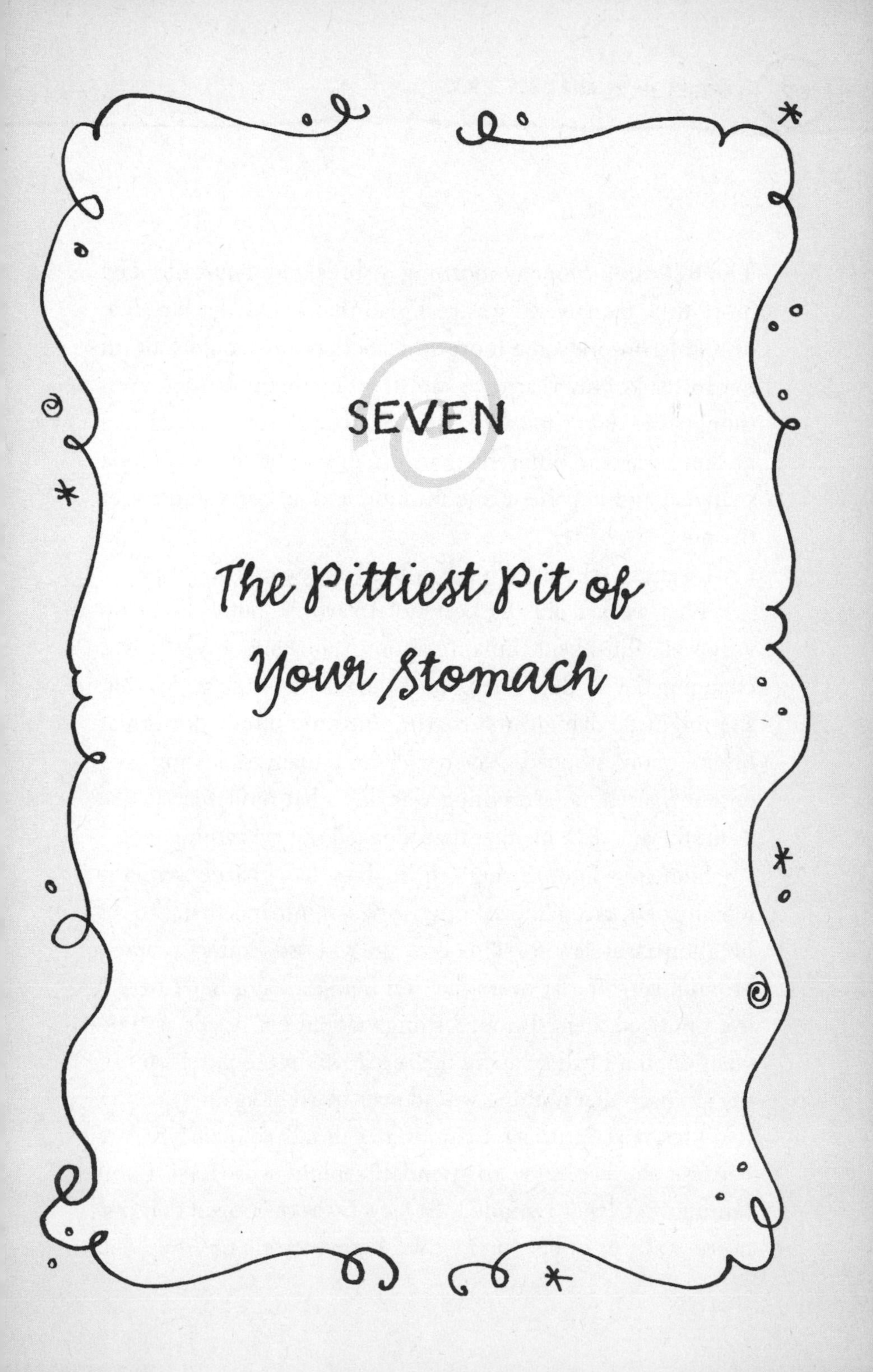

SEVEN

The Pittiest Pit of Your Stomach

The following Monday morning at breakfast, Mama looked more tired than ever. I was real glad that Daddy let Ian slide on the farmwork some more so Isabel's hubby could wait on her instead of my very own mother. For the most part, even though she didn't look like her usual self, Mama acted like nothing was any different than usual, except she was kinda snappish and impatient one minute, and all sorry and sweet the next.

I went to school feeling confused and scared about her.

That week I did my best not to worry, but I didn't do very well. I just kept thinking about Mama and how she was changing day by day. Then, once the very terrifying idea that she might be dying came roaring into my mind, all normal brain actions stopped. No matter how many times my parents reassured me everything was fine, that thought was like a smothering dark blanket that blocked out everything else.

Somehow I got through those days, but I hardly remember any of it, except more homework assignments than should be allowed by law for kids our age. Those Lotties roamed around, laughing at everyone and being a pain, but I barely even noticed them. I hoped things would get better as time went on, but I had an awful feeling down in the pittiest pit of my stomach that nothing would ever be right again.

That next Saturday, I couldn't even talk to ole Myra Sue because she had gone to spend the night with Jessica and Jennifer. Not that I minded. In fact, I was overjoyed that our house was free of her for a while. I tried to talk to Grandma, but she refused to discuss Mama other than to say, "If your mama says she's all right, then she's all right."

I thought about talking with Ian or Isabel, but I didn't do it for two good reasons. Number one: Isabel still slept a lot, and when she wasn't sleeping, she was complaining, and I had enough problems without listening to her gripe about her chipped teeth and where in the world would she find a "first-class orthodontist in this deplorable pit of the world." Number two: Ole Ian was still plumb worn-out, and I didn't have the heart to tire him even more.

Saturday afternoon, I just got to feeling so bad that I asked Mama if Melissa Kay Carlyle could come spend the night.

Mama was in the recliner with her head against the back and her feet up on the footrest. I had to stop and stare at her a minute 'cause seeing her relaxing like that is something I have not seen very often in my life. I felt kinda bad asking if I could have company, but I tell you, I needed another pair of eyes and someone of equal smarts who would listen and talk to me straight.

"You okay, Mama?" I asked.

Without lifting her head, she turned it and gave me a tired smile. She reached out and took my hand. "I'm fine, honey. Just taking a rest."

Hmm. Grandma looked up from where she sat in her rocker, sewing a button on one of Daddy's shirts. She didn't say anything, but she pinned a gaze on Mama for a bit.

"Mama, since Myra Sue's spending the night with Jessica and Jennifer, can Melissa spend the night here?"

She did not look as if the idea pleased her very much.

"Oh, honey, I don't know."

"She's not been here since early in the summer. And we'll be really quiet, I promise. We want to help each other with that awful, terrible math homework." I pulled a face that I was pretty sure looked ugly as all get-out, but it demonstrated how I truly felt about junior high math.

"Well . . ."

Good ole Grandma spoke up. "Let her have Melissa over. I'll be here, and it will give April some company. I want to use your sewing machine, Lily, so I'll be in hollerin' distance if they need something."

"We'll be really, really quiet," I repeated.

Mama thought about it a little longer. Then she smiled. "Okay then," she said. "You go ask if she wants to come over."

"Thanks, Mama! Thanks, Grandma!" I gave them both quick kisses on the cheeks, then galloped to the telephone and called up Melissa Kay Carlyle.

"Hey, whatcha doin'?" I asked as soon as she answered.

"Nothin'. Whatcha doin'?"

"Nothin'. Listen, Melissa Kay," I said. "You know how I've been doin' all this worrying over Mama? Well, I have a good idea. You think you could come spend the night tonight? Maybe you'll see something I've missed."

"I'd like to, but Mom probably won't let me. I haven't done my math homework yet."

Just the thought of math and nasty ole homework gave me a severe pain where the sun don't shine.

"Me either," I told her. "Maybe we can help each other."

There was a small silence in which I heard something rattle that sounded suspiciously like a bag of chips or cookies, then I heard that Melissa nibbling like a mouse on something. She crunched those chips or cookies right into my hearing waves, and I like to have come unglued, but I didn't, because what good would that do?

So I said, all nice and calm, "Why don't you go ask your mom right now?"

"Okay. Hang on." Half a second later, she screamed, "*Mom!*", hollering as if my eardrums were not hanging around right there. "*MOOOOOOMMMMM!*"

So, all right. This sort of behavior is probably why Melissa's mother is cranky so often.

"Hang on," she said again after a little bit. This time you could hear the clatter of the telephone as she clunked it down on the floor or the table or wherever she had clunked it. In a minute she was back and asked, "She wants to know if it's okay with your mom."

"Of course!"

"Hang on." In a minute she came back. "Mom says it's okay as long as I get my homework done."

That settled, I ran upstairs to be sure my room was completely tidy. I hung up all ole Myra Sue's clothes and emptied her overflowing trash can. I made good progress, and I felt pretty relaxed until Grandma walked into the room with her purse strap over one shoulder and her car keys in her hand. That could only mean one thing.

"C'mon, baby girl," she said, smiling. "Let's go get Melissa."

I gulped so hard, I nearly swallowed my tongue and

adenoids and all my molars. Grandma drives either slow, like she's taking a tour of the whole entire countryside, or all crazy, like she's wearing a paper bag over her whole entire head. One time we drove halfway to Cedar Ridge on the wrong side of the road because the highway department had just patched the highway cracks with hot-mix on our side. I reckon she'd rather we got blood and guts all over her white car instead of a little bit of tar around the wheel wells.

"Are you gonna drive?"

"Yep," she said, grinning.

Well, just when you think the world might be tipping a little bit more in the right direction, it flops over like an old, one-eyed rag doll with the stuffing hanging out.

"We'll even stop at Ruby's Place, and you girls can get yourselves a Pepsi slush."

Even the promise of a Pepsi slush didn't make me feel as good as it usually does, especially as I knew I had to risk life and limb to get it.

When we got back home, safe and sound with Melissa and her purple overnight case, I was finally able to breathe easy again. The worst thing on that trip was when Grandma blasted the car horn, stuck her left arm out the window, and waved at someone she knew like she'd never see them again. She ran right off the road, and we went bumping along the shoulder for a while. She like to have scared me and Melissa white-headed. I did not know who she was waving at, and I did not care, but when we finally got back on the road, I nearly offered to drive us the rest of the way.

Here's the deal. After all that wheedling I did, and after

taking my life in my own hands by riding to town with Grandma, I was bumfuzzled to see Mama act like her regular self that night when Melissa was over. She did not act cranky or seem dragged-out tired or anything.

While Grandma whirred away at the sewing machine on the service porch, Melissa and I followed Mama around like two puppies. She didn't seem to notice that we eyeballed her sharply every minute or two.

At one point, she looked up from peeling potatoes for supper and said, "Before it gets dark, you girls ought to play outside and get some fresh air."

Melissa and I were sitting at the kitchen table, where I was skunking my ole pal pretty good at Yahtzee.

"We aren't in the mood for outdoor activities," I told Mama.

"Yeah," Melissa agreed. "We like being in here. With you." She gave me a sneaky look that said we were in on this together.

"Seems to me you'd want to be out in the fresh air and sunshine. On Monday you'll be back in school, wishing you were outdoors."

Mama was right. Boy, oh boy, I would've loved to take a walk through the woods with my two best friends, Daisy—our white Great Pyrenees dog who is older than Methuselah's grandfather—and Melissa. We always loved to do that except for the time we got into the seed ticks. But that's a whole 'nother story, and I won't gross you out with the details. I did not want to leave Mama unattended, so we just kept playing Yahtzee.

Pretty soon Grandma finished sewing her new curtains

and came into the kitchen. She started helping Mama put supper together.

"You girls were going to do some math homework, I believe," Mama reminded us.

Melissa and me exchanged looks of severe torture.

"Let's get it over with," I said bravely.

"Yeah."

We picked up the Yahtzee cup, the dice, the nubby little pencils, and the score pads, put them all back in the box, and dragged our pitiful selves upstairs to sit in the middle of the floor of my bedroom and work on that awful, horrible homework assignment.

"April Grace," she said before we started, "your mom does not seem one little bit different than usual."

"I know she doesn't right now, but she has been." And I told her about Mama being cranky then sweet, and about her being tired and sleeping a lot.

"You know something?" Melissa said, staring thoughtfully into space. "They say kids go through phases, but I think mothers do, too. Mine sure seems to. Like right now she's in a knitting phase, and she's bought more yarn than you can shake a stick at." She looked at me. "I think your mom is just going through a phase."

There was a little flicker of hope in that statement.

"I sincerely hope you are right and she gets over it soon."

We settled down then and got to work on that math.

"You want to know what I think?" I said at one point.

"What?"

"I think anything that says $5(x+2) = 25$ should be illegal,"

I told her. "What is wrong with two plus two equals four, I'd like to know? Junior high is bad enough, but why do they have to make it worse by torturing us with this stuff?"

"I don't know. But going to school in that rotten old building with only one restroom for all us girls is bad enough. It should be illegal. And I think gym class should be outlawed, too."

"Me, too. Especially when Coach Frizell is our teacher. Of course, next semester Isabel is going to be teaching physical education. At least that's what they're calling her dance class."

"That doesn't sound like a barrel of laughs," Melissa said, "but it'll be better than relay races and sit-ups for the whole period like it is now."

"Yeah."

Neither one of us said anything for a minute. Then I came up with something else.

"I tell you what else ought to be outlawed in our school. J.H. Henry and his hair. He looks like he has been severely beaten with the wrong end of an ugly stick."

She giggled. "Yeah. And what about him wearing shoes with no socks?" she added.

"And him calling me 'babe' and 'foxy baby' and 'sweet red' and trying to sit next to me in every class and making those awful goo-goo eyes."

"I think he's in love with you, April Grace."

Now, right then I think I saw spots in front of my own eyes at the mere mention of such an awful thing. "Do not ever say that again, Melissa Kay Carlyle."

"But it's true. If it wasn't, he'd not always be winking and grinning at you."

"He makes me sick!" I hollered. "One of these times, when he points his finger at me and says, 'Hiya, hot stuff,' I'm gonna urp on his sockless feet."

I thought Melissa was gonna have hysterics right there in my room. "If you did that, I bet he'd stop bothering you," she said.

"Then I'm gonna do it!" I declared, not really meaning it, but I figured it might just be worth the mess to make that boy leave me alone.

Pretty soon, Melissa looked up from that stupid math book and asked me, "Does $5(x+2) = 25$ make a lick of sense to you yet?"

"Not a single lick."

I have to say, my friend and I would probably have had more fun if we'd had our teeth extracted by the dog dentist.

EIGHT

Mama Reveals Her Secret at Last

In Sunday school the next morning, Miss Chestnut went on and on about the wonderful privilege for us young people to be involved in this year's Christmas pageant.

"You gonna be in that pageant?" Melissa asked me during the break between Sunday school and church.

"Nope," I replied with all the confidence you can imagine.

When it was time for the service to begin, Melissa and I settled down in our usual pew. The choir had barely started to file in when Daddy and Mama stood up from their seats. Mama looked pale. It seemed like most everybody noticed them as they walked out of the sanctuary. I jumped up and went right after them.

"What are you doing?" I said out loud in the vestibule and did not care who all heard me. "Where are you going?"

"Mama's feeling a little queasy, so I'm taking her home," Daddy said quietly. "You ride home with Grandma."

"But—"

"I'm all right, honey," Mama said, "but my stomach is upset, and I think I'd feel better lying down at home."

"I'm coming with you."

"Don't argue, honey. Just do what your daddy said, and we'll see you as soon as you get home from church."

I could tell that if I said more, she'd feel worse, so I just nodded and watched them walk out the door. Then I stood at the door, cracked it open, and watched as they drove away. I just stood in that vestibule for the longest time. Pastor Ross was probably halfway through his sermon before I went back into the sanctuary and settled down on the back pew.

When we got home, I ran straight into the house and up the stairs to the room Mama and Daddy shared while Ian and Isabel stayed in the big master bedroom downstairs. Myra Sue followed me in a more ladylike fashion than the galloping flight up I'd taken. Mama was lying there in bed, her eyes closed. She was all pasty white. Even her lips looked pale.

"Mama?" I whispered.

She opened her eyes and gave me a weak smile.

"I'm okay, honey." She looked past me at my sister. "You girls run downstairs and help Grandma fix lunch. I'll be right as rain before long."

"You promise?" Myra Sue asked.

"I'll do my best."

We both gave her a kiss on the cheek and quietly went back downstairs. Daddy and Ian were helping Grandma in the kitchen.

"We'll set the table," I said, and Myra Sue nodded, and that's what we did.

Mama said she didn't want any food right then, so she stayed in bed. Isabel actually hobbled with her crutches to the table and ate with us for the first time since she'd gotten home. Guess what? That woman did not utter one complaint. I think she realized she was not the only fish in the fishbowl that day and that sometimes other people are more important than her own personal self.

"I hope Lily recovers soon," she said, and not one person disagreed with her.

I'll tell you something. That was the quietest Sunday dinner the Reilly house had seen in a long time—maybe in forever.

Later, Isabel scraped and stacked the dirty plates from where she sat. When she finished, Ian helped her up and led her down the hall so she could go back to bed. Of course he stayed right there with her.

Myra Sue and I cleared the table. As we carried those plates from the dining room and into the kitchen, I realized that my sister and I had done this exact same thing the week before because Mama hadn't felt well last Sunday either.

Maybe I should have felt better when, after we got the kitchen all cleaned up, Grandma announced she was taking a Sunday ride with Ernie Beason. You see, I knew Grandma would never go off that way if anything was seriously wrong. And the fact that Daddy said he was gonna go take a nap should have been enough to prove he wasn't all that worried. But I was still scared.

I went outside and sat down on the top step of the front porch. Good ole Daisy lumbered up the steps and sat on the porch next to me. She leaned against my side and breathed her warm, damp doggy breath all over my head and face and looked at me with her brown, understanding doggy eyes.

I tell you, I dearly love that dog. I slung one arm around her fuzzy shoulders and buried my face in her fur. I could feel the motion of her big body, which meant she was wagging her tail in sympathy.

"If you knew what was wrong with Mama, you'd tell me, wouldn't you?"

I pulled back and looked at her, eyeball-to-eyeball. Her wet tongue slid right across my cheek, nose, and part of my upper lip. This time I didn't even wipe away her canine kiss. I just hugged her up to me real tight.

"Daisy," I said to her, "I just don't understand why people can't be as understanding as dogs."

"April?" Myra Sue called softly.

She was standing on the other side of the screened front door, looking sadly at me. "Will you come in so we can watch a video together or something?"

"I'm talking to Daisy right now."

Her lower lip trembled, and not in the pouty, put-upon way she always tried when she didn't get her way. A big tear slid right down her cheek. "I don't want to be by myself right now. Please?"

My sister doesn't usually want to be with me, whom she has often called a brat, a dork, a geek, and the pest of the South. The fact that she asked me to spend time with her right then just proved she's human after all. I'll be purely honest with you: there have been many times when I've questioned that.

"Okay. But Daisy is coming in with me." I might be good company for Myra Sue right then, but Daisy was good company for me. "And I don't want to watch a video; I'd rather read. I'll read out loud, and you can listen."

"Okay," Myra said, holding open the screen door for us both. "Shall I fix us some lemonade or something?"

Any other time, I might think this was a trick and that she'd give me something disgusting, like Kool-Aid made with vinegar, but I knew that wouldn't be the case this time.

"Okay. And let's give Daisy a drink, too."

"But not lemonade," Myra said, leading the way to the kitchen.

"No. Just plain water."

A little later, in the front room with our lemonade and plate of cookies and Daisy stretched out and half asleep on the floor near us, I picked up a book.

Near the end of the third chapter, Daddy and Mama came into the room. Daddy was in his blue jeans and white T-shirt and Mama was in her pink pajamas and pale green robe. She settled down on the recliner, and Daddy sat on the sofa.

Myra Sue and I looked at each other, then at our parents. Mama rested her head against the back of the recliner and closed her eyes as if she didn't have the strength to keep them open a moment longer. I laid the book down, and my sister and I scrooched close together, grabbing each other's hands.

"Girls," Daddy said. "We want to talk to you."

Mama looked into my eyes. Then she looked into Myra Sue's. "Girls, you are so precious. Do you know that? God has blessed me and your daddy with the best daughters in the world. Hasn't He, Daddy?" She looked around us at Daddy.

"He surely has."

Even with all this praise and reassurance swimming around my sister and me like caramel goo, my imagination just wouldn't let go of trying to solve the puzzle of why Mama didn't look or act like herself.

I stared right into her face.

"Tell me straight out," I said, then swallowed hard so I

could force out my next words. "Are y'all gonna get a divorce? You and Daddy. *Are you gonna split up?*"

I know it sounded like the craziest thing in the whole entire world. But I had to ask. Otherwise that very idea would trail me just like the fear of Mama's death.

Mama's eyes couldn't have gotten any bigger if I'd pulled out Daddy's electric razor and shaved every hair off my head.

"Of course not! I love your daddy and he loves me. You know that. We'd never split up."

"That's right," Daddy said. He got up and grabbed one of Mama's puffy hands and planted a kiss in her palm. "Your mama is stuck with me for the rest of her life."

They smiled at each other. Boy, oh boy, how did I have enough imagination to even *suppose* such a thing as them breaking up?

"Well, girls," Mama said, "how would you girls like another person living here?"

"Another person?" I repeated, mystified. "Like who?"

Myra Sue and I looked at each other, then back at our mother, and I continued, "We got the St. Jameses sleepin' right down the hall. I think that's enough, don't you?"

Myra Sue was staring at Mama with her mouth wagging open like a dying fish. Then she shut it, gulped, and said in a strangled voice, "Mama? Are you . . . oh, *Mother*. Tell me no. You *aren't*. Are you?"

Sometimes my sister is not the most articulate person on the planet. Or even in the house.

"We're going to have a baby early next year," Mama said,

her full smile returning. "The doctor says sometime around the end of January or early February."

While they looked at my sister and me, the two of us just sat there gawking back. Myra Sue blinked fast about a hundred times.

"A baby," she repeated.

"Yes!" Daddy said with a grin. "What do you think of that?"

I couldn't even think straight, let alone repeat that word. All this time I had been worried and confused and scared out of my mind. Now I didn't know what to think. I was gladder than you can imagine that Mama was not dying and that she was going to be fine, but . . . a *b-b-baby*?

Good grief.

Myra Sue and I exchanged a glance. I could see she had a hard time swallowing this crazy news, and I'm pretty sure my face looked the same way. A baby. In our house. For forever. It was just too much for a human child with a bratty older sister to take in.

I wanted to hurl and nearly did.

I finally found my voice. "Do you mean that having a baby makes you this sick?"

"This time, yes," Mama said with a wan smile. She looked all pale and worn-out.

"Then why would you ever want one?"

"Well, honey, it was a surprise to us, too, but it's a blessing. Your daddy and I are very happy. As happy as we were when we found out you were coming along, and Myra Sue when we were expecting her."

I had nothing to say to that.

Ole Myra Sue's face gradually went from disbelieving and amazed to downright peculiar. I thought maybe she was getting sick, too, so I moved back in case she decided to lose her lunch in my direction.

She stood up. Stiff and straight as a flagpole, she blinked about twelve times, and then she gave our mama a sour little smile.

"I am so glad you aren't seriously ill, Mother," she said, so prissy it would make your gizzard curl right up, "and I hope that you will feel better soon."

She kissed Mama's cheek with the very tips of her pooched-out lips, then she walked like a robot out of the living room.

"Myra Sue Reilly!" Daddy said in a Tone of Voice he reserved for dreadful times such as these when anyone could see he was ticked off good and proper.

Mama, looking pale and confused, turned to me.

"April Grace, honey, what else do you have to say?"

It was kind of hard to think of anything at all except I still felt like I might be sick any second. I reckoned I might feel that way for a few years or until that baby grew up and moved out.

"I don't know what to say," I managed to get out.

"Don't you think you'll like being a big sister?"

I felt my eyes get all big and buggy, 'cause that was something I hadn't even thought of. Having been the little sister all this time and having been subjected to Myra Sue's meanness, I didn't want to be the older one if it meant I'd act like her. Being a drip has never been one of my goals.

"When it gets here, will I change?" I asked.

Mama frowned a little. "What do you mean?"

"I mean, will I have to be all snotty and snippy and bossy and pushy like Myra Sue? Is it required to act like a complete ignoramus to be a big sister?"

"Oh, April Grace," Daddy said, and I could tell by his voice that he was right disappointed with my answer. But, good grief, if they don't want to hear what you think, they shouldn't ask. That's my motto.

"You and your sister are two different people," Mama said. "You aren't going to change a bit."

"No, you won't. But you might change a diaper," Daddy said, joking.

"*Diapers?* Wet, poopy diapers? Me? No, sirree, thank you very much!"

"I'm really going to need your help, honey," Mama said, coaxing.

Well, I was aghast and agog with this whole unrolling saga, so I spoke up again, even though I figured the adults weren't going to like what I had to say.

"Mama, I'm happier than I can say that you are all right and not severely sick. You had me plenty worried."

She gave me a soft little smile, but I plunged on.

"But I have to tell you the honest truth: I think having a baby in this house is not a good idea. It's gonna change everything around here. And it isn't like a baby will be moving into its own house, like the St. Jameses are gonna do someday soon, I sincerely hope. Plus, getting sick like you've been . . . and all cranky and moody . . . Well, it just doesn't seem worth it, Mama. I wish you had talked with me before you decided to be pregnant, and I would have told you it was not the best thing you could've done."

After I said all that, it got so quiet in the front room you could hear the yellow wall clock in the kitchen ticking away.

"I see," Mama finally said.

"April Grace," Daddy said, his voice low and quiet like when he gets riled. The way he got riled at Myra Sue a minute ago. I reckoned I'd just made it worse.

"No, Mike," Mama said. "The girls have a right to feel the way they feel. It's been just the two of them for a long time."

"But, Lily—"

"It's all right, Mike."

A minute or two passed, and nobody uttered a mumbling word.

"It's okay," Mama repeated softly. "They'll get used to the idea."

She said it, but I didn't hardly see how we would.

NINE

How Myra Sue Spells Humiliation

☼

Daddy was mad, but as you know, Mama didn't let him scold or punish me or Myra Sue. He sent me to my room, and I went, right quick. I reckoned he did not want to look at me anymore for a long time.

Myra Sue was lying flat on the bed, her arms crossed on her chest like she was a corpse in a coffin. I woulda thought she was dead, but she drew in a deep, shuddering breath about the time I shut the bedroom door. She stared up at the ceiling and didn't blink once. Her radio played some dumb song by Madonna, a singer that I'm purely bored with, by the way. If my sister ever turned off that stupid radio, the world would probably stop spinning on its axis, and we'd all fly off into outer space.

I stood next to her bed and stared down at her remains until she finally looked at me.

"So?" I asked.

"So?" she replied.

"What do you think about all that mess downstairs? I mean, I feel awful that I feel awful, because Mama has been so sick, and we were so worried she was dying, but now that she isn't, is it okay to feel . . . Oh, I don't know! Myra Sue, I don't know *how* I feel."

She took in a deep breath and hauled herself up into the land of the living by sitting up. "Well, I know how *I* feel."

Good. Maybe she could help me. "How do you feel, Myra?"

"Like a doofus," she said flatly. I could hardly believe she admitted to such a thing, her being so high and mighty all the time.

"You *are* a doofus," I said, "but what does that have to do with Mama having a baby? You didn't have anything to do with *that*."

To tell you the honest truth, I don't know why Mama and Daddy ever wanted to have a second child once they got a load of ole Myra Sue. I would think she'd be more than enough for any parents, even if she'd been an only child.

"I *know* I did not have anything to do with it," she said, "but I'm old enough and sophisticated enough to have known about Mother's condition all this time. I mean, the signs were there. And why do you have that hideous look of disbelief on your face? I *am* sophisticated."

"Whatever you say, Myra. I don't want to argue about something that dumb. But if you know so much, tell me the signs that you, in your amazing *sophistication*, failed to see."

She moved around on the bed until she was sitting Indian-style, facing me. I did the same, facing her. "Remember when Mother first started being . . . well, a little grumpy this summer, not nice like she usually is?" she asked. "She has never acted all touchy and grouchy before. I mean, you and me give Daddy and her a pretty hard time once in a while, you know. But Mama never acted like it bothered her very much."

"Get real, Myra. Mama has always scolded us when we don't behave. But kindly remember that we never had them two St. Jameses living with us before. Them being here was major stress on everyone, especially Mama."

She rolled her eyes, then said, "All right, then, but let

me remind you that more recently, Mother has been sitting down in the kitchen instead of bustling around and never taking a break."

Yep. Sure 'nough, my sister had a point. I had been thinking it was strange that Mama had sat at the table and had coffee with Grandma a lot more than usual, even when there was work to be done.

"And then Mother started putting on weight," Myra added. "Even Isabel noticed."

"Oh brother!" I hollered, even though I had noticed Mama's puffiness, too. "Isabel thinks crowbars are fat."

"Don't talk mean about Isabel. She had to lie in the hospital, all pitiful and alone without us."

Sometimes I just wanted to smack that girl. "Isabel St. James and all her bangs and bumps will heal just fine," I said.

"And in a few months, Mother will have a crying little baby, and *she'll* be just fine!"

We glared at each other.

"Isabel St. James would never allow such a low-class thing to happen to her," Myra Sue said after a minute. "Besides, she doesn't want to ruin her figure."

"Is having a baby low-class?"

"Of course."

My sister obviously had not thought about this dumb idea for any length of time.

"Then I reckon everyone on the face of the earth is low-class 'cause everyone's mamas and daddies had babies once. And having a baby would not ruin Isabel's figure. She exercises so much, she'd just go back to looking like she always does."

Myra Sue narrowed her eyes at me. She was trying hard to think, I suppose. I hoped she didn't give her brain a hernia.

"Then I will tell you something else you have not considered," Myra Sue said after a bit. Her voice was all stiff and snooty.

"Pray tell," I replied, snootier than her, if that was even possible.

"Once that baby gets here, Mother will not have time for us."

"That's the dumbest thing you've ever said." This was an Exaggeration, because my sister has said more dumb things than can be contained in one book, but I needed to make a point. "What do you mean?"

"Babies take a lot of time and attention," she said, "and Mother will not be *our* mother anymore."

"Good gravy, Myra Sue! You have totally lost what's left of your senses."

"Oh yeah? Then you just think about it. A cute, soft, cuddly, helpless little baby who will get its own way every time it whimpers or moves, because that's what always happens. It will need to have its diapers changed umpteen times a day, and Mother will feed it every time she turns around, and if it cries, she will rock it to sleep, and when it sleeps, she'll just stand by its bed, looking at it. She will totally forget about you and me and Daddy and Grandma and everyone else. And that, April Grace, is the facts of life."

I just stared at that silly girl. Then, in spite of my resistance to her questionable brand of wisdom, Myra Sue's words started to sink into my brain, little by little. I could not see how Mama would neglect the rest of her family. She wasn't like that.

"You're wrong," I said, finally.

"Oh? Am I? Am I really?" She said all this with all the Extreme Drama you can imagine, as if she'd heard it from Isabel a million and twelve times. "Then let me tell you what happened to Alice Ann Reed. Her mother had a baby last year, and Alice Ann said her mom did nothing but talk about the baby before it was born. She pampered herself like a princess while she was pregnant, and when that kid finally got here, Mrs. Reed moved a bed into the baby's room and stayed in there. Poor Alice Ann had to do all the cooking for herself and her father and brother, and she had to clean the whole house every week! And her mother never did a thing but take care of that wretched little baby."

I frowned. "Myra Sue, for one thing, our mother is not like Mrs. Reed. And for another, I'm not sure, but I think calling a little baby wretched might be a sin."

Myra Sue's hand flew to her mouth. "Oh! You think it might be?" Her eyes were wide.

I shrugged. "Well, probably not a *sin*," I amended. "I'm no preacher, but I don't think you ought to say mean things about tiny little babies, anyway."

Neither one of us said anything while I thought about what she said about Alice Ann Reed.

"Did Mama do all them things when I was a baby?" I asked. "Rocking me to sleep and looking at me in my crib all the time?"

Myra Sue rolled her eyes. "How would I know? I was only two, but she probably did. You know how Mama is."

"But even if she did, I bet she did not neglect you and Daddy. Mama isn't like that."

"April Grace Reilly, sometimes you are the dumbest child alive. Mother is *old*. She is not going to want to cook meals or do the cleaning or drive us to any school stuff or church parties or *anything* anymore. She will want to put her feet up and cuddle that baby. That's what old women do!"

She clamped her mouth shut like she might bust out crying or something.

Now, here's the thing. I generally do not pay much attention to anything my silly sister might say because what she says usually has nothing to do with the real world. But that time she had a point. Mama *was* old—nearly thirty-eight. Expecting that baby had already been hard on her, and it hadn't even been born yet. Taking care of it was gonna be a nightmare.

I swallowed hard, realizing what all this meant. That baby was probably gonna cause more trouble than ole Ian and Isabel put together.

"I will never, ever tell Jennifer and Jessica about this," my sister moaned. "It will be just too, *too* utterly humiliating."

That seemed dumb to me. What are best friends for, anyway? I could hardly wait for school the next morning because I wanted to talk to Melissa face-to-face.

TEN

Dirty Details of a Rotten, Horrendous Day

When the bus pulled up to the unloading curb at the junior high building that Monday morning, I saw Melissa inside the big window by the front door. Her bus always gets to the school before mine, so she waits for me. It gave me some comfort that morning, I tell you, to see my best friend. After all that had transpired, I needed someone besides Myra Sue to spill all my troubles to.

"What's wrong with you?" she asked the minute I walked into the building. "Are you sick?"

Three eighth-grade boys shoved past us. They heard her and turned to look at me as if I had some horrid disease that was oozing out of my pores.

I scowled at them and shooed them away by flipping my hands. They sneered but kept walking. Boys! I'll never understand them, and to tell you the honest truth, I don't see what's so special about them, even though every girl in my class seemed to have a crush on one guy or another. Goofy girls.

I grabbed Melissa's hand and pulled her over to the wall, away from the crowd of the busy hallway, nearly spilling her books right out of her arms.

"I feel sick!" I said. "The most awfullest thing you can imagine has happened."

"Isabel St. James wants to adopt you?" she guessed, her eyes all big and gawky.

It was such a crazy, unexpected statement that I just stared at that girl for a minute.

"*What?*"

"Well, after all you've told me about her, wouldn't that be the most awfullest terrible thing you could imagine?"

She had a point, but Isabel St. James would rather adopt Daisy than me, I'm pretty sure.

"Listen to me," I said. "My mama is gonna have a baby."

Melissa's hazel eyes nearly popped out of her head. "Nuh-uh!"

"Uh-huh!"

She grinned really big and shrieked so loud, the ear wax nearly dribbled out of my ears.

"Really?"

"Yep."

"Wow! A new baby in your house. What fun, A.G.!"

I gawked at her. "Are you kiddin'? Mama is too old to be having babies."

"No, she isn't." She moved her books from one arm to the other. "She's old, but she's not *that* old. And your mama is so nice and she'll love this baby so much that I bet she'll want to have a bunch more."

I do believe if she'd had both hands free, that silly girl would have clapped after she said this. And here I was, hoping for a little sympathy and support. Was that too much to ask from a best friend?

The early bell rang, giving us warning that classes started in five minutes. The busy hallway nearly leaped right out of the building with so many kids breaking the rules by yelling and running and throwing pencils or books back and forth as they all rushed to their classrooms. I did not move because the reaction of my best friend stunned me stiff.

"You are out of your ever-lovin' mind, Melissa Kay Carlyle. Our family is perfect just as it is. We do not need a baby coming along messing up everything."

Some part of my mind told me I was falling into the thinking of my sister and all the silly things she said yesterday, but having had the night to sleep on it, I now realized that I tended to agree with her. That does not happen very often.

"Listen, Melissa. You don't know diddly about what a royal pain in the backside it is to have a sibling. Also, you weren't there for the Extreme Upheaval brought about by having Ian and Isabel St. James cluttering up our home and needing things and getting in the way of everyone, so you cannot possibly *begin to imagine* what having another intruder in the house will be like. And this one will poop its diapers and demand everyone's attention. Them St. Jameses, especially ole Isabel, like to have worn Mama down to a nub, having her run around doing things all the time. With a new baby, my mother most likely will fall apart, and our entire family with her. I don't want Mama to fall apart."

"I never thought about that," she replied slowly, after a bit. "I've never seen a baby that does all the rotten things you just said."

I huffed. "That's because the only babies you've ever seen are the ones in those goo-goo cute commercials on television, or the ones in the church nursery who are usually all dolled up and seem to sleep whenever they aren't playing or eating."

"But . . . but aren't those the only babies *you've* been around?"

She had a good point. However, I knew something she didn't. I knew about Myra Sue's friend Alice Ann Reed and what happened to her family. So I told Melissa all about the nightmare at Alice Ann's house when her mother had a baby last year.

"Oh," she said in a small voice. Then, a moment later, with more conviction: "But your mother is not like Alice Ann's mother. Not in the least! Mrs. Reed is kinda . . . well, self-centered."

Like Isabel St. James, I thought.

"Well, anyway," I said, "this baby is the reason Mama hasn't been herself lately."

"And she is *old*," Melissa reminded me. "This is bound to be weird for her, April Grace."

"I know."

"I'm sorry you're all upset about it."

"Thanks."

"And please don't feel bad. It'll be a good thing. You'll see."

I heaved a sigh. I'll tell you something. I tried talking Mama and Daddy into giving away ole Myra Sue once, and they wouldn't do it. I was pretty sure they wouldn't give this one away, either.

"I hope you're right," I said.

She smiled. "Me, too." She glanced around at the quickly emptying hallway. "We better get to class before we're tardy. Principal Farber has a real thing about tardiness, you know."

"So I heard," I said as we trudged toward our classroom.

"Don't you need to get your books from your locker?" Melissa asked.

That's when I realized all my books were still on the table at home. Oh brother.

Well, let me tell you something: some teachers have no heart.

Miss Jane-Nell Dickson, who teaches history and social studies and health, is one of them.

When Melissa and I got to class about two and a half seconds before the bell rang, she was already taking roll. I wanted to tell her that was about as unfair a thing as she could do, but looking at her broad face—which was the color and size of a round slice of watermelon—I decided not to utter a peep. She glared at my friend and me as we sat down in our seats.

"Open your books to page 24," she said without first saying very nicely, "Good morning, students." Not that she's done that yet, and I don't expect her to start.

Everyone opened their books. I sat there like a stump because I did not want her to notice me.

Oh well. She did.

"April Grace Reilly," she said, giving me a Teacher Stare. "Open your book."

"I can't, ma'am." Who would've thought my voice would've ever come out as squeaky as Betty Boop's? Everyone in that class laughed until ole Miss Dickson rapped her ruler on her desk. It sounded as loud and sharp and sudden as a firecracker.

"CLASS!" she roared, like we were all tearing the walls down or something.

Everybody shut up like you can't believe. I'm pretty sure no one breathed. I think our blood just sat unmoving in our veins, waiting for Miss Dickson to give our hearts permission to pump again.

"April Grace Reilly, why can't you open your book? Did you break your fingers?"

"No, ma'am," I squeaked like a squeegee on a clean window. "I left it at home."

Boy, oh boy, I thought that teacher's eyes were gonna pop right out of her head and roll across the floor to glare at me up close.

"Why did you leave your book at home?"

I swallowed hard. "I forgot it, ma'am."

"Forgot your history book? *Forgot your history book?* How could you do that?"

"Maybe she was too overcome with the barnyard smell," Lottie Fuhrman said.

Miss Dickson is known to be hard of hearing at times, and I reckon that was one time when she was because she did not blink or glare or say a word to ole Lottie.

"April Grace Reilly!" the teacher hollered. "You will write an essay on the importance of bringing books to class." She glared at everyone else. "In fact, you may all write an essay on the importance of bringing books to class. You will take out paper and you will do it now."

Oh good gravy. Now everyone was gonna hate me for the rest of the day.

And they did.

When Myra Sue and I got off the school bus, Daisy sauntered down the driveway to meet us. She sniffed Myra Sue, who reared back as if she was going to get dirty from Daisy's breath. Ole Daisy's tail never stopped wagging, though, and she came to me, sniffed all the school smells, of which there were plenty, believe me, then butted her head into my hip. I squatted down and gave her the biggest hug you can give a dog who is almost as big as a baby elephant.

As that stinky, noisy ole Bluebird school bus left us behind, I stood up and watched as it went on its way down Rough Creek Road. I was purely glad to see it go.

Then I looked all around at the scenery surrounding me.

Boy howdy, after a hard day, it's good to be greeted by someone like Daisy. And here's something else: it is always good to be home, even if you're just standing in the driveway, looking around. I have to say, when I hear the mockingbird and the cardinal and the meadowlark, or the soft, low moos from our cows, I don't want to hear the television or the radio or a car engine or any other man-made sound.

If you were here, you'd see how the big wooded mountains that surround our farm make you feel all comfortable and snugged in, like nature is hugging you and giving you shelter. The oaks, hickories, and pines grow thickly and throw cooling shade to make the hillsides look like green velvet. The sight makes me feel good all over.

Our house, an old, white, two-story farmhouse that has been in our family forever, has always been a sweet sight to my eyes, even with the St. Jameses living in it with us. I was happy to see that house. The big front porch beckoned me to come and sit in the swing and forget all about the day at school, but I wanted to go inside and see how Mama was feeling.

When I walked inside the house, there was no one in the kitchen, so I shot a glance into the dining room.

There sat my schoolbooks, stacked right on the corner of the table where I had left them that morning. The sight of them made my stomach clench, especially since I'd been sent to Mrs. Patsy Farber's office for leaving them *all* at home, and she said she was gonna call my folks.

Myra Sue was already chattering away with Isabel in her room, but I went to check on Mama. She was fast asleep when I peeked in on her. She slept quietly, as a lady sleeps, not snoring like a hibernating grizzly bear the way Isabel does.

From where I stood staring at her in the doorway, Mama looked young and fragile, not like Mama at all. I was aggravated at myself for being aggravated at her and that baby. I knew how babies were made, and I knew how they grew and how they were born, but I just never thought my mama and daddy would present the world with another offspring. I reckon Myra Sue and me weren't enough.

That was a disappointment that I couldn't quite come to terms with. Disappointment in *myself*, I mean. Maybe if I had been more careful to think before I spoke and had not been as sassy when I *did* speak, and if Myra Sue had been less prissy and uppity, our parents would not have thought they needed another child to make up for our rottenness.

Maybe Myra Sue felt the same way I did, but it sure

as the world seemed to me that she cared more about ole Isabel than she did her very own mother. Which just goes to prove my point. If I had not been so sad and so weary in body, mind, and soul, the whole idea would have made me downright mad.

I silently closed the door to the bedroom where Mama slept. In my own room, I changed out of my new jean shorts and blue-and-yellow T-shirt, and I put on a soft, scruffy pair of jeans that had been Myra's a couple of years ago and pulled on Mama's cast-off green T-shirt.

I knew I should go downstairs, get my schoolbooks, and do my homework. I knew Big Trouble awaited me if I did not. But I have to say, my bed looked purely inviting. I just crawled right up on it, scrooched down between the covers, and went to sleep in about five seconds.

The most awful racket you ever heard woke me up.

I had no idea where I was, what time it was, or what day it was. The color of late evening lay outside my window, which surprised me because it felt like I'd just lain down a few minutes earlier.

Then I knew what had awakened me. Voices. Voices in the hall outside my room and voices coming from the room next door. The room where Mama was. They were loud and scared-sounding.

My daddy was yelling, "*Lily! Lily!*" like my mama had fallen into a frozen river.

The sound of his voice terrified me worse than anything had ever scared me in my entire life. My heart stopped, and I couldn't think.

I tried to get out of the bed, but those covers seemed to have a mind of their own. They wrapped around my arms and legs and twisted around my torso like they were gonna eat me alive, and the more I growled and hissed and kicked and fought, the more tangled up I got.

"Hey!" I yelled to those voices. "What's going on?"

I finally freed myself from those crazy bedclothes and bounded to the door. I opened it up just as Daddy came out of the other bedroom, carrying Mama in his arms like she was a rag doll. Grandma tagged right behind him. I ran toward them, screaming bloody murder.

Someone scooped me up while I kept hollering, "Is she dying? Is my mama dead?"

I struggled in those arms, and a voice said right in my ear, "It's okay, April. It's okay."

Ian St. James cradled me like I was a little kid. His voice was quiet and soothing, but I did not want to be quieted or soothed. I wanted to know what was going on with my mama and why she looked lifeless.

"Daddy!" I screamed. "Where are you going with Mama? *What's wrong with her?*"

We followed him downstairs. Grandma was on his heels, and Ian carried me, though I wriggled the whole time. Isabel stood, propped on her crutches, at the foot of the steps, wide-eyed. Myra Sue stood real close to her. They wore the exact same expressions of fear and worry.

Grandma opened the front door for Daddy. She looked like someone had drained all the blood out of her body.

I reached out, tried to grab Daddy, but Ian held me back. Farmwork had made him strong and wiry.

"*Daddy!*"

He turned around.

"Honey, I'm taking her to the hospital. You need—"

"I am going with you! Put me down. *Put me down right now, Ian St. James!*"

Ian's arms just got harder than rocks.

"April!" Daddy said. "Sweetheart, don't make this more difficult than it already is." He glanced at Ian. "Hang on to her."

He turned to Grandma. "Mom, will you please explain to the girls what's happening? I'll call you when I know something."

Then he was out the door, gone into the black night with Mama in his arms. Grandma shut the door behind him.

Holding back all the snuffling and sobbing as best I could, I tried to reason with those three adults.

"I need to be with my mother," I told them. "She needs her daughter. Let me go *now*."

"Take her into the front room, Ian," Grandma said. "Isabel, honey, you need to get off your feet before you fall over. C'mon, hon, I'll help you." She guided Isabel to the soft old rocking chair, and ole Myra Sue trailed them like a lost dog.

Myra Sue settled on the floor right at Isabel's feet. Ian put me on the sofa, then sat on the edge of it. I heard the car speed out of our driveway and knew Daddy had taken my mama away.

Grandma sat in the brown leather recliner. She did not put the footrest up or recline the back of it. In fact, she sort of sat on the edge of it like she didn't plan to sit there very long.

"Okay, girls, let me tell you right quick what happened, then I'll give you a bite to eat. After I got supper fixed, I took a tray up to your mama, 'cause I knew she was feeling extra tired. I figgered it was a good idea to let her stay in the bed. When I got upstairs, though, I couldn't get her to wake up, so I started hollering for your daddy. Your daddy finally got her to wake up, but she passed right out again. He's taking her to the emergency room, and they'll find out what's wrong with her."

Myra Sue and I looked at each other, and I could see she was as scared as I was.

"Mike isn't taking her to that horrible hospital in Blue Reed, is he?" Isabel said.

Grandma nodded. "It's the closest one."

Knowing that, I felt sicker than ever. I hardly saw how going to Blue Reed General Hospital would help my mother, and in fact, it might cause more harm than good.

But Grandma made me feel better when she said, "If it looks like it's anything serious, Mike will insist they transport her to the Springdale hospital by ambulance."

"Well, that's a relief," Isabel said, heaving a deep sigh. "I hate to think of Lily in that odious place."

"Me, too," said Myra Sue, and I heartily agreed with her.

Right then, I did not like that baby and what it was doin' to my mama. Not one little bit.

Grandma cleared her throat, glancing at Myra Sue and back at me. "Girls, I need to explain something to you," she said.

Myra Sue and I exchanged looks. This sounded way serious, and I'd had about all I could stand of serious.

"You see, it's this way. Your mama has lost a couple of babies before."

I sat straight up, and Myra Sue kinda jumped a little.

"Huh? What?" I asked. "What do you mean, Grandma?"

"I don't remember any such thing," Myra Sue said, looking as mystified as I felt.

"No, you wouldn't remember, either one of you. You were little, and Lily thought it was best you never knew. She did not tell you girls about this baby early on because she didn't want to build up your hopes only to let you down if she lost it." She smiled, sad-like. "Babies are mighty sweet, and we get attached to 'em right quick. She didn't want you girls to be hurt and disappointed. That's why she waited to tell you this time."

"Is she losing this baby?" Myra Sue asked. "Is that why she's so sick?"

"Honey, I don't know. I hope not. Let's pray not. Let's ask God to spare this baby so's we can get to know it and love it and welcome it when it gets here."

"Do you think praying will do any good?" Myra Sue asked.

"I believe in prayer, Myra. You know that."

The St. Jameses, who are about as religious as a rotten old tree stump, did not say anything, for which I was grateful. Someday, maybe, they would believe in God and the good things He does. Maybe they would realize that there are things in our lives beyond our control, things that, if we trust and believe, will get better. I mean, they have had what some might call miracles happen to them since they moved to Rough Creek Road, such as showing up broke and alone and being taken in and cared for by strangers, and then having more folks who they don't even know agree to help them get their very own house fixed up. If that's not God working miracles for them, then I don't know what is. But they haven't realized it as such. In the meantime, I hoped they would kindly keep their mouths shut about not believing. It makes me sad for them.

"I will say prayers for my mama," I declared, "but I should have been allowed to go with my daddy."

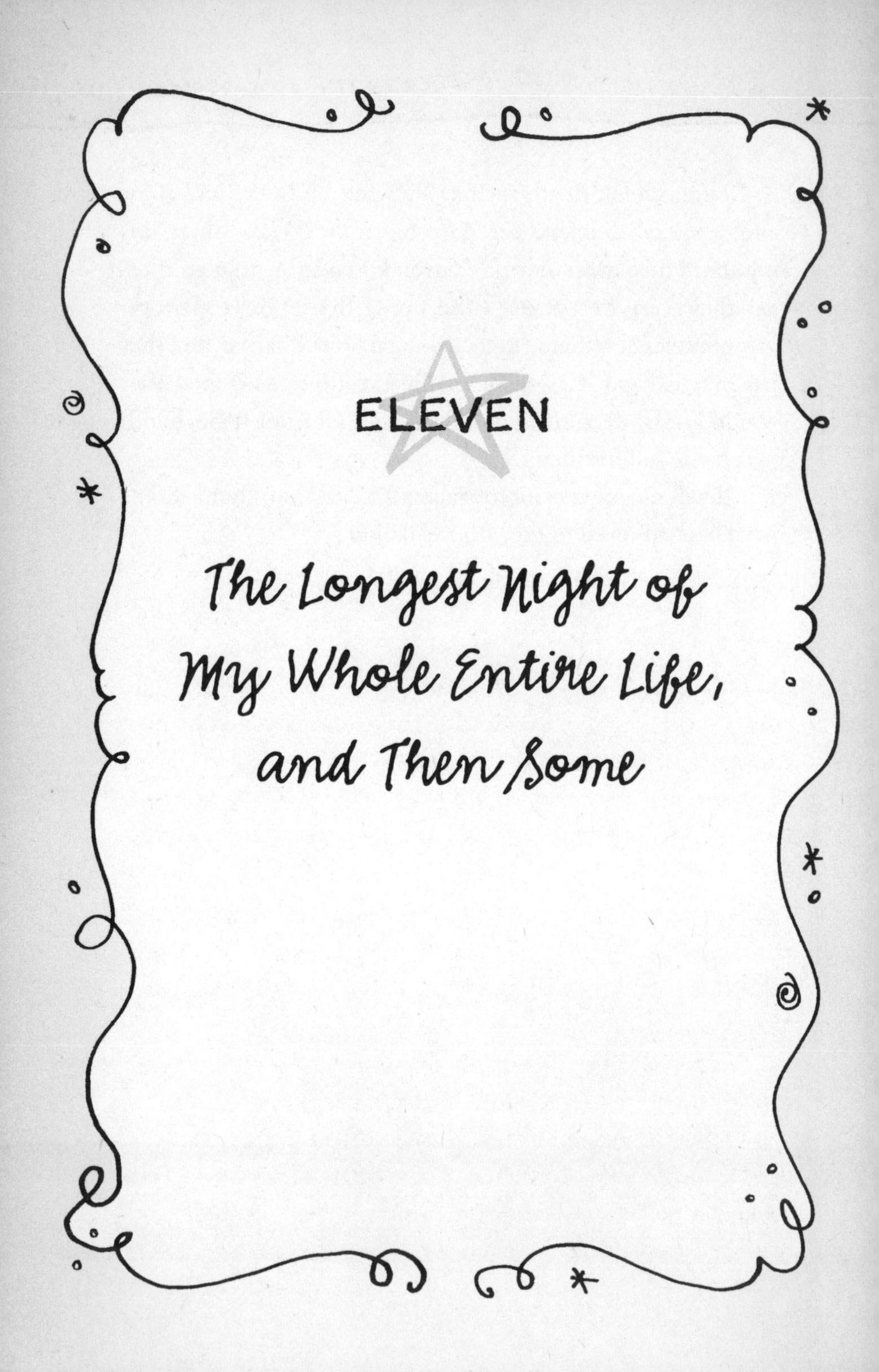

ELEVEN

The Longest Night of My Whole Entire Life, and Then Some

☆

At some point that night, I dozed off, and the next thing I knew, I was waking up, curled up on the sofa next to my sister. It was still dark outside, and I was wrapped in a tattered old quilt that I'd had since I was a baby. Myra Sue had her favorite pink blanket around her. We sat up but stayed right there, side by side. No one in that room, not me, not Myra Sue or Ian or Isabel, said a single, solitary word.

"What time is it, Ian?" I asked, yawning.

He glanced at his watch. "It's two."

I had never been up that late in my whole entire life, and I can't say that I liked it. Number one: It was pitch-black outside. Number two: The sound of the house that late is weird. And number three: My mama was in the hospital, and no one knew what was going on.

Grandma stayed busy in the kitchen, and I smelled food cooking. At one point she brought us a big pan of popcorn and mugs of hot chocolate. I couldn't stand the sight or smell, but I didn't tell her that. Ole Isabel sat in Grandma's rocker, cuddling her cup close to her chest. She shivered like she was ice fishing but refused the blue-and-white-striped afghan Grandma kept offering her.

Ian paced back and forth in front of the big picture window. No one bothered to draw the curtains, and the night stared in at us with empty, black eyes. It was creepy.

"Isabel, honey," Grandma said, "you shouldn't be up. Ian, make her go back to bed. She'll catch her death of cold."

I waited for Myra Sue to fly to her hero's side, but she just sat there and stared at her cold hot chocolate.

"I'm fine, Grace," Isabel said to Grandma. "If I went to bed, I'd just toss and turn with worry." She sipped her cocoa.

"Why hasn't my daddy called?" I asked anyone who cared to reply.

"He'll call when he knows something," Ian said. "Trust your dad to keep his word."

"Does anyone want a bowl of soup?" Grandma asked. "I have some nice potato soup I made earlier for Lily's upset stomach."

No one wanted anything, so Grandma went back to puttering around in the kitchen.

With Grandma out of the room and Ian nodding off, it seemed lonelier than ever. I leaned against my sister and rested my head against her shoulder. Any other time, she probably would have smacked me a good one upside the head and screamed for me and my cooties to get away. But she just sat there, staring at nothing.

"April Grace," Isabel said softly, "aren't you tired?"

I sat up long enough to reply politely, "No, thank you, ma'am. I'm fine."

"Little girls need their rest," she added.

"I slept for a little while." I sighed. "Besides, I'm in junior high now, so I'm officially grown-up."

Isabel laughed a little at that. "Well, you're growing up fast, I'll say. And, Myra, darling, you look exhausted."

Myra Sue finally lifted her gaze and looked at Isabel.

"I am awfully tired, but I refuse to sleep. Not until we know about Mama."

Isabel nodded. "I understand. But, truly, I think she'll be all right."

"How do you know, Isabel St. James?" I asked loudly. "How do you know that our mama isn't laying right there in that hospital, dead or dying, while those doctors and nurses run up and down the hall like a bunch of dizzy, headless chickens?"

Would you believe that Isabel grabbed her crutches, heaved herself up out of that rocking chair, and hobbled right across the room without so much as a groan? She sat on the sofa next to me and pulled me into the circle of her right arm. She cuddled me against her and stroked my hair.

Careful not to bump her broken left leg, I hung on to ole Isabel for all I was worth and didn't even mind that I could feel nearly every bone and vertebra in her body.

She spoke over my head. "Myra, darling, come over here on my other side."

My sister didn't leap or fly or bound, but she did get up, adjust her blanket, step around the coffee table, and settle into the circle of Isabel's other arm. The three of us stayed that way for a long time.

TWELVE

When the Good Lord Has a Happy Grin

At four in the morning, my daddy called. His voice was hoarse and tired-sounding when he told me, "Your mama's got a condition called preeclampsia, which means she has high blood pressure because she's pregnant. The doctor here has given her some medication, and she'll be just fine. And the baby, too."

"Is it serious, Daddy?"

"It's serious, but we'll just have to make sure Mama takes care of herself when she comes home. Okay?"

"Yes, sir. Are you coming home now?"

"Yes. We're leaving the hospital in just a minute."

"Mama, too?"

"Mama, too."

Inside myself, all my muscles and bones and blood and guts turned to mush. My knees went all soft, and I crumpled right to the floor from relief and exhaustion. Good ole Ian picked me up and carried me to my bed.

To tell you the honest truth, I don't remember another thing until I woke up with the sunlight pouring through the window. The house felt quiet.

Next to me, ole Myra Sue was breathing slow and deep and even.

Then everything from the night before rushed into my head. I shoved off the covers and sat straight up.

"Mama!" I yelled, and leaped off the bed. I ran to the room next door.

I went in without knocking, even though it was against the rules. Mama was lying there, sound asleep, just like I'd seen her yesterday when I got home from school. It was almost like she hadn't moved that whole entire time. I was so glad to see her that I had to force myself not to run to her bed and throw myself right on top of her.

"Is she awake?" my sister whispered, right behind me.

"No."

We stood there staring at her until Grandma came upstairs and called softly from the head of the stairway.

"Girls," she said, "come down and get some breakfast. You can see your mama after you eat."

We hesitated, then pulled ourselves away from the door to follow Grandma down to the kitchen.

Isabel, in her thin black robe, was sitting at the kitchen table, looking kinda worse for wear, pale and skinny, fading bruises still visible.

We sat down, and Grandma put bowls of oatmeal in front of us. Not my favorite breakfast, FYI. But I have discovered if you put enough butter and brown sugar on almost anything, it tastes better. Myra Sue curled her nose.

"I do not like oatmeal, Grandma," she said.

"Eat it, dear," Isabel said. "It's good for you, and your grandmother went to the trouble of preparing it."

My eyeballs about popped out, given that Isabel thinks lettuce and celery are the main ingredients for most meals. Without uttering another word, ole Myra Sue picked up her spoon and dug in. I picked up my spoon and reached for the bowl of brown sugar.

I was stirring the whole mess real good, to melt the sugar and butter, when I glanced at the yellow clock on the wall by the back door.

"Good grief!" I yelled before I could stop myself. "Is that the real time?"

In our concern over Mama, we had not even looked at the clock in our bedroom. Myra Sue's spoon clattered as it slipped from her fingers into the bowl.

"We've missed the bus!" she squawked. "We've missed half of our morning classes!"

She started to get up, but Grandma stopped her.

"You girls have the day off."

"Huh?" I gawked at her. "We have never in our whole entire lives got the day off from school unless it's a holiday. And this ain't no holiday, Grandma." I heard those words and changed them quickly even though Mama wasn't there to correct my grammar. "Er, I mean, today isn't a holiday."

"No, it isn't. But it's been a rough coupla days for all of us, and I want you girls to get some rest. Especially after staying up all night like you did. Now, eat your breakfast. When your mama wakes up, you can go spend time with her." She hoisted the coffeepot. "More coffee, Isabel, honey?"

Isabel smiled, showing the chipped places on her two front teeth. I wondered when she was gonna get those things fixed.

"Just a little, Grace."

"Grandma?" I asked.

"Woo?" It does my heart good when Grandma says

"Woo?" like that. Some grandmas just ignore you when you try to get their attention. When my grandma says "Woo?" I know she's listening.

"Has Mama had breakfast yet?"

"Not yet, child. Let 'er sleep. She needs her rest." She glanced at Isabel. "You oughta hop back into bed yourself, Miss Isabel, when you're finished with your breakfast. You ain't exactly mended yet. You don't want to lose all your spizzarinctum."

"My *what*?" said Isabel.

"All your energy," I supplied. *Spizzarinctum* is a Grandma word, and you might as well learn to use it, or at least know it, 'cause she uses it quite a bit. Sometimes she calls energy "your get-up-and-go."

"I'll go back to bed later," Isabel said. "I just can't rest until I know Lily is awake and doing better."

"Well, Lily is awake, and she's doing better," my mama said, coming into the room. She was wearing her thick purple robe.

"Mama!" I yelled.

"Hush that hollering, child! We ain't in the barn," Grandma told me, frowning. "Lily Reilly, what on earth are you doing out of bed and down here in this kitchen?"

"Oh, Mama Grace, don't fuss. Staying in bed has never been my forte, you know."

"Perhaps not, Lily, darling," Isabel said, "but these are exceptional circumstances. You absolutely *must* take care of yourself."

"Yes, Mother, darling," Myra Sue put in. "You *must* take care of yourself."

Mama gave her special smile to each one of us. "I'm taking care of myself," she said. "And right now I need my loved ones around me. Mama Grace, is there any oatmeal left?"

"I'll get you some, honey. And some good hot coffee."

"No coffee," Mama said. "Just a tall glass of nice, cool water."

"Doctor's orders?" Isabel asked.

"Well, he recommended only one cup of coffee a day."

"What else did he say?" Grandma said, giving Mama a bowl of oatmeal.

Mama sighed. "Use moderation and good sense, mostly. Watch the salt, fat, and sugar. Not too much of any of them."

"Mama," I said, "your diet sounds like an Isabel-diet."

Isabel blinked a few times. "I guess it does," she said, and the two women smiled at each other.

Daddy and Ian came in the back door. Grandma had their coffee poured and cups on the table before they had time to blink twice.

"Lily, why are you sitting at this table?" Daddy asked when he spotted Mama.

"Because I got lonely."

"Oh brother," I said. "If you wanted company, all you had to do was holler and I would've come right upstairs. I would've read to you, too."

"Yeah," said Myra Sue, forgetting to be prissy for a moment. "April is pretty good at reading out loud."

I looked at her and grinned. "Thanks!"

"Lily," Daddy said firmly, "you know the doctor wants you to stay off your feet as much as possible. No running around doing chores. Nothing jarring. *No stair climbing*." Daddy looked at Myra and me. "You girls help out as much as you can, you hear?"

We nodded.

"What about that Christmas program?" I asked. "Did the doctor say you could do that?"

"Oh, I didn't even think to mention it to him," Mama said as if it were no big deal. "That's a long ways off yet."

"But you and Pastor Ross have already been talking about it," I said.

We all waited to see what she'd say, and you know what?

"We'll see." That's all she said, even when Daddy gave her a look and said, "Now, Lily, honey . . ."

"I'll be just fine, Mike," she insisted.

"I'm serious, Lily," Daddy said.

"I know you are, honey. Thank you."

Then they smiled all dopey at each other and gave each other goo-goo eyes and kissy lips, at which point I looked at Ian, who was grinning at them from ear to ear.

"Okay, you lovebirds," Ian said. "Here's what we're going to do, and no arguments. Isabel and I will take the upstairs room, and you two can return to your bedroom down here."

Boy, oh boy, I'd never heard good ole Ian speak so strongly about something unless he was fighting with his little missus.

"Isabel has a broken leg," Mama said immediately. "She can't be going up and down stairs, either."

"I'll trade," Grandma said.

She plunked herself down at the table so that we were all sitting around it like an ancient rerun of *The Waltons*.

"You two pack up your clothes and whatnot and move into my house for the time being," Grandma said. "I'll take the room upstairs, and Mike and Lily can have their room back."

That was the best news I had heard in about fifty-two years, except it meant ole Myra Sue would still be sharing my room with me, messing it up and hogging all the space. And I'd still have to listen to her stupid radio.

"Oh, Mama Grace, absolutely not! You aren't moving out of your own house—" Mama said over the noise of everyone talking all at once.

"Lily!" Grandma said loudly, and we all hushed. "I am moving in whether you want me to or not. If Ian and Isabel prefer to stay here and use Myra Sue's room, then I'll just bunk down on the couch. But I am staying *right here*." She jabbed her pointy finger downward very emphatically. "And I'm taking care of you, and that is all she wrote."

"But, Grace," Ian said, "this is a huge sacrifice for you."

"Not a bit of it!" Grandma protested. "When everything else is swept away, love and family and friends are all that matter. Anything you do for that reason can't be a sacrifice."

"Well," Ian said slowly, looking at his little missus. "If you're sure, Grace, and it seems you are, Isabel and I would be happy to stay in your home."

Isabel nodded. "Yes. Absolutely."

I figured I should get out my red pen and circle this date on the calendar because those two St. Jameses agreeing on something hardly ever happened.

"I'll help you pack!" I said with considerable enthusiasm at the idea of them finally moving out.

"No, *I'll* do that," Myra Sue piped up, all gushy with excitement. "And don't you think poor Isabel will need someone to help her get around while Ian's out doing farmwork? I'll move into Grandma's house, too!"

Oh brother! As if Mama would ever let her do that in a million years. But surprises never end.

"I think that's a fine idea," Daddy said. "If Isabel and Ian are agreeable."

I wanted to get up and dance a jig for joy, but I very politely stayed right where I was.

Sometimes I was pretty sure God was sitting on His throne in heaven, grinning from ear to ear.

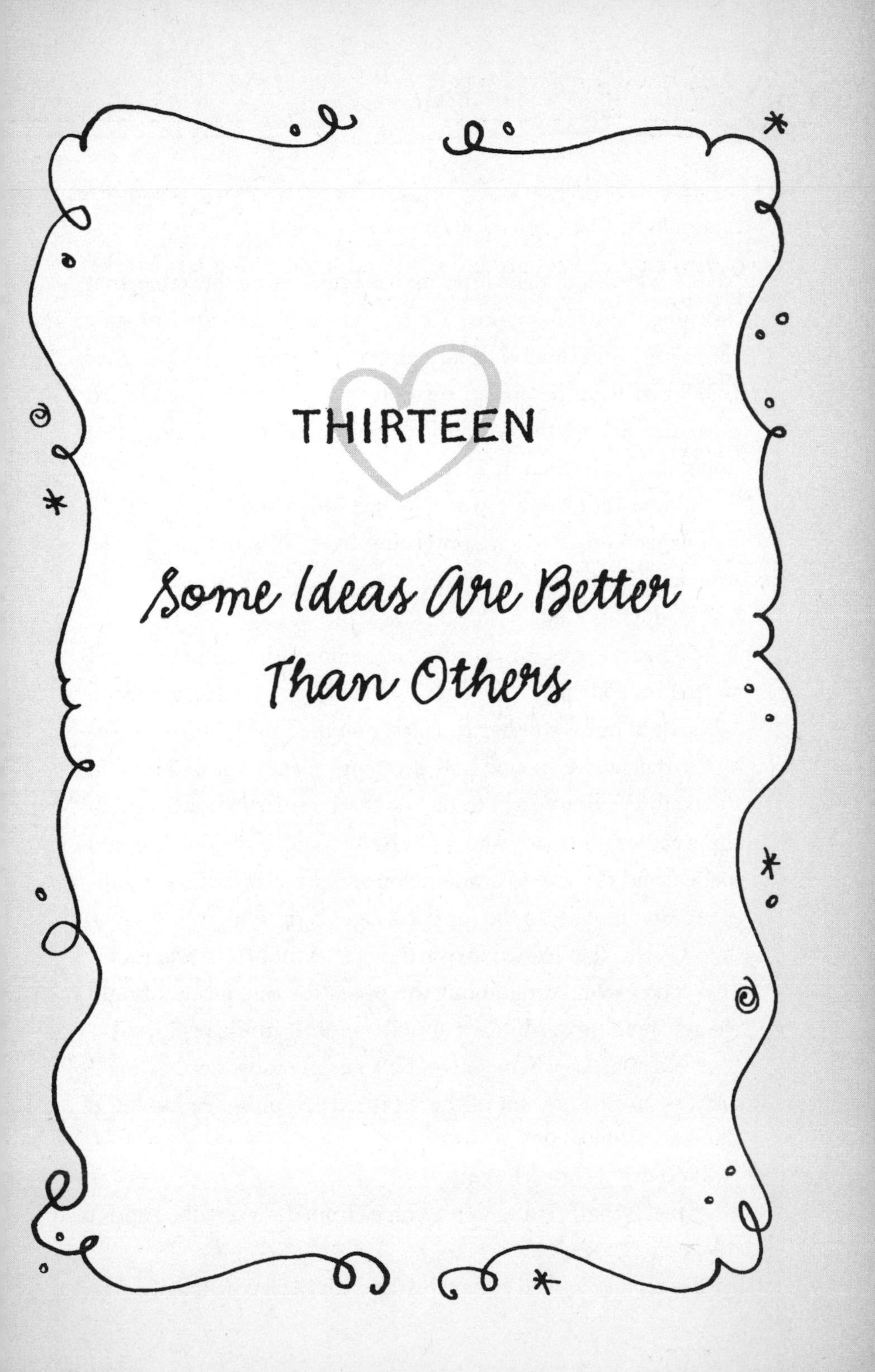

THIRTEEN

Some Ideas Are Better Than Others

♡

"Mike," Ian said a bit later as we lingered at the table that morning, "do you suppose we can move up the time to start renovating our house? The sooner it's finished, the sooner Isabel and I can be on our own and you folks can get back to normal. You have the new little skipper coming, you know; you don't need us in the way."

Mama didn't say a word, which surprised me because I half expected her to say something like, "No, no, please stay with us forever."

Daddy nodded.

"I believe we can do that, Ian," he said. "Before we get started on your place, though, we need to winterize our farm. We should make another run along all the fence lines, double-check that we've mended all the weak places apt to break in the cold. We don't want to be out there repairing fences when the weather gets bad. And we'll need to get firewood cut and hauled, and we have to drain the oil and diesel out of the equipment. Shouldn't take too long if we get right on it."

"Great!" Ian leaned forward, his eyes all bright and eager. "I've been wondering about the goats for our place. Should we get them now, Mike, or should we wait until spring?"

"No matter when you get them," Daddy said, "they'll need a place to stay out of the weather, so you'll need to build them a shelter first."

"*Goats?*" echoed Isabel.

"Yes, Isabel," Ian said, his voice clipped. "We talked about this once before."

Isabel just looked at her mister with her eyes all agog. We

all continued eating quietly, each and every one of us feeling a little awkward.

Finally, Isabel drew in a deep breath, took a sip of water, and abruptly changed the subject like we hadn't just been talking about goats. "I wonder about Lily's health," she said. "Riding on Rough Creek Road in her delicate situation is dangerous to her health and the baby's."

"It's not good for her," Daddy agreed. "She can't go anywhere except to the doctor's office for weekly checkups."

"Not even to church?" I asked.

"Not even to church," Daddy said.

Mama sighed. "It's going to be a long autumn, and an even longer winter."

"I'll try to entertain you, Mama," I offered.

"Doing what?" scoffed ole Myra Sue. "Even if you're a good reader, you aren't very entertaining otherwise. Mother, you can watch the soap operas with Grandma and me."

"Girls," Mama said, interrupting our bickering. "You clean the kitchen while Grandma and I help Ian and Isabel get their things together."

There arose a chorus of protest so loud and unifying that George Washington and all the rest of our founding fathers would have been proud.

"You will go straight back to bed, Lily Reilly." Daddy spoke for all of us. "The doctor said bed rest. A lot of it."

"Oh, Mike," Mama said.

"Isabel and I can pack up our things," Ian said. "Can't we, darling? I'll gather our clothes, you sit on the bed and fold them as best you can, and I'll pack them into our cases."

"Of course," Isabel replied, but her sour smile said she'd

rather let Someone Else do it. Poor ole Ian. He practically had the words *Someone Else* tattooed on his forehead.

"And while the girls are cleaning the kitchen, I will run over to my house and get it spruced up for you." Grandma looked at my sister and me. "When you two are through here, you can pop across the field and help me."

♡

Myra Sue did not pop over to Grandma's with me. She stayed and helped Isabel and Ian, for which I was grateful. If she'd gone to Grandma's house, she would've moaned and whined the whole entire time about being there.

While Grandma and I dusted and swept and moved things around that afternoon, the thought of returning to school the next day to see those smirking Lotties and eat slimy spinach and instant mashed potatoes for lunch and listen to teachers yammer about paying attention and about being eager and responsible made me downright queasy.

As Grandma and I put fresh sheets on the bed, Queenie, that spoiled cat, kept rubbing against my legs even though she knows she gets on my nerves Big-Time since she does *not* like to be petted. If I had tried, I'm sure she'd lay open a vein on my arm with one claw.

"Get away from me, Queenie," I said in the nicest voice you can imagine when you're talking to a cat who drives you right up the wall.

Grandma shooed her out of the room while we kept working.

I had come up with what I thought was a grand idea to solve all my problems.

"Grandma?"

"Woo?" She was slicking her hands over the top blanket to get all the tiny little wrinkles out. I guess she thought ole Isabel was a princess who feels tiny little wrinkles in the blankets. Maybe she was.

"Would you please homeschool me?"

She stopped smoothing to gawk at me like I'd just announced I was going to grow a beard.

"Homeschool you? What kind of notion is that?"

"'Cause I know there are kids around here who have never, in their whole lives, set foot inside that Cedar Ridge Junior High School. They get taught at home."

She straightened up and rested her hands on her hips. "What on earth are you talking about?"

"Well, for one thing, I'd like to spend more time with you before everybody gets all busy with that baby." Other than being the endangered passenger in her car while she drove to Cedar Ridge, I loved being with Grandma. Once that baby got here, though, I'd probably never see her again.

"So what d'ya say?" I prodded. "Will you?"

"Teach you at home?"

I nodded eagerly.

"No."

I felt my face fall, and my heart went right down with it.

"For one thing," Grandma said, "I only have a high school diploma, and for another thing, I forgot most of the things I learned in school, and for another, there's been so much new that's happened over the years that I couldn't possibly teach it to you nor nobody else."

"But, Grandma, you tell me all kinds of nifty junk, like for instance about nature and the plants and wildflowers and animals when we go on our walks."

She narrowed her eyes at me. "You hate school that much this year?" she asked.

Boy, oh boy. I wonder if someday, when I'm a grandma, I'll be able to read minds, too.

"Hmm?" she persisted.

"Kinda." I refused to meet her eyes.

"Your principal called yesterday before your mama got sick, if that's what this is all about. I was the one who talked to her."

I felt my eyes get big. "I ain't never been sent to the principal's office in my life," I whispered, and I didn't care about grammar right then.

"Well, I know that. And I talked with that lady quite a spell. She's a real nice woman. You kids are lucky to have her."

My eyes bugged out more.

"Mrs. Patsy Farber? *The* Mrs. Patsy Farber?"

"Well, I'll swan, April Grace," she said, frowning at me. "Why are you acting that way?"

"'Cause, Grandma. She's scarier than a two-edged sword. If you were in sixth grade, you'd feel the same way."

"Well, mebbe so. But I told her about your mama, and how things were kinda in upheaval around here, and she was real nice and understanding. She said she saw no reason to upset your mama and daddy, and if you take your books from now on, pay attention in class, and be sure to do all your homework, she'd just forget the whole thing."

"She said *that*?"

"Yep."

Well, what do you know? Ole Mrs. Patsy Farber might be human after all.

FOURTEEN

One's Own Personal Space

❀

Grandma and I stowed all her stuff into her car. Right before we left, Grandma stood in the middle of her kitchen and gazed at Queenie, who lounged on the dining table in the kitchen like she was prime rib on a china platter. Boy, oh boy. If Myra Sue ever got a load of that, she'd keel over from the mere thought of cat germs.

I wondered what Isabel would think about Queenie in the same house with her, especially as ole Isabel was afraid of everything with more than two legs. It was gonna be a test of wills. But I knew one thing: if Queenie bit Isabel, the cat would probably be the one that got sick.

"Maybe we oughta take 'er with us," Grandma murmured.

"*Queenie?*" I said, trying hard not to choke. The cat opened one eye and glared at me. I thought fast. "Grandma, I read somewhere that cats don't like to move. They don't do well with change."

She nodded and chewed thoughtfully on her lower lip while she eyed ole Queenie, who lay there twitching the end of her tail and glaring at us. That cat did not blink one time.

"That's true," she said. "Queenie doesn't even like it when I move the furniture to sweep."

I pressed my advantage. "Well, there you go, then. What if Queenie got all scared and creeped out by being in a new place, and she ran off?"

"Oh my!" Grandma pressed her hand to her mouth. "We wouldn't want that! No, we'll just leave Queenie right here, safe and sound in her home. She'll be good company for

Isabel when Ian is working and Myra Susie's at school." She reached out to tickle Queenie under the chin. "But Mommy's gonna miss her widdle puddy tat, won't she, baby?"

Queenie laid her ears back the way she does when she's fixing to either bite you or swat you, so Grandma dropped her hand.

I didn't say a word. I just heaved a sigh of relief that the crazy feline would not be living in our house.

We drove down the short stretch of Rough Creek Road between Grandma's driveway and ours. When we got to our house, Ian was putting suitcases in the bed of the old pickup truck. He helped Grandma and me tote her things into the house.

"Temple showed up with some teas and such for Lily," he said. "I put everything on the kitchen counter."

Ick. Nothing was much worse than Temple's "teas and such" that you had to drink or eat. For her teas, she boils things like leaves and roots and flowers, and she probably throws tree bark and creek mud and spiderwebs in there, too.

We had supper together, us Reillys and the St. Jameses, just like usual. By then, all that moving and shifting-people-around business was done. Daddy and Mama had their old room back, Grandma was settled upstairs in Myra Sue's room, and the St. Jameses had moved their belongings into Grandma's house. Best of all, starting that very evening, ole Myra Sue would be out of the house until Isabel was able to take care of everything herself.

Boy, oh boy, if returning to school had not loomed like a rolling black thundercloud right smack above my head, I would be happier than you can imagine to have my grandma in the house and my sister out of it. Of course, there was the ever-present promise of that baby eventually coming along to make a mess of things.

"In all this hubbub, I plumb forgot to go to town today," Grandma said while we ate supper. "I think this is the first Tuesday I've missed going into town since I moved to Rough Creek Road. Not that I coulda found the time, anyway, even if I hadn't forgot."

"Wow, Grandma," I said, agog at such an idea. I gotta say, I was glad she had not thought of it or found the time to go, 'cause more than likely I would've been the one to ride shotgun while she drove like a madwoman to town and back.

Isabel looked at Myra.

"Do you have your things unpacked over at Grandma's, darling?"

"Yes!" my sister answered, glowing like a Christmas candle. "Two suitcases stuffed full."

"You won't need that much," Mama told her. "You aren't staying with Ian and Isabel very long. Just until Isabel is on her feet."

Myra Sue looked utterly pained, as if she had planned to move in, bag and baggage, forever until she died. As much as I liked that idea my own personal self, I don't think Mama or Daddy would've been too pleased about it.

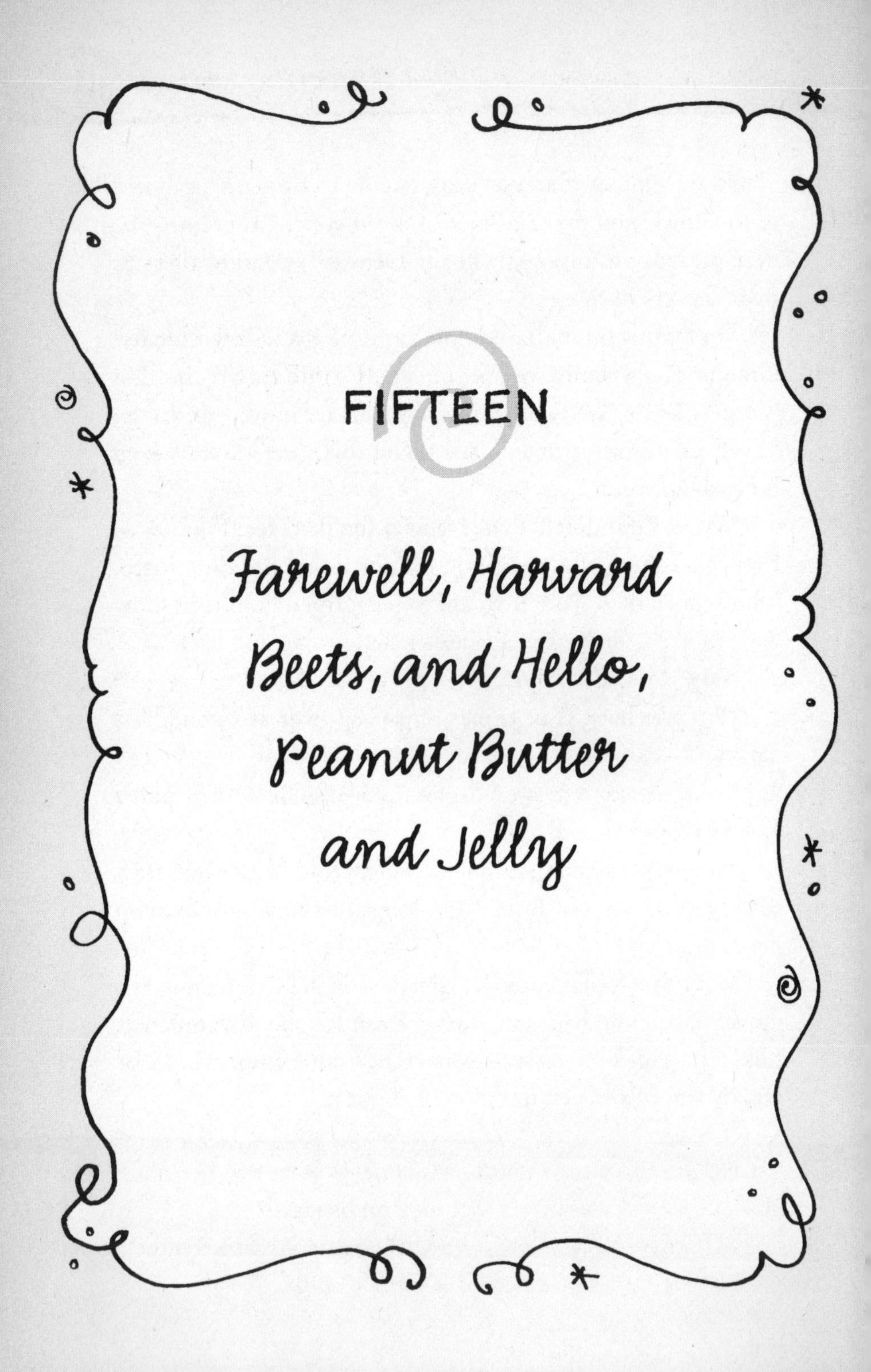

FIFTEEN

Farewell, Harvard Beets, and Hello, Peanut Butter and Jelly

The very next afternoon, when the school bus stopped at our driveway, Myra Sue refused to get off.

She called up to the driver, "I am in residence at the house next door. You may drop me off there, *s'il vous plait*."

La-de-da. As if she were a French lady living with the queen, or maybe with Ronald and Nancy Reagan in the White House.

When I got off the bus, I pulled the mail from the mailbox and hugged Daisy, who had ambled down the driveway to meet me. She wagged her fluffy white tail the whole time we walked to the house.

An unfamiliar dark blue car sat in our driveway near the front porch. I eyeballed it as I crossed the front yard. That car was a Buick LeSabre, and it looked pretty new. It sort of reminded me of Ian and Isabel's shiny black car they drove when they first moved here. They sold that car pretty quick so they'd have some money to fix up that old house they bought. I surely hoped that Buick had not come bearing a fresh shipment of snooty new neighbors since we had just gotten rid of the first batch.

I shot up the front steps and yanked open the screen door.

Grandma came out of the kitchen, smoothing and fluffing her short hair.

"Hi, Grandma. How's Mama? And whose car is that?"

Her cheeks were all pink, and her eyes were bright. What had she been doing to put that look on her face?

"That's Rob's car. He's in the kitchen having a little coffee."

I twisted my mouth but politely said nothing.

"Your mama's doing fine," Grandma continued. "Go see her; then come to the kitchen and get you a snack." She looked past me and out the door. "Where's your sister?"

I put my books down on the dining room table and made a face.

"She thinks Isabel needs her more than Mama."

Grandma didn't say anything for a minute, and when she did, all she said was, "Well."

I trotted down the hall to Mama and Daddy's room. The door was open, and the radio was on, playing that old music from the 1970s that Daddy and Mama like so well. Mama was sitting in the bed, propped against a mound of pillows. Her curly hair, pulled back in a clasp behind her head, was coppery and pretty against the white pillowcases, and her eyes were the color of the soft moss that grows in the woods. She looked beautiful, even with a little round tummy pooching against the covers.

I tell you, it was nice to have that room back to normal after all those weeks of the St. Jameses living in it. Not that they messed it up, but I liked seeing a pair of Daddy's shoes next to the closet door and Mama's things on the dresser instead of Isabel's tons of makeup bottles and fingernail polish.

Mama was frowning slightly as she read a thin book in her hand.

I knocked softly on the door frame.

"Mama?"

She looked up, her face losing the look of concentration.

"April Grace, honey!" She held out both arms, and I ran to her. "I thought I heard you a minute ago, but then I wasn't sure." She hugged me, then said, "Where's Myra Sue?"

There was *no way* I would ever tell my mama that my sister wanted to play nursemaid to ole Isabel St. James instead of coming to see her, so I said, "She'll probably be here. Mama, how do you feel?"

"Oh, I'm fine. And the baby has been moving a lot today. You want to feel?"

No, I did *not* want to feel! I eyeballed her round tummy and moved back a little. "That's okay," I said. "I might—oh, I don't know—wake it up or something."

She laughed. "You won't wake him."

Him? I hoped to goodness that baby was not a *him*.

"How do you know it's a him?" I asked suspiciously.

She laughed again. "I don't know." She laid her hands on her stomach. "It might be a girl."

What would we do with a little "him" running around, doing rotten little boy things like pulling Daisy's tail or spitting on the floor? I'm not a priss like my sister, but I'll tell you one thing: boys have no couth.

"Do you want a boy instead of a girl?"

It seemed logical that she did since she had already called it a "him." After all, she had two girls, and maybe she was sick to death of so many females underfoot.

"I want whatever God gives us," she assured me, squeezing my hand.

But I still had a feeling she'd rather have a boy.

"What's that?" I asked, pointing to the book she'd been studying so intently.

She handed it to me, and I saw the title was *Three Angels for Bethlehem*.

"It's our Christmas play. I haven't had much of a chance to read it, and Pastor Ross wants to discuss it."

I thumbed through that book. It was thirty-five pages long, with two acts, two changes of scene, and lots of dialogue spoken by several characters. I could tell right away this was no simple program with someone reading the second chapter of Luke and little kids singing carols before and after.

"Mama!" I said, trying to sound like a stern grown-up. "You absolutely cannot direct the church pageant this year, especially this play. It's too much!"

She took the script from my hand and looked at it. "There's a lot to it," she admitted.

I huffed. "You will have to tell him that you cannot—"

She patted my hand. "This is nothing you need to worry about, honey. There is plenty of time, and I'll figure out something. Just put it out of your mind. Okay?"

Well, what would you say if it were you? I could tell she would refuse to discuss this topic, even if I set it to music and danced a jig. She was right about having plenty of time—it was mid-September, after all. But I hoped and prayed she started feeling better soon. I sighed deeply.

"Okay."

Mama smiled. "Good! Now. Tell me about school. Did you have a good day?"

I shrugged. "Better than Monday, anyway."

"Oh? Did you have a bad day at school on Monday?"

I could've kicked myself, spilling the ugly beans that way. Wouldn't you agree that my mama had enough to worry about, what with that baby making her sick and her having to stay in the bed most of the time and the preacher expecting her to be a regular Broadway director? I surely did not want to worry her about rotten ole junior high and all that junk. Grandma knew about all that mess, and that was enough.

I thought fast, and luckily my brain works under pressure, unlike some people in our family with the initials of Myra Sue Reilly.

"School would be a whole lot better if I could take my own personal lunch!" I declared. "I'm pretty sure they just open up cans of Alpo and dump it on our plates."

She laughed. "Oh, April Grace. You're just used to my cooking."

"Listen. That food at the Cedar Ridge Junior High ought to be reported to the Department of Health."

She laughed harder. "Now you sound like Isabel."

My mouth dropped open. "Mama! What an awful thing to say!"

Mama may have had a point, but one thing you can take to the bank: I wasn't going to call the White House and demand catered gourmet lunches like Isabel would probably do in my situation.

"Well," I said, "I reckon PB and Js would be fine as lunch for the rest of my life while I'm in junior high, if you don't mind me taking my own."

"I don't see a problem with that, honey, but you may have to put it together yourself from time to time. Just be sure you have something in there besides cookies or pie."

I felt so good I nearly split my face a-grinnin'.

SIXTEEN

When Rivals Arrive

☆

When I walked into the kitchen to pick out what I'd pack for lunch tomorrow, I found ole Rob Estes sitting at the table with a large pile of Russell Stover candy on the table in front of him.

I'd never seen him at our house, let alone at the kitchen table, let alone at the kitchen table *with a pile of chocolate candy*. Rob is a retired pharmacist, but he still owns the drugstore, and the Estes Drugstore has carried good ole Russell Stover chocolates for as long as I can remember.

Forget about Rob Estes for just a minute because here is something you should know. My grandmother and I love chocolates more than any food God ever created. And Russell Stover is Grandma's all-time favorite. And the Russell Stover chocolates Rob brought over weren't just *any old* chocolates. They were Mint Dreams. And Mint Dreams are the best kind of Russell Stover chocolates. I love Mint Dreams almost as much as Kraft Caramels.

"Wow!" I said, ogling all that deliciousness and temporarily dismissing the fact that Rob Estes was another of Grandma's boyfriends and therefore on my list of Suspicious Persons until I decided otherwise. "Is *that* my after-school snack?"

"Sure," Rob said, smiling and shoving about two pounds of chocolate my way. He shot a look at Grandma. "If Grace says it's okay."

Rob was younger than Grandma by about ten years, but I'm not supposed to know that, so don't tell anyone I told you.

I put on my best "please, please, please" face, but Grandma twisted her mouth as she thought about it, and I knew that wasn't a good sign. Otherwise, she would've said, "Why, sure, have some."

"With supper in an hour and a half," she said, "I think an apple and a glass of milk is a better idea."

"Oh, Grandma," I said, bitterly disappointed. "I love Mint Dreams, and there is a whole mound of 'em right there, all wrapped in their shiny silver-and-green wrappers. Maybe I could have a couple of Mint Dreams out of that whole entire box *full* of Mint Dreams."

"After supper, for dessert, instead of cake."

"*Grandma!*" Boy, oh boy, I didn't know Myra Grace Reilly could be so hard-hearted.

"Maybe I shouldn't have taken the candy out of the bag," Rob Estes said, his face all droopy.

"Oh no!" I assured him, sitting down and staring at that wonderful hill of chocolate. "I like to look at it anyway." I sighed.

Grandma took an apple out of the refrigerator, and while she was washing it at the sink, Rob leaned toward me and whispered, "How about if I give you an entire box of Mint Dreams for Christmas?"

I felt my eyes widen.

"*Thank you!*" I breathed. He was fast getting himself off my list of Suspicious Persons and onto my list of Approved Gentlemen Callers, which so far had only one name on it, and that was Ernie Beason.

"Don't spoil her, Rob," Grandma said, giving me the apple.

"I'm not spoiling anyone," Rob told her stoutly. "But if I have a large stock in the drugstore, I might as well share them with special girls who have shiny red hair."

I liked him better and better. He was genuinely nice, not fakey nice like that rotten old man Rance, who tried to win me over one time with a Kraft Caramel he had pulled, warm and squooshy, from his jeans pocket.

Grandma set a glass of milk in front of me. You'd think with all that candy staring us in the face and me not having any of it, she would have at least put in some chocolate syrup for comfort's sake. But she didn't.

"How's your cold?" I asked Rob.

"All gone now," he said.

"Yeah, so's Grandma's." I looked over the rim of my milk glass at Grandma's blushing face. If I thought being sassy was gonna get me a Mint Dream or even chocolate milk, I thought wrong.

Out in the front yard, good ole Daisy barked. She hardly ever barks unless a strange car drives up the driveway, and sometimes not even then. She's old, so she sleeps a lot and misses things going on.

With all the windows open on that warm September afternoon, voices outside came right into the house. The voice I heard right then sounded mighty familiar.

I knew Grandma heard it, too, because her face went red as fire, and she looked downright caught.

Who do you think was out there? Ernie Beason, that's who. Grandma's other—and, so far, her *only* April Grace–approved—boyfriend, even if Rob brought chocolates.

Well, this oughta be good, I thought as I heard him knock on the front door. I got up to go let him in.

"Here," Grandma said, shoving *two* Mint Dreams at me. "Eat these. *I'll* get the door."

She hurried to the front door, but Rob stayed right where he was, blissfully ignorant that his rival was only a few yards away. Didn't he hear Ernie's voice telling Daisy she was a good girl? I reckon not. I sure hoped he wasn't hard of hearing like old man Rance. I don't think I could have put up with hollering in another man's hairy old ear holes ever again, for as long as I live.

Not one to waste the opportunity before Grandma realized what she'd done, I ripped the shiny wrapper off of a Mint Dream and bit into it. That thick milk chocolate cracked softly between my teeth and released its fluffy, gooey, creamy mint filling. Both tastes melted together on my tongue and slid sweet and smooth down my gullet in the best way you can imagine.

"Yummm," I said, closing my eyes for a moment so I could taste it and feel it for as long as possible. I licked a bit off my upper lip and took another bite.

"Like it, do you?" Rob said. I could hear the smile in his voice.

"Yup," I said as best I could with a mouthful of dreamy candy.

Footsteps came toward the kitchen.

I popped open my eyelids and hid the rest of that Mint Dream and the other one in my lap. There came Grandma with the most peculiar and guilty look on her face, and right behind her followed good ole Ernie with his arms full of groceries. He was smiling real big and talking as he came down the hallway.

". . . and since you didn't come into the store, I figured you'd be wanting your usual order. I added a few things I thought you'd like—" He broke off as he came into the kitchen and caught an eyeful of Rob and his big ole pile of Russell Stover candy.

"Well now," he said, stopping all of a sudden. "Well now."

Those two men just looked at each other for the longest time while Grandma stood there with a frozen smile on her face. The steady *tick-tick* of the yellow clock on the wall sounded real loud.

You see, I'm pretty sure each man had a suspicion he was not the only feller in Grace Reilly's life but probably had never let himself think about it to the point he'd admit such a thing out loud.

Now, I don't hardly see how this could be, because both men live in Cedar Ridge, and Cedar Ridge is a small town, and Rough Creek Road is a small community, and only a few miles separate the two. Everybody knows everything about everybody else in both places. This whole bit with those men coming face-to-face with my grandma caught right in the middle was bound to happen sooner or later.

I wonder if either one of 'em knew she'd been getting quite a few phone calls lately from Reverend Jordan, the Methodist minister.

"Well now," Ernie said one more time. Then he put those four paper sacks full of groceries on the countertop and said, "How do, Rob? You been keepin' well?"

Rob looked steadily into Ernie's eyes, and it was like those two guys tried to read each other's minds.

"I'm doing fine, Ernie. How about you?"

Ernie nodded. "Same."

They just kept staring at each other, and in the background Grandma watched, flashing her gaze from one to the other and back again. I couldn't tell if they were gonna start swinging punches, or if they were gonna sit down and have some coffee and candy.

Finally Grandma moved toward those groceries, laughing kinda loud and crazy. "Well now, Ernie, this was real thoughtful. Look here, Rob, what Ernie did. I couldn't make it to town yesterday, so he brought all these groceries out to me. And lookie there, Ernie. Rob brought us all some chocolate. Get you some, Ernie. Want some coffee? Rob, you want some more coffee?" Grandma was talking a hundred miles an hour and pulling groceries out of the bags like there was no tomorrow.

"No, thanks. I need to be getting home," Rob said, standing up at the same time Ernie moved toward the doorway, saying, "Thank you, no. I have to get back to the store."

"Well, you don't have to hurry away," Grandma said to no one in particular. She started stuffing that food into the cabinets without any rhyme or reason. She even put a dozen eggs where the plates go, for Pete's sake!

Boy, oh boy, right there was a big fat reason never to have a boyfriend, let alone two of them. They just mess up everything.

"You think they're gonna slug each other?" I asked Grandma as soon as those men left.

She sent me right out of the room, so I hightailed it into Mama's bedroom to tell her what was going on.

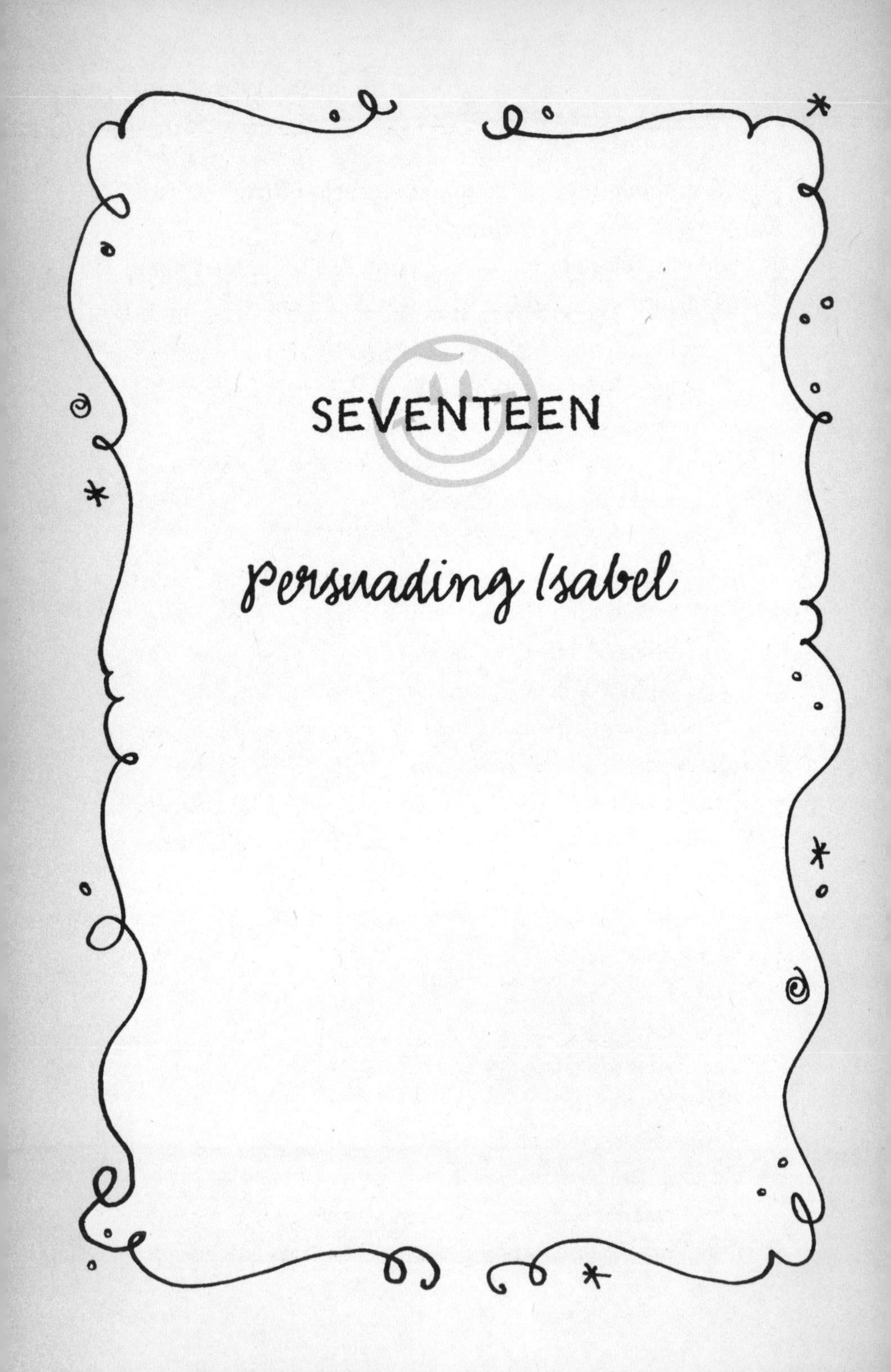

SEVENTEEN

Persuading Isabel

☺

Mama laughed till she cried when I told her about Grandma's love triangle a few minutes later. Right then, Grandma was still at the living room window, watching those two men leave.

I handed Mama my other Mint Dream and sat on the edge of the bed while she unwrapped it.

"Mama," I said in an undertone, "what about Reverend Jordan from the Methodist church?"

"What about him, April?" she asked, still giggling.

I sighed. "You know he's been calling her. And I don't think he's inviting her to church twenty times a week, either. All I know is that, after last summer and all that mess with that ole goofball Jeffrey Rance, the last thing my grandma needs is three boyfriends." I held up my hand and extended my fingers one at a time as I counted. "One. Two. Three."

Mama shook her head and bit into that candy. She chewed it all slow and dreamy-like, then she said, "Honey, I think you're worrying needlessly."

I changed the subject before it got sticky and I'd say something I shouldn't.

"Mama?"

"Yes, honey?"

"Are you getting enough rest?" I asked her.

"More than plenty."

"You want me to read to you?"

"I'd like that, April Grace."

"I read part of *Head into the Wind* to Myra Sue the other day."

"Oh?" said Mama, smiling wide. "That was my favorite

book when I was about your age. I read it more times than I can count. Go get it, and let's read it to each other."

So that's what we did until Grandma came to the door with Mama's supper on a tray.

"Supper's on the table, April Grace," Grandma told me.

Mama glared at that tray for a minute.

"No!" she said unexpectedly and pretty loudly. "I am *not* eating supper in this bed again tonight. I'll sit at the table like a civilized person."

Boy, oh boy, Mama doesn't often get all fired up, but she did right then.

"Now, Lily, you know—" Grandma began, but Mama shook her head.

"Mama Grace, I've been in the bed almost *all day* for two days. It won't hurt me to sit at the supper table."

"The doctor said—" Grandma said.

"The doctor said a *lot* of bed rest," Mama said, raising her voice slightly, "not *complete* bed rest."

"But still . . ."

"Now, *Mama*," I said. I crossed my arms, hoping I looked and sounded as stern as Mrs. Patsy Farber.

"Get off the bed, honey. We'll read more later. I'm going to enjoy Grandma's good supper with friends and family tonight and every night until the doctor tells me to do otherwise."

☺

With the St. Jameses living in Grandma's house, it was good not hearing so much of Isabel's fussing and complaints. School was bad enough, what with the homework and the Lotties and the smell of that rotten ole hallway, but at least home was more peaceful.

Two bright spots outshone everything else. Number one: Mama and I spent quite a bit of time sitting on her bed, reading aloud to each other, and number two: Myra Sue was still at the St. Jameses'.

Every single day, Grandma went over there to check on them and take them food for breakfast and lunch, and to spend time with Queenie. Every single day, I half expected her to come back to our house with that silly cat because I just couldn't understand how Isabel, Myra Sue, and Queenie could live together—which is funny when you think about it, because the three of them were so much alike in so many ways.

Every morning after the chores were done, Daddy and Ian went over to the St. Jameses' house and worked on it while Mr. Brett made sure everything on the farm was still going smoothly. Most every day, some of the men from the church came to help. Every afternoon, those two men came home all dusty and dirty and tired, but grinning like monkeys.

"We finally got the last of the drywall put up today," Daddy would say. Or Ian would tell us, "I hope I never see another tub of spackle."

All in all, it seemed to me like fixing that old house was going pretty well.

On Saturday, the first weekend in October, the preacher called Mama on the telephone while I was dusting her room. I listened to every single word she said, and it was plain as day they were discussing that Christmas program.

Mama apologized for being unable to follow through, and she and Pastor Ross talked for longer than you can imagine about how they could possibly salvage the program that year.

Well, I'm not called April Grace Reilly the Queen of Brilliant Ideas for nothing. Something began to flicker in my brain, and by the time Mama hung up the telephone, I had cooked up the best idea I'd had in a long time.

With her hand still on the telephone receiver, Mama stared down at it with worry on her face. One of the things the doctor said she was *not* supposed to do was worry.

"Don't fret about that Christmas play, Mama."

She looked up as though surprised I was in the room.

I gave her a big hug and a whopping huge kiss, smack-dab on the cheek.

"Leave it to me." I dashed to the door, paused, and looked over my shoulder. "I'm gonna go see how Isabel is doing today. See ya later!"

And I took off faster than you can blink, happy as a bear with a honey pot.

I got a little chilly running across the hayfield to Grandma's place. The days were usually mild in October, but you could feel a change in the air. The sky was bluer than any blue you can imagine. Beneath my feet, the field grass had begun to tuck itself back into the earth. In a couple of months, the ground would be firm and brown and cold to the touch, but in spring, it would be soft and tender again with new grass.

I could smell the scent of the pine trees that grew near Grandma's house, and I slowed my steps to a walk just so I could suck in that beautiful fragrance. Boy, oh boy, I've said it before and I'll say it again: there is nothing as good as living in the country.

I shivered a little as I stepped into the shade of the big old oak tree in Grandma's front yard and wished I'd grabbed my denim jacket.

"Hey, Isabel!" I hollered as I bounded up the porch steps and opened the door.

She was lying on the sofa, and Myra Sue was sitting cross-legged on the floor, facing the television. Isabel's crutches were leaning against the wall near them. She wasn't gonna need those things much longer, but I think she'll probably have to use a cane for a week or two. I hope she doesn't gripe about it.

"April Grace Reilly, don't you know enough to knock before you come bursting into someone's home?" Myra Sue said, as snippy and uppity as you can possibly imagine.

To prove there are some things I have learned in algebra, I gave her back a look that was equal to, or greater than, the one she gave me.

"When Ian and Isabel move into their very own home, I will knock on their door when I go for a visit. But I have never, in my whole entire life, knocked on my grandma's door, and I don't intend to start now, Miss Smarty-Pants Myra Sue."

I crossed my eyes then, dismissing my sister.

"Hey, Isabel!" I said again. "I have a great—"

My words dried up on my tongue because I saw something like I have never seen in my whole entire life. You know what it was? I'll tell you. Queenie lay all stretched out and comfy on Isabel's scrawny chest while Isabel stroked that dumb cat's fur like she thought it was a mink coat. Grandma's cat doesn't even like *Grandma* to pet her, for crying out loud! And Grandma has been trying for *years*.

I do here and now declare that if the TV had been turned off, I would have heard Queenie purr, which is something I have not heard before except once when she had caught a poor ole robin. That Queenie is not the sweet widdle puddy tat Grandma says she is.

"How in the world . . . how did you . . . ? Isabel, I have never seen Queenie do that!"

Isabel looked at that cat and got a dumb smile on her face. "She's a dear little kitty."

Oh, good grief.

"But how'd you get her to like you? She doesn't like *anyone*!"

Isabel sniffed. "She hissed at me, and I hissed back," she said with a little flip of her hand.

That was the craziest thing I'd ever heard.

But I put that thought out of my mind when I remembered what I'd come over for. Now, here's what I think. I think ole Isabel would probably feel a lot better if she didn't have so much sympathy and hand-patting and catering-to. She's the type of person who needs something she can sink her teeth into, something she can get all carried away with, even though she was a big fat pain when she did it. And I knew just the thing for her.

"I have one of the best ideas you've ever heard of."

The look she gave me was only mildly interested. "You

always have ideas, child," she said with a small smile. "What is it this time?"

"You must come to supper tonight. It's going to be a Special Occasion. This idea concerns *you*."

One eyebrow went up. "Oh?" she said. "I was thinking I would just stay here this evening."

"Please?" I asked, putting on my best face.

She regarded me solemnly, then said, "All right, since it seems to mean so much to you."

"Good!" I clapped my hands.

"But your idea better be a good one."

"Oh, it is!" I said to Isabel. "See you at supper."

I hightailed it back across the field. I told Grandma, and only Grandma, about my plan and asked if she could make an extra-special supper for Isabel, which she did with a lot of help from yours very truly.

For supper we had baked salmon with herbs, spinach salad, a fresh fruit salad, steamed green beans with almonds, and rice pilaf. Now, I'll be the first to say I'd rather have fried catfish and hush puppies, but in the interest of having certain kinds of meals for Mama's sake, and because Isabel likes a healthier kind of diet, I dove in with as much gusto as I could muster for something that did not crunch when I bit into it.

After supper, Isabel looked at me. "All right, April Grace," she said. "What's this idea of yours?"

All the grown-ups and ole Myra Sue looked at me in curiosity.

I sat up straight and put on the most adult expression I

could. "Isabel, how would you like a project where you can use your stage experience?"

A flicker of interest shot across her face, but she masked it with caution the way adults do when kids have interesting ideas. "What *kind* of project, pray tell?" Isabel asked.

"Yes," Myra Sue put in, "pray tell what?"

"Well, the thing is, our church always puts on a play every Christmas."

She blinked at me a couple of times.

"Mama has always been responsible for it," I went on.

Isabel glanced at Mama, then back at me. She lifted one eyebrow, so I continued.

"Well, this year she can't. She isn't supposed to do anything that is stressful, you know."

"Yes, I know. You are taking care of yourself, aren't you, Lily?"

"Of course," Mama said, smiling. "I'm going to have a happy, healthy baby, even if I have to sit around and do nothing but get plumper and plumper."

"Well, this year," I said, "Pastor Ross has chosen this big play, with scenes and costumes and actors from the youth group and everything."

Aha! At last I saw real interest flare in her eyes.

"I saw that script for that play, and believe me, it will be a lot of work. And Mama can't do it, not this year," I added.

"However," Grandma said, looking right in Isabel's brown eyes, "someone with *your* talent and experience can handle it. In fact," she added, leaning forward, "I'm sure you are the *only* person in this area who can do the job right."

Isabel looked at me, then at Grandma, and then she drew in a deep, deep breath.

"My dears," she said, all serious and dramatic as you can imagine, "I am completely flattered that you feel I should do this, but truly, directing a church play is, well, it's not something I believe I can do."

Now, that surprised me. I thought ole Isabel would have jumped up and danced around on her one good leg at the mere thought of producing a play.

"Sure you can!" Daddy said.

"Of course you can, lamb," Ian said with an encouraging smile.

She glanced at the men and shook her head.

"Why not?" I demanded.

Her mouth dropped open as if she thought I was nuts. "Because, my dear child, I have been seriously injured."

"You can't be serious!" I hollered before I could stop myself. This was no way to win her over.

Isabel blinked three dozen times.

"I'm sorry, Isabel. That's not what I mean. Yes, you've been injured, and we're all real glad you're getting better every single day. You've done such a good job of healing that you're gonna get your cast off next week, and all you'll need is that cane instead of those ole crutches! And pretty soon you won't need that, either."

She sniffed. "Well. You do have a point, I suppose. But kindly remember, I am not a church person."

"You don't have to be a church person to help out," Daddy told her.

"That's right, Isabel," Mama said.

"But I know *nothing* about church people."

"Church people are like everyone else," Grandma said.

Isabel shmooshed up her lips, but at least she did not blink, and that was a good sign.

"What if they don't like me and they refuse to listen to a thing I say? I've noticed you Ozarkers tend to go your own way, even when someone who knows more tells you you're doing it wrong."

I sighed and all but rolled my eyes. That attitude right there was exactly why no one around here wants to listen to newcomers. But we weren't there to debate Isabel's misguided logic. If there was one thing I had learned about ole Isabel, it was this: if you want to get through to her, you have better luck when you appeal to her vanity, of which she has plenty, believe me. I'm pretty sure Grandma knew this.

"Isabel, you're an expert in drama and dance," she said. "You got the experience. Folks'll listen to you. And they'll take real kindly to you helping Lily, because they all love Lily Reilly."

Isabel's eyes took on a new, thoughtful expression, a flicker of hope and interest. I could almost see the gears finally starting to turn in her brain.

And I topped off the whole shebang by adding, "If you really want to pay Mama back for all that she has done for you, this is your chance. One good turn deserves another. That's my motto. And, Isabel, you've had a lot of good turns."

At this point, along with Grandma's help, my job was done, and I was happy to let the adults take over. Besides, a goodly portion of my supper was still on my plate, and I was hungry.

By the time we'd finished our orange sherbet, Isabel had almost agreed to my idea. But wouldn't you know, she just had to be an Isabel St. James about it and throw a monkey wrench into the whole thing.

"April Grace," she said in that precise voice she has, "I will agree to direct the play on one condition."

I eyeballed her suspiciously, not liking this bit at all. What if she wanted to—oh, I don't know—have me move into their house when it was ready as a live-in maid and cook, or something like that?

"What's your condition?" I shot pleading looks at Mama and Daddy, but they just sat there, curious and waiting.

"You and dearest Myra must be my assistants through the entire process."

"Are you kiddin'?" I hollered at the same time ole Myra Sue gushed, "Oh, that would be dee-vine!"

Help Isabel with the Christmas program, when I knew she'd be all bossy and dramatic and with Myra Sue right there, cheering her on? Right about then I almost wished I had no imagination and no way of cooking up good ideas.

EIGHTEEN

The Preacher Comes to Our House

❀

The next afternoon, Pastor Ross came to our house. He was in a pair of jeans and a plain white T-shirt and denim jacket.

Mama had put on a brand-new maternity outfit of dark green with a pattern of lavender violets on the collar. Grandma had bought it for her, and it looked real pretty. She and Daddy greeted Pastor Ross at the door, invited him to sit down, and then Mama sat in the recliner and put her feet up. Daddy settled on the sofa while Pastor Ross took Grandma's rocking chair, which was a little too short and small and girlie for him, but he didn't seem to notice. Grandma wasn't there to help because she was out for a drive with Rob Estes, looking at the fall colors. Boy howdy, if she wasn't with one boyfriend, she was with another.

"Would you like some sweet tea, Pastor?" I asked.

"That would be real nice, April Grace. Thank you."

As I fetched his drink, I could hear him and Mama talking. They talked about how she was feeling, how much she was missed at church, and how much she missed being there. When I returned, they were discussing the weather.

"I hope we have a mild winter again this year," he said, taking the glass from me. "Thank you, April Grace." He took a sip, then said, "Now, Lily, when you called last evening, you said you wanted to talk to me about Isabel St. James directing the church play. Would you give me some details about that?"

I didn't know Mama had called him last night, but that did not diminish my interest in this conversation, not one little bitty bit.

So Mama explained Isabel's background and experience and concluded with, "They've hired her to teach at the school, and I think she'll be a real asset to the Cedar Ridge school system."

"That's fine, that's fine." He nodded and sipped, and I thought he looked a little nervous.

"Mike. Lily," he said, clearing his throat. He glanced at me. "This is a rather . . . delicate subject, isn't it?"

"Delicate?" I echoed. "I bet you think ole Isabel might be a great big pain in the patootie, don't you?"

"April Grace!" Mama and Daddy both scolded at the same time.

I winced. "Well."

Pastor coughed softly and rolled the glass between his hands, watching the motion.

"Folks, my concern is not so much about Mrs. St. James directing the play, per se. I'm more than willing to give her a chance. Do I wish she attended our church? Of course I do. Is it absolutely necessary that she do so to work on the program? No." He shifted in the rocker, put the glass on the little table next to it, and looked at Daddy, then Mama. "Please understand when I say I don't want to pass judgment on Mrs. St. James, but I'm afraid her abrasive personality presents a problem."

"I didn't know you knew Isabel," Daddy said.

"I don't. But knowing she was a friend of yours and someone who lived in your home, I did call on her while she was in the hospital."

That was news to me.

"Her behavior toward me is unimportant. I've been

spoken to far worse, believe me." He paused to smile at all of us. "However, in the few minutes I was at her bedside, I saw her interact with staff; that is, a nurse, a cleaning woman, and the orderly who brought her meal."

"Uh-oh," I said because I couldn't help it.

Pastor Ross glanced at me, winced a little, and nodded.

"Yes." He turned to my parents. "And I have to say, folks, that I'm none too eager to have our church family spoken to the way she talked to the staff."

"Oh my," Mama said faintly. All of a sudden she wore that worried expression again.

"Pastor," she said, looking at him earnestly, "if Isabel does not direct that play, I just don't know what we'll do. I called everyone I could think of, and while many expressed their willingness to help, only Isabel wants the responsibility of directing. It's quite an undertaking."

"Yes, yes," Pastor Ross said with all the sympathy and understanding you can put into those two words.

There was complete and utter silence in that room for a time.

"Isabel has already said she'd do it," I said in a quiet voice. "In fact, she's all excited."

Pastor looked at me.

"Oh?"

I nodded.

"I think she *needs* something in her life that excites her and gets her involved," Mama said.

"We all need that," Pastor Ross said softly.

"We do!" Daddy agreed. "In our family, we have each

other and all this love. We have our home, our friends, our church. Above all, we have God in our lives. We forget what it's like for someone who has none of that."

"This would be a good step for Isabel," Mama added. "A way to get her involved in the community and the church."

You could see Pastor Ross wanted to do the right thing, but he wasn't sure what the right thing was.

That man seemed at a complete loss for words.

"Pastor Ross," Mama said, "you can count on April Grace to help Isabel interact with our church folks in a way where no one gets upset."

The preacher looked at me like he could read my mind and was gonna write down all my thoughts. That was a little scary because sometimes I have thoughts I don't want the whole world to know. But finally he smiled, turned his attention to my parents, and nodded.

"Well, on your recommendation, we'll give it a try, Lily. I know you have only the best interests of our church in mind."

"You can count on that, Pastor," Daddy said. He gave my mama the sweetest smile you ever saw. I had to look away before I ended up with high blood sugar.

❀

Mama called Isabel and asked her to come over, without Myra Sue, to talk with the preacher, and then she and Daddy sent me upstairs to my room.

I guess they thought I didn't need to be in on the next part, but I'll let you in on a secret. I sort of like to hear things that aren't intended for me to hear. Okay, so I eavesdrop. You know that about me already, and it's not such a secret. But that's how I find out things, especially things grown-ups refuse to tell me.

So I hung around at the top of the stairs, out of sight, but I could still hear the conversation. Daddy introduced Pastor Ross and Isabel, and those two greeted each other with all the politeness you can imagine. For all I know, Isabel was rolling her eyes and squooshing up her lips, but I sorta doubted it. She was so jazzed to do that play, I figured she'd be nice to the person who could veto the whole thing.

Here's what happened. The preacher explained everything he'd talked with us about—except the part where I'm supposed to keep an eye on her—and he wrapped it up by saying, "The church kids are good kids. A little rowdy at times, but good. A kind word and respectful tone of voice will go a long way with them. I'm sure you will get one hundred percent cooperation if you remember Christ's teaching about treating others as you would have them treat you."

There was the tiniest silence in which I am sure Isabel blinked thirty or forty times. But when she replied, her voice was quiet and respectful.

"I understand. I assure you, Reverend, the people in your church will have a Christmas program of which they can be proud. In fact, the entire town of Cedar Ridge will be pleased to attend."

Again, silence hung around for a moment or two.

"That's wonderful, Mrs. St. James," Pastor Ross said. "Just bear in mind, there will be a period of adjustment in which patience might be tested all around."

"Well," Isabel sniffed. "I am the very *soul* of patience, so you may put your mind at rest."

I wanted to scream out, "*Oh brother! Are you kidding?*" But I didn't for a few reasons. Number one: This was all my bright idea in the first place. Number two: If Isabel did not follow through or Pastor fired her, Mama might feel like she'd have to direct that play, even against doctor's orders, because that's how devoted to the church she is. And number three: I was not supposed to be hearing any of this.

"Well, that's fine. That's fine," Pastor Ross said maybe just a tad too enthusiastically.

"Remember, Pastor," Daddy said, "Isabel will have the assistance of our girls, and they'll be a big help to her."

"Yes! Yes, that's right. They will!" The relief in his voice rose from downstairs like the good smell of bread baking in the oven.

But I'll tell you one thing: I hoped I had not cooked up a recipe for disaster.

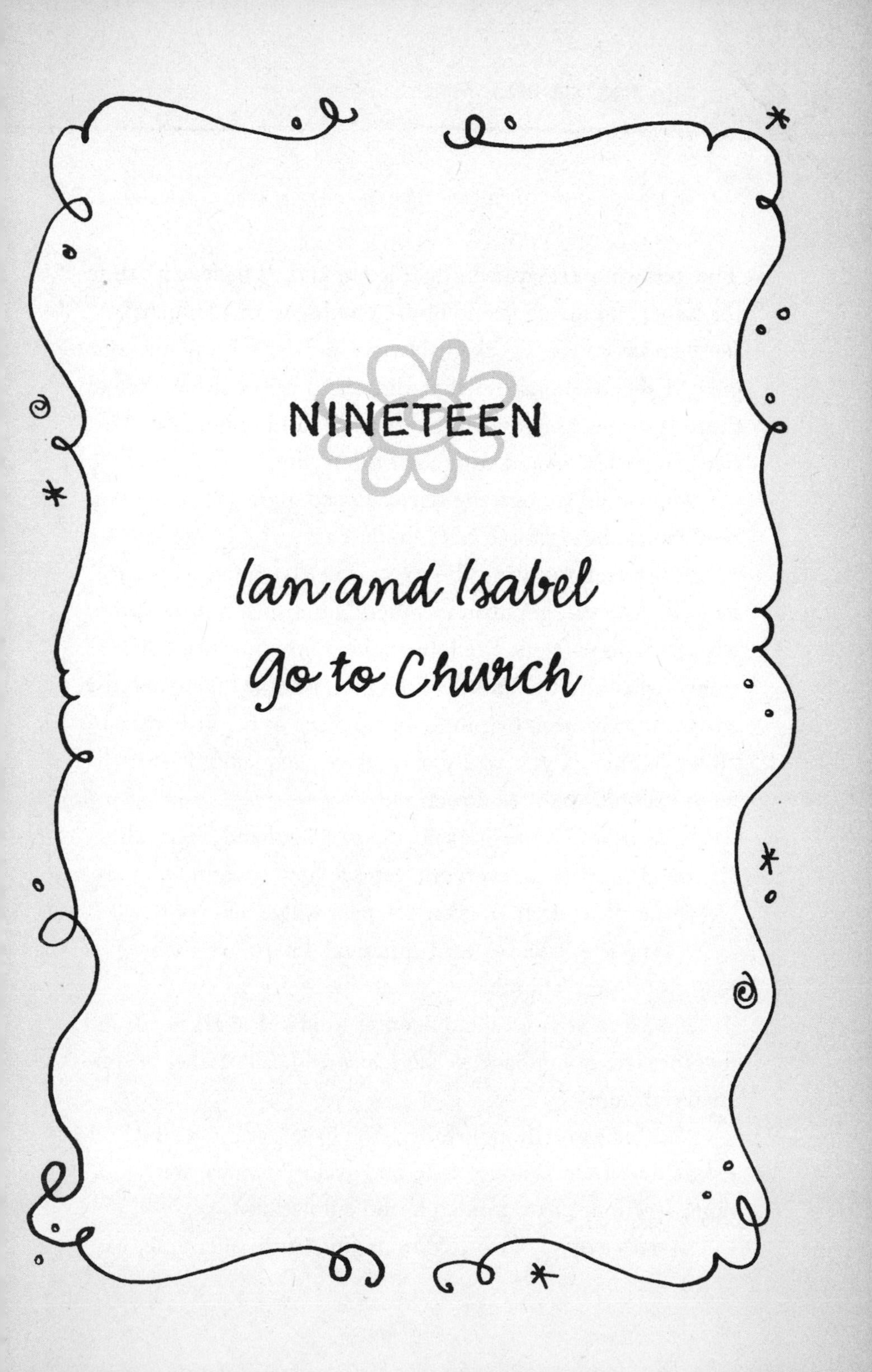

NINETEEN

Ian and Isabel Go to Church

❀

The following Friday evening, ole Ian said, "I believe it's time for Isabel and me to attend church with you this Sunday."

I know you're shocked, but try not to fall out of your chair. I reckon he chose that time because he'd have us all there as witnesses in case Isabel tried to clobber him. Not that our being there would stop her from trying.

You should've seen the narrow-eyed glare she pinned on him, but he just ignored her.

"With Isabel getting the cast off her leg a few days ago," he said, "she can get around much better, just a little slowly with that cane of hers. We'll be moving into our own house in a few weeks, and we'd not be doing it if not for the men at the church who've been helping." He glanced at the little missus. "Plus, lambkins, you really should get acquainted with the young people you'll be directing."

"Oh, Isabel!" Myra Sue said, clasping her hands to her chest. "If you go to church, everyone can see how beautiful you are! No one at the church, or even in Cedar Ridge, has your style."

"Myra Sue," Mama said quietly. "There are many *good* reasons to go to church."

But Myra Sue's idea had been planted in Isabel's head, and there was no going back to the real world. Ole Isabel brightened right up.

"Yes," she said thoughtfully. "You have a point, dear Myra. I should let them witness style and grace *before* we start auditions. It will inspire confidence and emulation."

"That's a lovely idea!" Mama said. "And, of course, with

Isabel being much recovered, Myra Sue can come back home."

Ole Myra looked like the world had just collapsed, and I sorta felt that way, too. I sure had liked having my room all to myself.

❀

Sunday morning, Daddy, Myra Sue, and I went to church in our Taurus. It was a nice car, so we didn't use it for knocking around the farm. It was used for going to church and weddings and funerals and visiting folks.

"I don't know why I couldn't ride to church with Ian and Isabel!" my sister said in the car on the way. She pooched out her lower lip about twelve yards. "They need me to show them how to get there. What if they get lost?"

"Oh brother!" I hollered. "As if anyone can get lost in Cedar Ridge."

Daddy glanced at my sister, who was sitting in the front seat where Mama usually sits, but where she hasn't sat for a long time.

"If I can't have all three of my girls going to church with me, honey, I'd sure like to have at least two of them," he said, smiling at Myra. "It's not so bad, is it, riding to church with your old papa?"

She kinda rolled her eyes, but then she kinda smiled, too. "Oh, Daddy."

A few minutes later, Myra Sue spoke up again. "Hey, Daddy?" she said. "Do you think I could move into the

St. Jameses' house and take care of Isabel a little longer? I think she might still need me."

"She's on her own two feet now," Daddy said to Myra Sue. Since Isabel was recovered enough to get out and about, ole Myra Sue would be moving back to our house that afternoon, and she was not happy about it, let me tell you.

I kind of don't blame her for wanting to move into the St. Jameses' house 'cause it looked pretty good now. It had a new roof, new siding, new gutters, and new windows. According to Daddy, the kitchen cabinets and bathroom fixtures still had to be installed, and the walls still needed paint, and the very last thing to be done was to have the old wood floors refinished. That house was gonna look real good when everything was finished. They'd be moving into it in two or three weeks.

❀

The three of us waited outside in the church parking lot for Ian and Isabel to arrive so they wouldn't feel like two butter mints in a bowlful of purple gumdrops.

When they showed up and got out of the pickup, those two St. Jameses looked like they were going to a party in some big city. Ian wore a dark blue three-piece suit, white shirt, and dark blue tie. His shoes were so polished, Isabel probably used them for mirrors when she put on her face that morning.

She wore a long-sleeved, knee-length black dress that was straight and narrow as a pencil, and I don't hardly see how she balanced her skinny self on those thin black towers she called high heels, especially as she'd just been out of her cast a few days. I bet if her doctor knew that, he'd have a duck fit. I just hoped she didn't fall and break herself all over again.

Good ole Ian kept his arm around her waist as she staggered across the parking lot to the church door. Bedroom slippers might have looked funny with that dress, but they would have been a lot more practical.

Daddy had to catch Myra Sue by the arm to keep her from running to Isabel's side like a kid going after Santa Claus.

I reckon it would've looked odd to some people to see Daddy shake hands with them since they see one another every single day, but you know what? That's what people do when they go to church. They shake hands when they greet you. They do it again during fellowship time. And then when we have a brief greeting time after the first song, and then again when church is over and you're filing out the door. It's my opinion that if someone would invent an automatic handshaker to pass around, it would save a lot of time and sore fingers.

Once inside, people greeted ole Ian and Isabel with a lot more warmth than you might think, especially as Isabel's uppity reputation apparently had spread itself through the community like cow doodie over the vegetable garden. A lot of men already knew Ian, either from seeing him in town at the farm supply store, or in the Koffee Kup having lunch, or because they'd been working like crazy to help him and Daddy get the St. Jameses' house fixed up. I think most of them liked him pretty good.

Everyone was friendly enough, but they eyeballed Isabel like they expected her to do something crazy. Of course nearly everybody expressed interest in her recovery and health. Several of the women complimented her hair and her dress, and they exclaimed over her shoes. Well, boy, oh boy, if you wanted to get on Isabel's best side, the folks at the Cedar Ridge Community Church sure knew how to do it.

During church, Melissa and I sat in the pews where kids our age sat, and the St. Jameses sat with Daddy four rows from the back. Lottie Fuhrman was not in Sunday school that morning, but she did come in late for church and sit on the very back row with two of her followers, Aimee and Brittany, on either side. I figured they'd had a sleepover and Lottie brought them to church as her guests. I hadn't been to Lottie's for a sleepover since sometime last spring. Not that I wanted to at this point. But still, it felt weird that I'd probably never spend the night at her house ever again.

Those girls must have sneaked off to the Cedar Ridge Dollar and Dime down the street where everything cost $1.10 no matter what it was, because they had a sack full of candy and snack cakes. They rattled that sack around, munched those treats, and whispered like crazy. They made so much noise I thought for sure Lottie's mother or stepdad would turn around and give them the Dirty Eyeball.

Now, if you've never been to church and sat with your friends instead of your parents, you might not know what the Dirty Eyeball is. I will tell you.

It's when you're whispering and giggling and passing notes with your pals during prayer or while the preacher is preaching, and you act like you forget you're in church instead of at a slumber party, and then you look up and you see your mother or father has turned around in the pew where they're sitting and they are Looking At You, and then your liver shrivels right up. *That*, my friends, is the Dirty Eyeball. And let me tell you, if you don't sit up, straighten up, hush up, and listen up, your mama will get up and come right back to where you are and escort you to her pew, and there you will sit beside her like you are three years old.

Lottie's mom and stepdad were sitting, all slicked up and shining in nice clothes, in the second pew from the front, and they never, not even *once*, so much as *glanced* at that girl and her friends. Some of the old ladies turned around and glowered, but you know what Lottie did? She gave one old lady the snootiest, smart-aleckest look you can imagine, then stuck out her tongue like a big fat brat. Lottie always could be a little bit of a smarty-pants, and she sometimes said hateful things when she got her feelings hurt, but she had never been such an out-and-out brat like she was now. It was almost like her feelings were hurt all the time, except she didn't act hurt. She just acted, well, *bratty*.

I was completely embarrassed that Lottie and her crew acted like such knotheads on the very first Sunday Ian and Isabel attended church. But the St. Jameses never even glanced at those girls, so maybe they didn't hear them. Maybe me and Melissa and the old ladies were the only ones who noticed, and maybe I wouldn't have noticed so much if Lottie had not continued to be such a stuck-up, snobby pain in the neck at school, not speaking to hardly anyone and acting like if you got too close to her, she was gonna catch germs or something.

Right before the benediction, that trio of girls scooted

out of the sanctuary, and after that, I had no idea where they went. Nor did I care.

After the final "amen" had been said, Isabel smiled without looking like someone yanked up both sides of her mouth with fishing line. Ian seemed so relaxed it was like he had been going to church all his life. You'd never know those two had curled their noses up at the very idea of church and church people just a few weeks ago.

It took a while for us to get out of the building because of all the fellowshipping and handshaking and yakking, but once we got outside, I saw Lottie and her friends sitting on the edge of the brick wall around the flower garden.

"I bet ole Lottie's folks don't know she was late for church or that she snuck out like a sneak before church was over," Melissa said.

We both stared at those girls where they sat giggling and sneering at everyone who came out the church door, like a trio of High-and-Mighty Nincompoops.

"I think we're better off without Lottie Fuhrman," she added.

"Well, I don't like the way she is now, that's for sure, but I miss how much fun we used to have."

Melissa thought about it. "Yeah, me, too."

Just about then we spotted the Tinker twins peeking around the corner of the church house. Micky stepped out and took a few swift steps. His neon orange peashooter lifted, and he blew into it. The little, round plastic pea hit Lottie right smack-dab on the back of the head. Before she had time to jerk around with her hand on her head to see what happened, those two boys had leaped back behind the corner, out of sight. This happened two more times—once for Brittany and once for Aimee. Melissa and I were grinning like two monkeys when Lottie spotted us.

"Who's doing that to us?" she yelled.

We did not answer.

"April Grace Reilly and Melissa Kay Carlyle," she screeched, "who is throwing things at us? And you better tell me right this minute!"

If it'd been me who was being pelted with peas, I woulda jumped up and looked for the culprit; then I woulda found him and jerked a knot in his tail, even if it was Sunday and we were at church. I reckon those girls were too lazy to find things out for themselves.

Through all my snickering, I was able to yell back, "I'm sorry, but us hicks aren't allowed to speak to the Lotties."

Melissa and I like to have broke our ribs laughing when those girls got up and flounced off toward Melissa's stepdad's brand-new car. Since it was big as a boat, they had plenty of room to barricade themselves in the backseat and pout. But if it had been me, I'd've gone after those boys 'cause logic would have told me Micky and Ricky Tinker are the only boys in our church with nerve enough to shoot peas at someone with a million adults milling around.

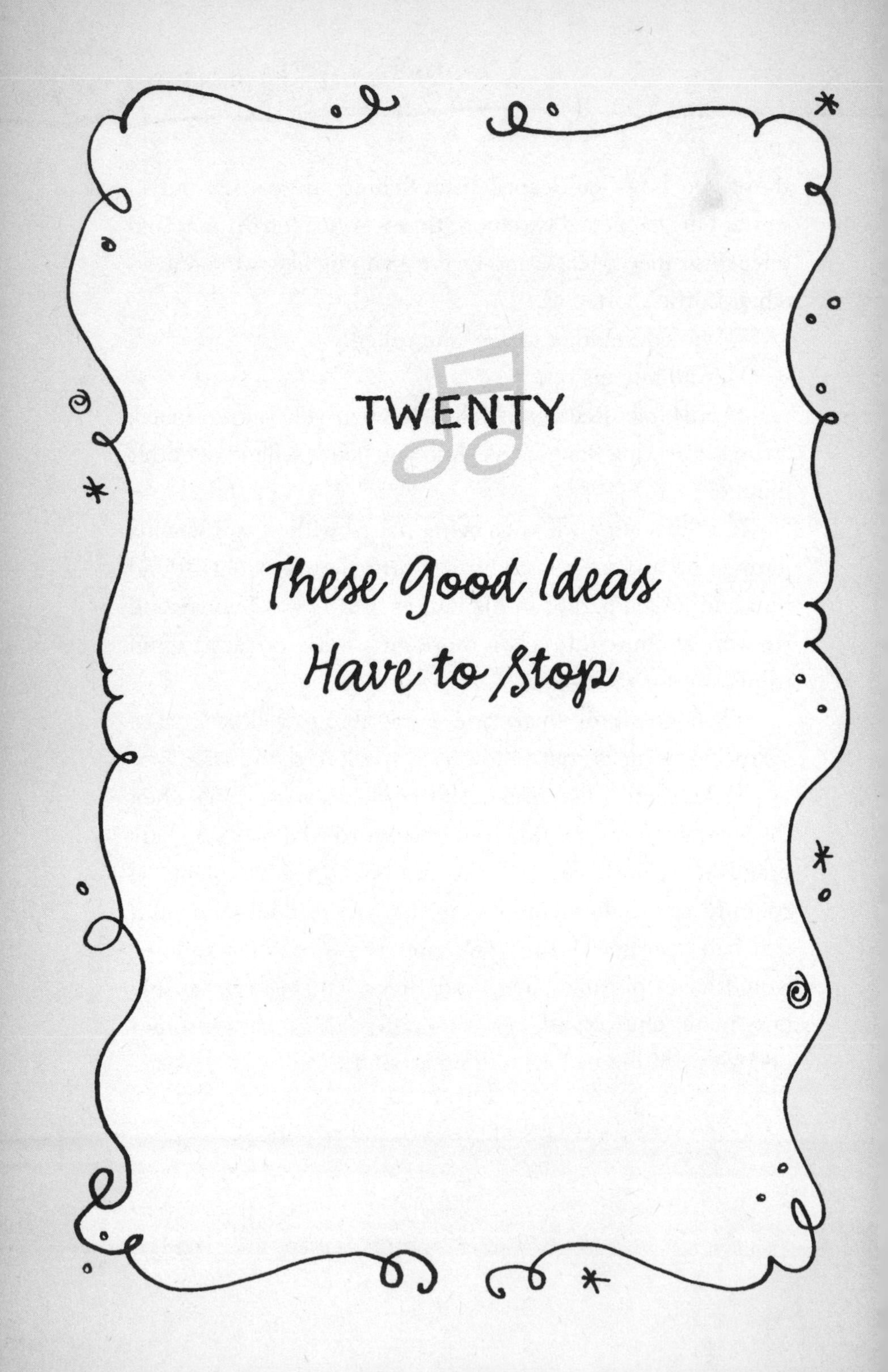

TWENTY

These Good Ideas Have to Stop

♫

"Did you two enjoy church?" Mama asked with a smile as we ate dinner.

"I was surprised by how many people I knew," Ian said. "And they were all so friendly. I was afraid we'd feel like fish out of water, but actually it wasn't awkward at all."

Isabel dabbed at her lips with her napkin. "Well, darling, they want us to come back."

"Of course they do!" Mama said. "They want you and Ian to be a part of our community. Oh, I wish I'd been there! I really miss church and seeing all my friends. Did anyone say anything to you about the Christmas play?"

Isabel shook her head.

"Not one word. I found that a little odd. When you want to be in a play, you want the director to be familiar with you."

"I know we're going to have a great program this year, thanks to Isabel," Daddy said. "Why, just think of it! Our church will have the very first professionally directed play ever seen in Cedar Ridge."

If ole Isabel had been a bird, she would've preened.

That afternoon, after dinner, Grandma went for a drive with Rob Estes in his blue Buick LeSabre. I hoped Ernie Beason, who drove a Jeep and often took his dog, Rascal, on rides with them, did not call while she was gone, but if he did, I hoped I wasn't the one who answered the phone.

Daddy excused himself to go take a nap, and Ian went off to Grandma's house for the same reason. Me, my own personal self, I don't like wasting a perfectly nice day sleeping, so I figured I'd go for a walk with Daisy. Maybe we'd go down by the creek after Myra and I got through washing the dishes.

Isabel and Mama sat at the dining room table with the play script, notebooks, and pens. They would've got started a lot quicker if ole Isabel didn't have to puff a cigarette or two on the front porch first.

"Now, if you feel tired, Lily," I heard Isabel tell Mama, "we must move our conference into the living room where you can put your feet up."

Just the two of them at the dining room table was a "conference"?

"May I be of assistance?" Myra Sue asked them, all prissy, as we came out of the kitchen.

"Sure, honey," Mama said. "You may sit right here by me."

"Here, darling," Isabel said. "Use this pen and notebook, and take notes for us."

My sister smiled all over herself until Isabel glanced at me and said, "April, dear, would you help, too? I can always use a plan of action, and you have the best plans."

Boy, ole Myra Sue gave me a look that said she wanted to snatch me bald-headed. I don't think she liked it that Isabel wanted me there, too.

You know what I thought about that? Tough cookies, that's what.

"Sure," I said, pulling out a chair. "I'll help, but I want to go on a walk with Daisy, so I hope I don't have to hang around too long."

"Now, Lily, darling," Isabel said, ignoring my comment,

"you've examined this script completely. Tell me what this play is about. I do hope it isn't excessively religious."

"I'm not sure what you consider excessively religious, Isabel," Mama said kindly, "but it's a fairly simple story. It is set in Bethlehem, Kansas. There is a young family, the Millers, who find themselves facing hard times. They have three children. He has lost his job, she's expecting another child, and their bills need to be paid. They are in desperate circumstances that test their faith, but help comes from unexpected sources—"

"Hence this title, *Three Angels for Bethlehem*, I assume? Angels flutter down from heaven, strumming harps, with wings flapping, delivering pots of gold?" Isabel said this with some derision.

I did not like her tone or her smirk. "Isabel, your idea is the craziest Christmas story I ever heard of!" I declared.

Mama shook her head at me, and I hushed.

She answered Isabel, quietly and with courtesy, but also with the tiniest edge in her voice: "No, Isabel, angels do *not* flutter down and give them gold. The three angels are actually three regular people who cross the Millers' paths: an elderly woman, a homeless man, and a blind girl. There are also four people who have the ability to help but do not—a store owner, a banker, and their wives. The three who have the least give the most and make a difference not only in the lives of the family, but in the whole town. By the end of the play, the merchant and banker and the wives begin to understand what true giving is."

Isabel rolled her eyes. "Goodness, what a concept."

"What do you mean?" Mama asked her.

The two women met each other's eyes.

"I was expecting a more—oh, I don't know—something deeper, something richer, something with significance," Isabel said.

"I will grant you, the story is fairly simple," Mama said. "We don't want something too complicated or lengthy, but you will find this play *does* have rich significance."

Isabel blinked a few times, then said, "Very well. Let's take a look, shall we? And, of course, I will take this book home and study it thoroughly."

We all watched as she scanned the pages.

"We'll have a casting call," she declared when she finished. Her eyes were all bright and sparkling. "I shall put it on the radio and television. We'll get auditions from all over the state—"

"Whoa, Isabel!" Mama said, laughing. "Slow down. This is just a church play, for the community. And it's starring *kids*."

"It's *quality* I'm looking for, Lily," she was saying. "Good actors who can bring the story alive. Some young people are good actors."

"Like me, Isabel?" Myra Sue said, all fluttery.

"Yes, darling, I'm sure you are *excellent*."

In a weird kind of way and in spite of her being hardheaded in her ideas, it was good to hear ole Isabel get all excited about something. But here's what I have decided: there'll probably always be something to get her all worked up, so it would be better for us all if we could keep her focused on something without going off the deep end.

"Isabel?" I said.

She dragged her intense gaze from Mama and said, "Yes?"

"If you try to make this a bigger deal than it is, no one will cooperate with you."

"Well." She blinked some more and shmooshed up her lips.

"I think a casting call is a perfectly marvelous idea!" Myra Sue said, sighing wistfully. "In fact, I wrote it down."

Oh, good grief.

"This is gonna be the youth group, not the grown-ups, *remember*?" I said. "A casting call would be a Dumb Thing to do."

"April Grace," Mama said, reproving. She turned back to Isabel. "The way we usually do it is to simply assign the parts—"

Isabel sat up so straight, it was like someone had poked her with a sharp stick. "Oh, my dear. That is *not* the way it's done."

"No, Mother," Myra Sue said. "*Not* done that way at all!"

I saw no reason for my sister to be so snooty to our mother.

"Then why don't *you* tell us how it's done, Myra?" I asked her. "Educate Mama and me, would you?"

Well, I reckon Mama did not like that, or maybe she didn't like my personal snooty tone, because she gave me the Look. She did not chastise me aloud, but to tell you the honest truth, I couldn't understand why it seemed she didn't hear ole Myra Sue being snooty and uppity.

"Your idea of merely assigning parts will never work," Isabel said. "Lily, if the wrong person plays a certain role, the entire play will bomb. This little play is . . . well, it's not the most intriguing story line I've ever heard, so the acting *must* carry the play. We simply *must* have auditions. If you want me to direct this play, then it really has to be done the right way. I insist."

The two women sat there silently, eyeballing each other. Maybe each was waiting for the other one to give in. Mama was the one who caved.

"I'm sure it'll be just fine, Isabel, if you want to have the kids audition. And I'm sure the girls will encourage their friends to try out." She looked at us. "Won't you, girls?"

"Of course!" Myra Sue said, all but clapping her hands.

"Hmm," I said. I was not at all thrilled at the prospect, but as long as I, my own personal self, didn't have to try out, I was all right.

"Now, where is our stage?" Isabel asked. "I really prefer auditions on the stage rather than dry readings elsewhere."

"It's the church platform," Mama said, "not a regular stage."

"I beg your pardon?" Isabel said, all aghast-sounding.

"The play will be staged on the platform in the sanctuary," Mama said.

"You aren't serious."

"That's the only place we can do it," I piped up. "Unless you want to have it outside in the parking lot."

"April Grace." Mama gave me a third look that said my sassy suggestion topped her list of Unapproved Suggestions.

Isabel blinked twenty-eight times, or thereabouts, then heaved a big sigh.

"Well, I'll need to scc it again. Then I must go through the props and costumes."

Was she kidding?

"Oh dear," Mama said, laughing a little. "Isabel, I hope

you won't be too disappointed, but the church has very little money for theatrical productions. We've just always made do with what we can scrounge up at home."

Isabel made an O of her mouth.

"Well, we'll see about that," she said finally, about halfway muttering. "I intend to bring some culture to this backwoods, and no one is going to stop me."

Oh brother. I was beginning to regret Big-Time what had seemed to be a good idea just a few days ago.

TWENTY-ONE

How Crazy Does a Two-Edged Sword Have to Be?

Well, I tell you what. Sometimes I think Isabel is crazier than a two-edged sword. Here is what happened after school the very next afternoon after she agreed to help with the program.

Isabel took me and Myra Sue with her to meet with Pastor Ross at the church.

"This church is the *absolute* worst place for a performance," she groaned as the three of us stood on that platform so she could "get a feel for the arena." Isabel St. James has some mighty weird ways of saying things, in case you hadn't noticed.

"On the contrary," Pastor Ross said, "the Cedar Ridge Community Church Christmas program has always played to a full sanctuary. A packed house, you might say."

When he mentioned "packed house," Isabel got all pleased-looking. She slowly made a complete turn, like rotisserie chicken without the skewer, eyeballing the entire sanctuary, taking in the overflow rooms and the choir loft. Muttering about acoustics, she studied the height of the ceiling and gazed down at the dark red carpeting on which we stood.

She pointed to the railing that separated the choir loft from the sanctuary. "That thing must go."

Pastor Ross followed her pointing finger and looked at the choir rail as if he'd never seen it before.

"I'm sorry," he said, "but if we do that, it will ruin the carpeting. You see, it was—"

"Wonderful!" she said. "For the sake of our acoustics, rip it out! Carpet absorbs the voices and dulls projection. The play will be better without it. We must have acoustics!"

Pastor Ross gaped at her. "Mrs. St. James, we can't rip up the carpeting."

Ole Isabel blinked about twenty times. "I fail to see why not. You can put it back down when the play is finished."

He shook his head. "I'm sorry. That is out of the question."

Her eyes got all big and buggy. "You refuse to help?"

"Help? Mrs. St. James, I'm happy to do anything that is reasonable to help you, but pulling up a brand-new carpet that has been down less than three months is costly and unwise."

Had ole Isabel lost her cotton-pickin' mind? I looked at Myra Sue, who was watching the whole crazy scene with her mouth slightly open and her eyes all big.

Isabel's lips thinned. "Is that your final word on the matter?" she asked.

"Absolutely."

"Very well. Since you're so uncooperative, I must make do." She sniffed with all the uppity, snooty sniffiness you can imagine. "I do assume you or someone can build our sets."

"Sets?" Pastor Ross echoed.

"Yes. Sets. Plays take sets. Scenes. Backgrounds. Rooms and landscapes. *Sets.*" She spoke to Pastor Ross as if he were two years old.

"I know what sets are, but I'm not sure about having them built—"

"What about costumes?" she snapped.

"I hardly think you'll need costumes," he told her. "The play is contemporary. The kids can wear their own clothes."

"So no one will be making costumes?"

"I hardly see the point."

"We must have stage lights," she bit off, like biting the tops off of the words.

"I'm sorry?"

All this time you could see, plain as day, that good ole Pastor Ross was trying to be a gentleman about this whole business. But I'll tell you something: I saw his left eyelid twitch. I think Isabel was getting on his nerves just a wee bit. Or maybe a lot.

She blinked at him, and her face got redder and redder. I'd seen her look at Ian in just that way, and I knew, sure as shootin', she was gonna blow.

"Isabel?" I said. "I'm thinking we can—"

"Why are you trying to derail me, you wretched, wretched man?" she shouted, waving her fist at him like he was a dirty old dog in the street.

We gawked at her. I knew she could be a stinkpot, but I didn't know anyone would ever yell at a good preacher the way she yelled at him.

"Isabel, the pastor is not trying to derail you," I said as fast as the words would come out of my mouth.

"Of course not, ma'am," he said, with his face pink, his body tense, and his left eyelid twitching like crazy. "Our church simply does not have the budget for what you're asking."

As he went on to explain church finances to Isabel, Myra Sue inched closer to me and whispered in my ear, "But if he won't let her have what she wants, then he's messing up everything."

"No, he isn't," I hissed. "She's wanting something far and away more than what she needs for this play. She's being a complete Isabel about the whole thing."

Myra Sue gave me a look that told me I did *not* understand anything.

"And even if I sanctioned all these things you want, Mrs. St. James," the pastor was saying, "the church board would put its foot down. Hard. I'm sorry to disappoint you, but that's just the way it is."

Steam practically came out of her ears.

"Then I see no reason to continue this . . . *travesty* in the face of all that is refined!" she announced, turning on her high heels and stomping off.

She was halfway toward the back of the sanctuary before I could find my voice 'cause I'd never seen or heard someone act so crazy in my life, unless it was all those other times when she said and did crazy things.

"*Isabel!*" Myra Sue shrieked, reaching out her arms, as if her Highly Esteemed Role Model were being dragged off to prison, where she'd have to live off bread and water for the next sixty-eight years.

That skinny, angry, ungrateful woman did not stop, turn, or slow down.

"Isabel," I hollered. "Wait!"

She kept marching.

"Isabel St. James, do you want to kill my mama?" I yelled at the top of my lungs. My words echoed acoustically off the church walls and high ceiling.

I hoped God would forgive me for bellowing like a wounded woolly mammoth in church.

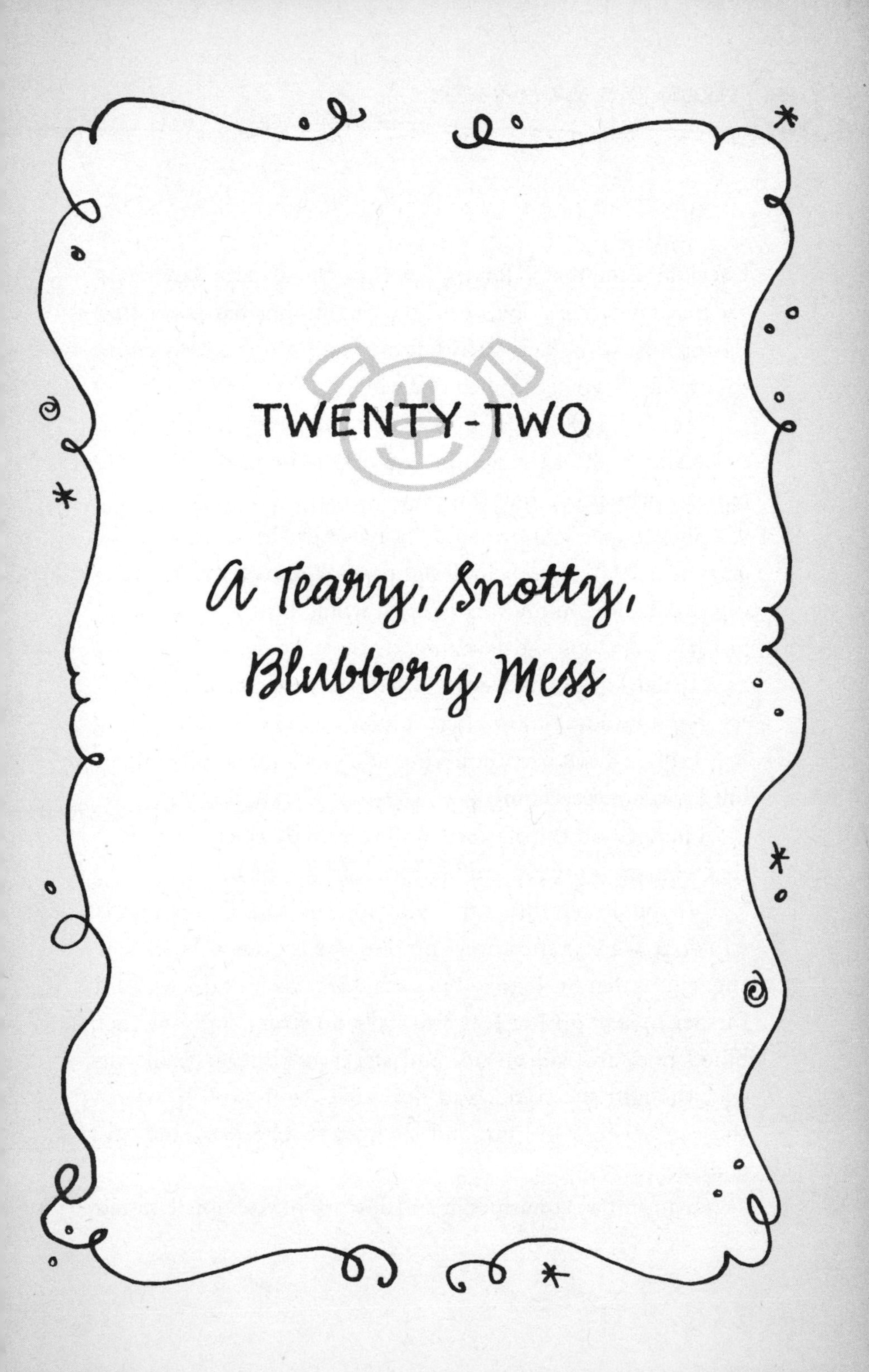

TWENTY-TWO

A Teary, Snotty, Blubbery Mess

I reckon after that I forgot I was in the church sanctuary. Or that my sister stood nearby, wringing her hands, or that Pastor Ross with the twitchy left eye was right there, listening to my yelling voice. I yelled anyway.

"You will kill Lily Reilly, the best friend you have in all of Arkansas, in all of the South, and maybe in all of the whole entire world, if you quit this play."

She stopped and turned. Her eyes were hard and narrow, and she fixed that steely look right smack-dab on me. I'm telling you, I thought my very gizzard would bust a blood vessel just from the look she gave me.

"Child, I do not understand what you are screeching about."

Now, I want it known here and now that I was not *screeching*. I might have been hollering and screaming and yelling, but I was not screeching.

I jumped off the platform and trotted up the aisle toward that woman. If my gizzard bled to death, so be it.

"If you do not direct this play for our church, my mama will do it because she knows no one else is gonna. You know she will, Isabel St. James. *You know she will!* Her doctor said for her to stay off her feet and have no stress, and now her blood pressure will go up, and she'll get puffier than you ever thought she could, and her ankles will swell to where she can't even stand up, and she'll get sicker . . . and . . . and . . ."

To my utter astonishment and downright vexation, I busted

out bawling like a big fat nincompoop baby, and that was not what I meant to do at all.

"Oh my!" Isabel said, her eyes big and round.

"April Grace," said the preacher, hurrying toward me.

I looked at his concerned, kind face and blurted, "If that dumb ole baby doesn't kill my mama, then Isabel St. James is gonna. That's what's gonna happen."

And then I set up the awfullest, howlingest sob-fest you ever heard and didn't know how to stop, even though I wanted to more than you can possibly imagine.

"Well, forevermore!" Isabel said, sounding exactly like my grandma. I reckon she really had gone nuts, 'cause she'd never say such a country-sounding thing if she'd been in her right mind.

"April Grace, what on earth is wrong with you?" Myra Sue said.

I caught a glimpse of her between my teary-gooed eyes, and she looked all horrified and embarrassed. Well, let me tell you, she couldn't feel any more horrified and embarrassed than yours very truly. But I could not stop bawling.

Pastor Ross led me to a pew and sat me down. He blotted my cheek with a tissue, then handed me an entire box of them he'd picked up from the pew in front of us.

"Whatever is the matter with that child?" Isabel fretted. "Is she having some sort of breakdown?"

"Oh, I hardly think so," Pastor said, wiping my face again. "Here, April, blow your nose."

Ewww. Blowing my nose in front of everyone, especially

our very own preacher, was gross, but I did it 'cause stuff was running out of every hole in my face.

"I don't—" I hiccupped and tried again. "I don't want my m-mama to d-d-die."

"Of course you don't," Pastor Ross said.

"Is G-G-God gonna make her die?" I asked. "Did He make her have that baby s-s-so she'd die?"

"Oh, April Grace!" Isabel sank into the pew right in front of me and looked at me over the back of it. "I thought you believed that God is love."

I took in a deep, shuddering breath, and if I hadn't been so upset, Isabel's statement might've surprised me, her being so critical of church and God and everything. "I don't know what I think about Him right this minute."

"Listen to me," the pastor said kindly. He tipped my face up so I had to look at him. I bet I looked a mess, too, all teary and snotty and blubbery, but he didn't seem to notice.

"Listen to me," he said again. "Women have some problems with pregnancies all the time, but these days they have good medical care to help them. Your mother has a good doctor that she and your father trust, doesn't she?"

I nodded.

"And she's taking care of herself, isn't she?"

I nodded.

"And she has you and your sister and your father and your grandmother to watch over her. Right?"

Again I nodded. He took my left hand in one of his and covered it with the other, and he looked right into my eyes.

"I'll tell you something, April Grace—something that I

know in my heart: God loves you and your mother and your whole family. He understands that you're scared and has wrapped all of you in His love. Right now He is holding you and your family—even that new baby—close to His heart."

I gulped down my sobs until I nearly strangled myself and stared at him because I wanted to believe what he said.

"Really?"

"Really. When times get tough, like what's going on with your family right now, God is the strength that holds it all together. Even when He seems far away, April Grace, He isn't. In fact, He's with us all, not just now, but all the time."

I thought about it, and then I thought about it some more. I liked what our preacher had to say to me, but I was still scared. Even though God always does the right thing, sometimes people don't. That's what scared me right then. Maybe Isabel wouldn't keep her end of the bargain.

"But, Pastor Ross, Mama has done the Christmas programs since forever. If Isabel quits, Mama will get right up off her sickbed and take over. And if she does that . . ." I could feel all that squalling and blubbering trying to start up again, and I did my best to swallow it back down.

"Oh!" Isabel huffed like she'd been insulted. "That is *not* going to happen."

Pastor and I both looked at her, and she stared back as if we were aliens with strange ideas.

"I will *not* allow Lily to endanger herself or her baby. I shall direct that play, even under these primitive, backwoods conditions."

I felt my eyes get as big and round as Myra Sue's.

"You will?"

She nodded. "I will." She stood, drawing herself as thin and straight as a broomstick. "I shall soldier on!"

My tears dried up, and I grinned so big I nearly threw my jawbone out of joint.

"Oh, Isabel!" Myra Sue said from where she still stood on the platform. "You are wonderful!"

"Yeah, Isabel!" I said.

"Yeah, Isabel," Pastor echoed, beaming. That just shows what a nice guy he is, being happy even though ole Isabel was such a pain. His left eye wasn't twitching right then, either.

"Spread the word," she declared, waving one arm dramatically. "Auditions will be one week from tonight, and I expect every young person in this church to be here!"

TWENTY-THREE

Not-So-Silent Night

*

Monday night was the night for auditions. The lucky kids who got the smaller parts in the play wouldn't have to memorize or do a whole lot. But those big parts—well, all I can say is, if you were gonna play a lead, you better have had a good brain 'cause it was gonna be full of things to memorize and recite. This is why I wondered if ole Myra Sue knew what she was getting into when, at the supper table that Monday evening before we left for tryouts, she announced that she wanted to play the Absolute Lead.

Isabel gave her a brilliant smile. "Darling girl, I can almost guarantee you'll be the best. But we must have our auditions, you know."

"Yeah," I put in. "That's the way it's done. Remember?"

Myra Sue narrowed her eyes, and I figured her pinchy-finger was coming toward me. I skittered sideways, just in case.

"Girls," Mama said, "if you're finished eating, run upstairs and get cleaned up for the tryouts."

"Yes," Isabel said, all parental. "Please don't take too long, children. I simply *must* be there early."

We trotted off upstairs and did that Cleaning Up thing that my mother thinks we have to do for everything, even if we were going to muck out the barn. Of course, ole Myra Sue did more than clean up. She changed every bit of clothes she had on, and she sprayed her hair with junk and spritzed it with another kind of junk, and then she grabbed it in her fists and pulled it up and sprayed it some more. She called it "scrunching." I tell you, if that girl had run her head into a brick wall, that wall would've crumbled like the one around Jericho, with or without the trumpets. When we were going downstairs, I poked it and like to have broke my poking finger.

We got to the church so early, Pastor Ross wasn't even there yet. We had to sit in the pickup and wait, so while we waited, Isabel smoked three cigarettes, one right after the other, right there in the church parking lot. I hung my head out the passenger window and hoped I didn't get cancer from all her puffing.

"Excuse me," I said finally, sure I was gonna choke plumb to death from smoke. I got out of the pickup and wandered over to the brick wall that encircled the flower bed—the same wall that ole Lottie Fuhrman had decided was her own personal church space because she always plunked her carcass on it to wait for her folks after church, and she sure enough did not want any of the rest of us to sit with her. But she wasn't there right then, so I settled down on it. It was cold against my backside and a lot harder than the seat in the pickup, but I stayed there even though full dark lay across the landscape and the air was chilly. At least it smelled better.

Have you ever noticed that when the air is crisp and clean, the stars sparkle like a gazillion diamonds? Staring up at that sky, I sighed. Now, here's the thing. I am *not* someone who likes to get all dolled up and powdered and perfumed and fluffed, but I decided right then that someday, when I become a grown lady, I want a deep, dark midnight-blue velvet dress with sparkling bits scattered over it. I would call it my Winter Night Dress, even though that night when I was looking at the stars was only late October. I would wear that dress as often as I wanted to, even if no one was around to see it. I smiled happily at the prospect.

Pastor Ross drove up right then and parked his white Chevrolet Celebrity next to the pickup. He greeted Isabel and Myra.

"Didn't April Grace come with you?" he asked, looking around.

It might have been my imagination, but I thought I heard a note of panic in his voice, so I popped up from where I'd been sitting and dreaming on that cold wall and hollered, "I'm right here, Pastor!"

He turned, and even in the dark I could see he was smiling. Probably with relief that he did not have to deal with Isabel and Myra Sue all by himself.

"Let's go in the church where it's warm," he said to us all, and we followed him like a flock of sheep, then waited while he unlocked the door and turned on the lights.

The minute Isabel stepped inside, she slid out of her coat that looked like fur but probably wasn't since the St. Jameses would have had to sell fur coats and diamond necklaces and gold watches when they lost all their valuables. I wondered why she was wearing such a heavy coat, anyway. Boy, oh boy, if she thought an evening in October was cold, she was in for a Big Surprise around the second week of January.

You know what that woman did? I'll tell you. She handed that coat right to Pastor Ross, as if he were the church butler or something, then she marched off into the sanctuary without so much as a "Thank you, sir, for opening the door, turning on the heat, turning on the lights, and taking my coat."

I could see ole Myra Sue was fixing to do the same thing with her pink jacket, but I bugged my eyes out at her, telling her inside my head that if she was that rude, I would personally tell our very own parents about it. I bet she'd never watch another soap for as long as she lived if I tattled. She hung up her own jacket on the rack near the door and then trotted off after Isabel like a baby calf going after its mother.

"Let me have Isabel's coat, Pastor," I said, taking it from him. "You got better things to do."

"Thanks, April Grace. I guess I better see what Mrs. St. James will be needing."

I hung up that dumb coat and my jacket, then hurried into the sanctuary to help our poor preacher.

Ole Isabel was hollering, "I need a spotlight! I need a spotlight!"

"I'll turn on the overhead pulpit light," Pastor Ross said. He showed her where the switch was on the wall near the choir loft.

"I'm not sure that will do," Isabel sniffed.

Pastor looked at her kinda funny. "It will have to do," he said. "It's what the church has."

She looked down at me, bunched up her lips like a dried-up old rosebud, then sighed heavily out of her nose. I sure was glad she wasn't smoking right then. The leftover smell of it was bad enough. I bet her lungs smelled worse than Temple's armpits, if you want to know the honest truth.

TWENTY-FOUR

There Are No Small Parts

The vestibule door opened again, and Christy Sanchez came in for her audition. She's a couple of years older than Myra Sue, with pretty black hair and eyes and a big, bright smile. Before she was halfway to the front of the church, the door opened again, and the Tinker twins galloped in like two wild mustangs. Melissa showed up just a little bit after that, looking kinda nervous.

In fact, she sat down on the pew right behind me, leaned forward, and whispered, "This kinda makes me feel queasy."

I nodded, because I knew what she meant. "Have you decided what part to try out for?" I asked her.

She sighed. "I think I want to be one of the children. Or maybe the banker's wife."

"They hardly get to say anything," I told her.

"I *know*! I don't want to do this, but Mom said I have to."

"I'm Isabel's assistant, so I have enough to do," I said, happy as strawberries in May.

Pretty soon, Chuck, Brenda, and Madison Holt arrived, and on their heels came Holly and Joy Burnside. Before long the entire youth group, except for Lottie Fuhrman, was in the sanctuary, hollering and laughing and acting goofy. Since I was there to help Isabel and not be a kid, I tried my best to act grown-up. Which is not easy to do when someone is passing out watermelon bubble gum and you want a piece of it in the worst way.

Another awful, terrible thing happened right about then. Ole J.H. Henry, the Un-heartthrob of Cedar Ridge Junior

High, came strolling into the church with his hair all bunched up and his jacket sleeves pushed up to his elbows. He swaggered down the aisle to the front like he was the hottest thing in a pair of Nike sneakers. When he saw me, he winked as big and bold as an elephant and pointed at me, grinning like an ape. I wanted to smack him. Instead I just shook my head like I thought he was Dreadful and looked the other way.

Why was J.H. there, anyway? As far as I knew, he had never darkened the door of our church in his whole entire life. I reckon ole Lottie invited him because she acts like he's the greatest boy in the whole world and always has, even before she became one of the Lotties. I never understood why. Ick. Dumb girl, and she wasn't even there yet.

As ole Isabel's assistant, I sat right beside her on the front pew, so when she lifted her wrist to look at her watch, I peeked and saw it was seven thirty, the time our church bulletin had announced we were having tryouts. Of course, Isabel had insisted on calling them *auditions*, but that's Isabel for you.

Isabel took in a deep breath, got up, stepped onto the platform, and faced everyone.

"*People!* May I have your attention?"

I gotta say, she spoke so loudly and with such authority, every one of those kids shut their yaps and looked at her. Melissa and I glanced at each other. Ole Isabel was almost as scary as Mrs. Patsy Farber, the junior high principal.

"We have exactly eight weeks." She held up eight fingers. "*Eight weeks*, people, to get this show on the road."

She looked at everyone through squinched-up eyes, as if she were piercing us all with tiny, sharp knives, and it was *our* fault that all we had were eight weeks to prepare for that play.

When she finished with the staring, she paced from one edge of the platform to the other and then came back to stand under the pulpit light. We all just sat there, frozen, watching her. Boy, oh boy, this was not going to be pretty. In fact, it was downright scary. Isabel had become someone else right there before our very eyes.

"You will learn your parts," she said. "You will attend every rehearsal, you will be here on time, and you will stay until I tell you that you may leave. You will emote, enunciate, project, and pause.

"Please pay attention, young people." As if to demonstrate, she paused, stared out at us, emoting for all she was worth, and, being sure to enunciate, she projected the following: "I assume you are familiar with all the parts in the play. I will call for a certain part, and those of you who seek to play that role will step up here on this stage, beneath this light, and read." She paused again. "No one in this group will be talking, laughing, or wandering about during auditions." She paused once more, emoting, projecting, and scaring the liver out of all of us. "Is that clear?"

I think every single one of us murmured a "Yes, ma'am"—even the Tinker twins, who think speaking softly is shouting off the rooftop of City Hall.

"Well, I certainly hope you speak up more than that when you audition, or we'll be without a Christmas program."

At that moment, I figured every last one of us would be more than happy if the Christmas program was canceled.

But I knew Mama would not be happy, and I knew that just couldn't happen.

Isabel stepped off the platform and settled her skinny self down in the front pew between me and Myra Sue again. She picked up the playbook and opened it up to the cast of characters. Already, she and Myra Sue and I had highlighted the parts in the books for everyone so that no one would have to go hunting for his or her speeches. They were already there, all nicely bright and yellow.

"All right," she said. "Who would like to audition first for the role of Rosemary Miller?"

Let me tell you, not one person made a move. Rosemary Miller was the lead female role, and I knew Myra Sue wanted it in the worst way. And yet, right next to Isabel St. James sat Myra, hands folded in her lap and big eyes staring straight ahead. Well now. Something had to be done.

I scrooched up real close and hissed in her ear, "Isabel St. James, you better soften up, or no one will cooperate. You've done scared everybody speechless."

She blinked at me at least fifty times.

"Look at 'em, Isabel. You got the entire youth department of the Cedar Ridge Community Church too scared to move."

Like a stiff little windup doll, ole Isabel looked around. Now, you'd think every teenager and preteen there would've already stood right up and walked out the door they came in. Maybe their parents had threatened to ground them until January 12, 2099, if they didn't cooperate. Whatever the reason, you never saw such a quiet bunch of kids in your whole entire life, and probably won't if you live to be 194 years old.

She faced forward again.

"Very well," she muttered out of the corner of her mouth. "I will do my best."

She stood, turned around, took a deep breath, and smiled. Now, let me tell you something. When Isabel gives you a real smile, it changes her whole face. But when she gives you a pretend smile, like she was doing right then, it sort of looks like she might have rabies or something, 'cause she pulls her lips back, and all you see is teeth.

"Aren't you gonna read?" I asked my sister.

Ole Myra-darling looked around; then she stood up and trickled on up to the platform, looking terrified. Not of Isabel, of course, but of all the rest of us. Isabel smiled for real as she picked up the playbook on which the name of Rosemary had been written in black marker across the front cover.

She handed it to my sister and said, "Turn to page 3, darling, and read Rosemary's part. I will read George's part."

As she read, ole Myra Sue's voice shook so bad, she sounded like she was in the spin cycle of a washing machine. The other kids snickered nervously.

I turned around and gave them all a dirty look. If anyone was gonna laugh at my sister, it would be me.

Isabel had a funny look on her face that seemed to say she was confused by my sister's efforts. When Myra finished reading, she gave Isabel a pleading, sick look. You could see ole Isabel was trying to be kind to her darling. She gave her a tight little smile and said, "Thank you, dear.

You may sit down." She looked over her shoulder at the others. "Who's next?"

Well, right about then the vestibule door opened, and guess who strolled in, like they owned the world and everyone in it. Yep. The Lotties, that's who. Well, two of them. Lottie and Aimee. Brittany, Ashley, and Heather were not there. I guess Lottie must've invited Aimee to try out, like she did J.H. Boy, oh boy.

I'll tell you something about Aimee. She has been snooty ever since we were little kids, so all this uppity Lottie business is nothing new to her. Her clothes have always been real nice, her blond hair has always been shiny and pretty, and she has never needed braces on her nice, even teeth. And something else you should know: she used to pick on Lottie. So what changed? I haven't got the foggiest idea, but maybe someday, like when I am grown, I'll figure it all out.

Laughing and talking loudly, they sashayed into the sanctuary.

"We're here!" Lottie announced as if we'd been waiting breathlessly. *As if.*

Isabel did not seem to be impressed by those girls. She stood up and watched until they sat down in the very back pews.

"You are late," she said, all snooty. Then she glanced at me and strained out that smile again. As far as I was concerned, she could have saved the bother and just reamed out those girls like she was hollering at everyone else earlier.

"Please have a seat up here with the rest of us, girls," she told them. "And hereafter, remember to arrive on time if you are cast in this play. Punctuality and reliability are of utmost importance to pulling off the best play ever."

Lottie and Aimee rolled their eyes and stayed where they were, but when steam started to shoot out of Isabel's ears, they got up and sauntered to the front. Of course they sat *apart* from the rest of us. Maybe they thought when Jesus said, "Come ye apart," He meant they needed to stick their noses in the air and be separate. I'm not a preacher, but I'm pretty sure He did not mean that. In fact, if I'm not mistaken, He does not care for that stuck-up, I'm-better-than-you behavior *at all*.

When Lottie and Aimee had settled down, Isabel gave everyone a nice, big, sorta-scary smile that wasn't as scary as the other one.

"Now. Who else is going to read for the part of Rosemary Miller?"

Holly Burnside timidly raised her hand, and so did Christy Sanchez and Madison Holt, even though Madison was a year younger than me and way too short to play a married lady.

I have to tell you, all three of those girls read that part so much better than ole Myra Sue, I actually felt sorry for my sister.

Isabel went down the list of characters. George Miller, Rosemary Miller, Jim Burke, Nancy Burke.

Then she did something that nearly made me lose my supper. She handed me the book that had the part of Nancy Burke, the wife of the storekeeper.

"I want you to audition for this role," she told me.

"Oh, Isabel," I choked out, "I can't. I . . . I . . . I'm your assistant, remember? You need me to run errands."

"Just read it, dear. I think you'd be really good playing this part."

Well, I tell you what. I'm not sure which I felt the most: petrified or insulted. You see, the role of Nancy Burke is not a nice one. In fact, she's the rottenest character in the play, all bossy to the storekeeper and demanding that he not give any help to anyone.

"*Isabel!*" I whispered in my most pleadingest voice. "Let Myra Sue read for this one. *I can't.*"

Then I heard that rotten ole Lottie snicker like there was no tomorrow, like she did not care if Isabel ate her for breakfast. She snickered like she knew I was a big fat chicken too scared to do anything.

I looked over at Lottie's and Aimee's smirking faces, and I couldn't stand it. I grabbed up that book.

"What page?" I asked Isabel.

Then I went up there on that stage, stood under that spotlight, and read the part of Nancy Burke as if I were Nancy Burke herself.

Guess what?

Isabel assigned that part to me.

Guess what else?

She assigned the part of Jim Burke, the storekeeper and Nancy's husband, to none other than J.H. Henry. I thought I might as well lie down and die right there, but that did not happen.

One more thing.

Isabel gave the part of the banker's nearly silent wife to Myra Sue.

Later that night, ole Myra bawled her head off in her pillow.

"I am devastated," she wailed with way more than a hint of drama. "Isabel gave the part of Rosemary Miller to that Christy Sanchez when she knew how much I wanted it, and she didn't even give me a second chance!" She howled some more. "I didn't know she could be so cruel. She even gave *you* a better part than she gave me!"

I almost felt sorry for her 'cause I know how much she wanted that part. I wished Mama could come upstairs; I wished Daddy didn't go to bed so early sometimes. I wished Grandma wasn't taking a bath. Any of those adults could've probably helped Myra Sue stop crying, but they weren't around right then.

I wasn't sure what to say.

"Myra Sue, I'm sure she didn't mean to be cruel to you. She *loves* you," I finally said. Now, that sounded pretty good when it came out.

"It's just too, too humiliating," she blubbered. "I don't get to do anything but walk around on stage most of the time. I don't even get to say anything except a few words."

The bathroom door opened down the hall, and I was purely glad to hear it.

I said, "Wait a minute." As if she was going to move an inch from where she was scrunched up in a little ball, all pathetic-like.

I ran out into the hallway and grabbed Grandma's arm before she got to her room. Her hair was damp and combed back from her face, and she wasn't wearing a dab of makeup. Her red-and-blue-plaid robe was about a million years old.

"Grandma, come in here and talk to Myra Sue. She's all upset, and I don't know what to tell her."

A little, worried frown settled between Grandma's eyebrows, and she hurried to our room.

"Myra Susie," she said as she sat down on the edge of the bed. "What's wrong, child?"

With a new sympathetic onlooker, my sister set up to wailing again for a minute or two; then she tapered off that mess and poured out her heart and soul about Isabel and that ole play.

"I was so scared when I read for the play that I made a big fool out of myself, and now I am just utterly and totally humiliated. Isabel will never want to speak to me again."

"Well now," Grandma said, smoothing back Myra Sue's tangled, sweat-damp curls, "you know Isabel thinks the world of you, honey."

"That's what I told her!" I said.

"I think she hates me. She gave my part to Christy."

Here came the waterworks again, and I trotted off to the bathroom and got a fresh roll of toilet paper for her to mop her eyes and nose. She grabbed it from me and unrolled about three hundred yards and blew her nose for a good five minutes. Which grossed me out some, I have to say.

"Tell me about that part you're gonna play," Grandma said.

"It's nothing but a walking-around part. I'm the banker's wife."

"At least you get to walk around and wear fancy clothes and look pretty, Myra Sue," I said. "You'll like that."

She hushed blubbering for a couple of seconds to think about it.

"Listen, honey," Grandma said. "I read that play when your mama had the book here, and it struck me then that all the parts are important. Ever' last one of them. The banker's wife, even though her role isn't large, represents something. All that walking around in fancy clothes and saying hardly anything shows the indifference a lot of people have toward the Christ child."

Myra Sue gulped back a sob and hiccupped a time or two, but she was looking at Grandma in a hopeful kind of way. "Really?"

Grandma nodded. "Yep. You get up there on that stage and act as cool and uncaring as you possibly can, and folks watching can't help but understand what your part means."

Myra swallowed hard. "But what if I get up there and get scared and make a fool of myself again?"

Here's the thing. Isabel has yakked about being onstage ever since she moved to Rough Creek Road, and believe it or not, some of what she's said has stuck with me.

"Hey, Myra," I said. "Who is the most uncaring person you know?"

"Binkie Shumacher," she said immediately. She sniffed hard and raked her palms across her eyes. "Why are you asking me about that brat?"

"I don't know a lot about this acting stuff, but most of it is just pretending, isn't it?"

She sorta shrugged and said, "I suppose you could call it that."

"Well then, just pretend to be Binkie Shumacher pretending to be the banker's wife."

She gawked at me for a minute like I was a Christmas elf, then she sat up straight.

"Yes! April Grace, yes! It's called method acting, and Isabel would say it just that way." She narrowed her red-rimmed eyes at me and looked at me all suspicious. "Have you been hanging around with Isabel behind my back?"

Oh brother.

"No way. And why would I?"

"Because you usually are not so smart."

Sometimes I just wanted to smack that girl.

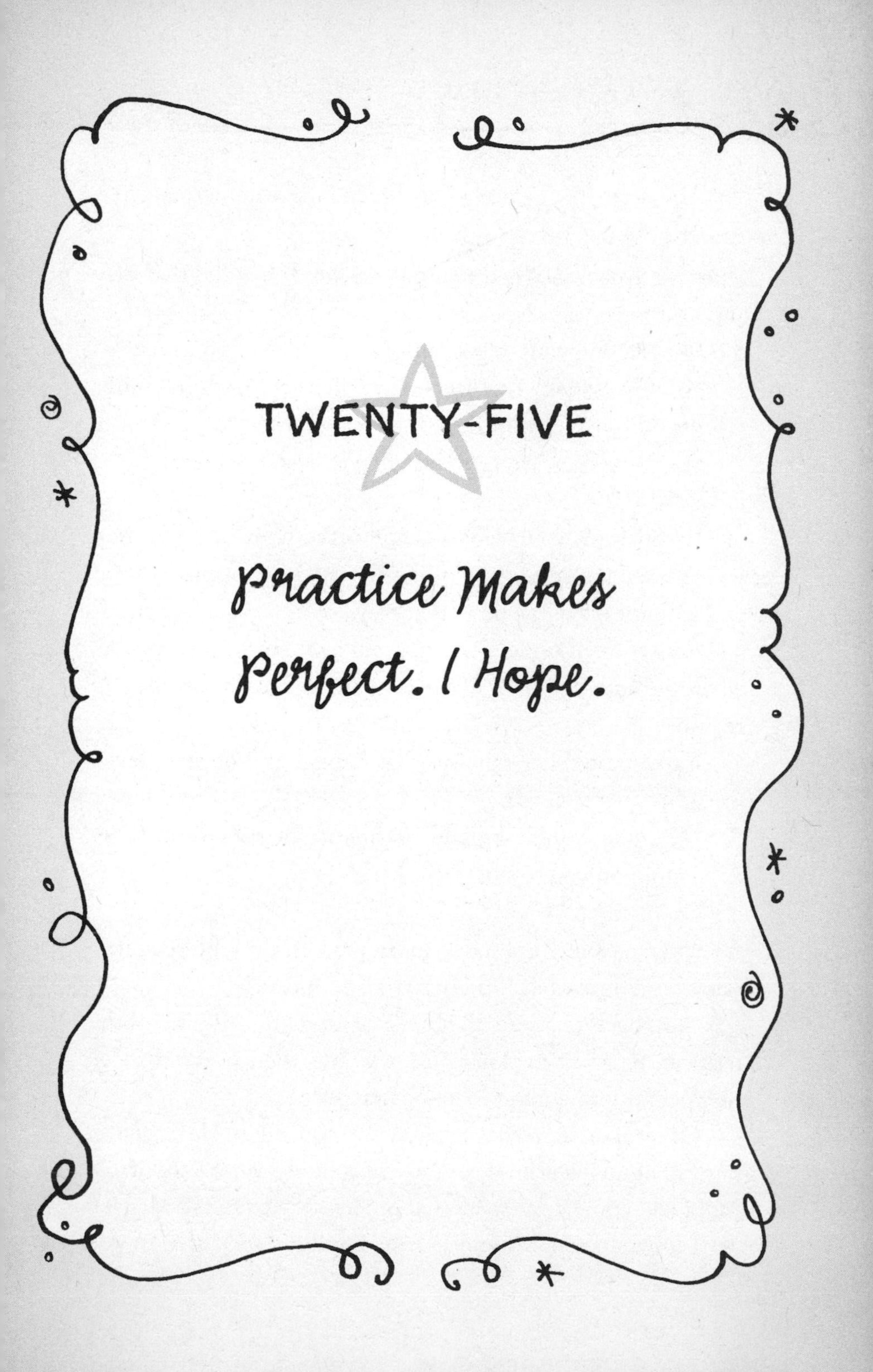

TWENTY-FIVE

Practice Makes Perfect. I Hope.

☆

Once ole Isabel assigned that part to me, I dreaded that play and all the rehearsals leading up to it every waking hour of the day. I kept trying to get out of it.

"Listen, Isabel," I said at supper the very next night after tryouts, "I'll make you a deal."

She looked up from her salad and raised one crazy eyebrow. "Oh?"

"I will wash your windows and make your bed and mop your floors and scrub your toilet for the next twelve years if you will not make me be in that play."

"Why, April Grace!" Mama said as if she was surprised, when she *knew* I did not like getting up in front of people and reciting.

Isabel patted her lips with her napkin and blinked seven or eight times real fast.

"My dear child," she said, all important-sounding, "I am depending on you to carry that part."

Oh brother.

"Nancy Burke is a nasty, mean person. I might be a little sassy sometimes, but I'm not nasty and mean."

"You have to *pretend*," Myra Sue piped up. "Think of the nastiest, meanest person you know and then pretend to be that person pretending to be Nancy Burke."

Ole Isabel clasped her hands and looked at Myra Sue in pure delight. "Darling! You are absolutely right." As if ole Myra had come up with all that on her very own. Good grief.

I looked at Mama and Daddy, hoping they'd step in and

say something like, "Isabel, April Grace really shouldn't be getting up in front of people because she might throw up or pass out."

But they didn't. They just smiled. As far as I was concerned, a gigantic volcanic tornado-blizzard could come and carry us all to Oz or the North Pole, whichever was closer.

☆

The following Sunday afternoon, I rode along to church with Myra and Isabel, dreading the whole entire first practice that was about to take place. I envied ole Melissa, who got to play the part of one of the Miller children, and she did not have to say a single line except "Merry Christmas."

When everyone got to the church for that first rehearsal—and I do mean everyone 'cause I think they were too scared to stay away—Isabel had us stand in a circle on the platform and read. We read that whole entire play from first word to last. We were purely awful.

When we were finished reading, before anyone had a chance even to sneeze or sigh, ole J.H. stood up all straight and tall and spoke like he was about forty instead of in junior high. Do you want to know what that rotten boy said? Well, I'll tell you.

He said, right out loud in front of that entire bunch of kids, "Mrs. St. James, ma'am, I think in that one place where Jim Burke gives his wife, Nancy, that diamond necklace she'd been wanting, he should kiss her. I mean, it would make the whole scene more realistic."

Isabel didn't have time to answer because I narrowed my eyes at him and yelled, "J.H. Henry, if you even *try* to kiss me, I will slug you so hard, you won't come back to earth till you reach the Texas border. I promise you I will."

He looked at me all surprised, like I shoulda been dying to let him smooch me, but *no thank you very much forever*!

Well, you can imagine how everyone laughed and howled at all that, but I just kept staring at ole J.H. with my fist ready for action. He looked around at all those snickering kids, then he got all smirky his own self and winked at ole Lottie. I glanced at Lottie, and she was giving me the dirtiest, meanest stink-eye look you ever saw.

Let me tell you a little something about J.H. Have you ever seen that old, old TV show *Leave It to Beaver*? If you haven't, you should, because J.H. is exactly like Eddie Haskell, who thinks he's way cool, but is in fact a Total Creepazoid. For instance, both Eddie and J.H. swagger instead of walking like normal humans. And they both are real polite to adults but all smirky behind their backs.

Why Lottie Fuhrman clearly likes J.H. Henry is beyond me, but as far as I'm concerned, they can have each other.

"*People! I will have silence!*" Isabel projected so loudly, the overhead lights shivered in fear. "There will be no kissing whatsoever, on this stage or off it, during these rehearsals. You, young man." She fixed a poisoned-dart glare on ole J.H. "You'd better behave yourself."

We all stood in our circle and stared at Isabel. You know what? I figured ole Isabel was not going to have one bit of trouble controlling her dance classes at school next semester.

I figure if you can scare teenagers just with dirty looks and projecting loudly, you have a natural gift.

The next thing we did that afternoon was read the script again, but this time, Isabel broke us up in little groups, where we practiced the same bits over and over. By the end of that practice, I think everyone kinda was beginning to know how to say their parts.

Before she dismissed us for the day, Isabel said, "Begin learning your lines, people. Soon you will not be reading from your books." There went that Look again. She passed it to every one of us, even me and Myra Sue, then she said, "Next rehearsal will be Sunday afternoon."

On the way home, ole Isabel said, "April, dearest, you were wonderful! I knew you had a natural talent."

"Thanks," I said, sorta sadly, because I did not want her to get the idea that I was all enthused about being in a play, 'cause I was *not*, I promise you!

Ole Myra Sue crossed her arms over her chest and pooched out her lower lip.

"What about me?" she said, all dreadfully despairing and utterly undone.

"Oh, darling," Isabel said, glancing from the road to Myra Sue, "you'll be fine. Don't be afraid to project."

"I thought I *was* projecting!" she said.

"Perhaps you need some brush-up lessons, Myra, darling. We'll drop April off at your house, then you come home with me and we'll work on that."

Ole Myra brightened so bright, you would've thought the sun was shining inside that old pickup.

TWENTY-SIX

Ian and Isabel Go Home

☺

I tell you what. I needed something to take my mind off my problems, because it seemed all I could do was think about stuff that made me mad, sad, or ticked off.

My mama. That play. School. And the Lotties. Those goofy girls were getting on my nerves Big-Time, prancing around in their identical, oversized, padded-shoulder outfits and acting like they were God's gift to Arkansas.

"Make way for the Lotties!" one or the other of them always hollered as they strolled through the junior high hallway, even though there was a school rule against hollering in the halls. You know what? Everyone, even those smarty-marty eighth graders, got right out of their way like a bunch of ninnies.

The Lotties made fun of everybody except a few kids they chose to be nice to, like J.H. and his bunch and the basketball players and the cheerleaders. One day, ole Lottie followed behind Portia Wilkes, holding her nose and rolling her eyes while everyone laughed like it was the funniest thing in the world.

I'd stepped right up and said, "Lottie Fuhrman, you're mean."

And that just made everyone laugh harder. Luckily, Portia never knew what was going on.

Aside from the Lotties, there was math, which drove me crazy and which I do declare here and now that I will never understand unless someone with some good sense explains it where I can understand it, which I don't think our math teacher, Eugene Lesko, ever will.

You know what that teacher does during most of the time he's supposed to be explaining equations? I'll tell you. He talks about science fiction books. Who knows? He's kinda pale and glassy-eyed. Maybe he's an alien or a robot.

Lottie and Heather, the only two Lotties in that awful math class, draw pictures of him and pass them around during class, but ole Mr. Lesko has never caught on. Now, I don't like him much, but I don't think that's funny, my own personal self.

Of course, you know that Christmas play hung over my head like a rotten ole cloud, and at night I dreamed I was in front of a huge audience in only my underwear. That dream just never goes away, and it's a pure nightmare.

And let's not forget that baby. By November, Mama was getting rounder than a butterball, and that baby's due date kept creeping closer and closer like the approach of winter.

"I can't believe I still have almost three months to go," Mama said one night at supper. She looked at Daddy and said with a laugh, "Mike, honey, you might need to bring in the wheelbarrow before long to haul me around the house."

I eyeballed my mama's plumped-out figure and wondered if she'd ever look like Mama again.

☺

The first week of November, the St. Jameses moved themselves, bag and baggage, into their very own personal house. At last.

We helped them move, of course, and it was an adventure, let me tell you, because even though ole Isabel was more than fully recovered by that time, she did not want to break her long red fingernails or get her hands dirty. Not that I minded doing work too much. It kept my mind off other things.

You should've seen the St Jameses' place. All that hard work everyone had done really paid off. That house was no longer the falling-down old wreck that it had been last summer, with broken windows, a holey roof, and a saggy front porch surrounded by a weed-infested yard. Now Ian and Isabel were moving into a snug, cream-colored house with shining new windows, a red front door, and a nifty front porch big enough to have two wicker chairs. The men had cut and cleared out the overgrown scrub, trimmed dead tree limbs, and prepared some flower gardens that would bloom next spring.

All in all, you would have thought Isabel and Ian would've been happier than two pigs in slop to be in their own pretty house. Ian was satisfied, because he said he had always been a country boy at heart. Ole Isabel was probably happy, too, but she rolled her eyeballs every time he said it.

I was rather glad to help sweep and dust and lay shelf paper and all that kind of stuff to get Ian and Isabel's house ready for them. Isabel looked on in her pretty, pale yellow living room and ordered everyone around like Marie Antoinette. I hoped no one's head would roll.

The St. Jameses did not have furniture until right before they moved in because they had to sell everything before they came out here from California. You know all about that mess, so I won't go into it again, but the good folks along Rough Creek Road and at church all pitched in and donated things so Ian and Isabel would have everything they needed.

Grandma donated a nice recliner that she had bought when old man Rance was hanging around, but once he was out of our lives, she never used it. Mama and Daddy gave Ian and Isabel their own big old comfy bed and bought themselves a new one in Harrison. Ian and Isabel had slept on that bed so long, it was like it was theirs, anyway.

Mr. and Mrs. Hopper, an old couple down the road, gave them a rocking chair and a couple of cast-iron frying pans. Pastor Ross donated a small dining table and chairs that someone had given to him a few years ago.

All in all, they ended up with enough furniture to fill that house, and not only that, folks gave them pictures and curtains and lamps and a TV and rugs and a refrigerator and blankets and sheets and everything. Nothing matched, and most of it was used. I figured ole Isabel would curl her nose up at it, but if she did, I never saw it.

We threw a celebration party for them on the second Friday night in November. Grandma and Mama cooked it up. Grandma and me and Myra Sue and Temple were the ones who put most of it all together, although Mama did sit in bed and write out invitations for everyone. I about halfway figured the only ones who'd show up would be the Reillys, the Freebirds, and the St. Jameses, and maybe good ole Pastor Ross. Everybody was supposed to bring sandwiches and chips and cookies and such like. Of course, Temple balked at that, and she said she was gonna make big double batches of her nature cookies and bark bread.

All I could say about that was I was glad we were gonna have ham sandwiches and chocolate chip cookies because that stuff Temple makes is purely awful. Nobody would eat any of it, I knew, because everybody had been well-educated the hard way about Temple's snacks. But I'd be sure to eat one just so she'd know somebody was brave and loyal. Mama probably would, too, if she was sure one of them nature cookies wouldn't hurt the baby.

Since Ian and Isabel's house was only a short way down the road, Mama insisted on going to that party.

"There's no sense in trying to make me stay home," she told us all, "because I have not been out of the house except to see the doctor for *weeks*. I'm going, and that's that."

Shortly before it was time to leave that night, there was an Awkward Situation, and it was all because Grandma is more popular than she ought to be. Ole Ernie Beason knocked on our door, and he'd no more than come inside when someone else knocked.

I opened that door, and who do you think stood there, grinning all happy as he could be? I'll tell you. Rob Estes, that's who.

I reckon my ole eyeballs got bigger than two full moons when I saw him. If he noticed, he did not say anything. Instead he handed me a box of Mint Dreams.

"You share those with your sister, okay?" he said.

"Yes, sir. Thank you very much." I was thrilled with the gift, but I also had my eye on this whole boyfriends situation as Rob walked into the living room.

You know what? Rob smiled at Daddy, then he smiled at Ernie just like he wasn't a bit surprised to see him, and they shook hands.

Mama waddled into the living room, dressed in a dark blue maternity outfit with a lacy white collar and wide pant legs. She was wearing a pair of Grandma's ugly old shoes because her own shoes were too tight on her puffy feet.

When she saw both men, her eyes got big for a second, then she gave them both her pretty smile, just like this was not an Awkward Situation at all.

"April," she said, glancing at me, "would you run upstairs and tell your sister to hurry along?"

I was pretty sure she wanted me to inform Grandma of her two gentlemen callers while I was up there.

I dashed upstairs to knock softly on the door of Myra Sue's bedroom.

"Woo?" Grandma called.

"Grandma!" I screamed as loud as I could while whispering at the same time.

She opened the door, and would you believe she had false eyelashes on one eye but not the other? She was holding the other strip of lashes between the thumb and forefinger of her right hand like it was a spider she'd just plucked from the back of the closet.

"Grandma, who are you going to the party with tonight?"

"Going with? Why, I'm ridin' along with your mama and daddy and you girls. Why you asking?"

She went back to the mirror and made the awfullest face, with her eyebrows raised way high and her mouth drooping way open, and she poked those fake lashes on her eyelid.

"'Cause Ernie and Rob are *both* in the living room this very minute, *waiting for you*," I said in a loud whisper.

She was so startled, her hand jerked and those dumb eyelashes ended up on her forehead. She whirled around and gaped at me.

"*What?*" she squawked, like a strangled duck. "Why are *they* here?"

"Well, I don't know, Grandma. They are *your* boyfriends, not mine."

"Oh, hush that!" She scowled at me and bit her lower lip, thinking. "What am I gonna do?"

That was a good question.

"I think if it was me," I said, "I'd at least take my eyelashes off my forehead."

"What?" She spun back around and looked at her reflection. "Oh, good gravy!"

She set about removing those eyelashes and fixing her face, but she looked all wide-eyed, and I could tell, plain as day, she wasn't thinking about that dolling-up she was doing.

"Okay," she said finally as she put on some shiny black pumps, "here's what we're going to do."

"We?"

"Yes. *We*. I can't go down there and tell one I'll go with him and leave the other behind, so you and me and Myra Sue will ride with both of them."

She grabbed her coat out of the closet. Her face was pinker than strawberry Jell-O.

"All in the same car?" I hollered before I could stop myself. "Are you kiddin' me?"

"Hush, I said! And, no, I am not kiddin'."

"Grandma, I don't want to go with you—"

"You are going, and that's that. Get your sister, and we'll all go downstairs together. There's safety in numbers."

Oh, good grief.

Rob had the biggest car, so he drove. Grandma hustled me and Myra Sue into that backseat. Then she plunked herself down back there with us. That left ole Ernie to ride in the front seat with Rob.

Nobody uttered one mumbling word that whole entire trip. That was about the most awfullest, uncomfortablest car ride I've ever been on. I wished Rob would at least turn on the radio so we'd have some music to listen to instead of all that quiet. You know what else made it bad? I'll tell you: the amount of time it took to drive that short distance, that's what. Up ahead, Daddy drove Mama in the Taurus, and he was as careful as anything going over the bumps and rocks and ruts. Following along behind the way we were, it took us about a decade to go that half mile from our house to the St. Jameses' place. There was nothing to do in the car, and it was dark outside, so I couldn't even look at the landscape.

When we arrived at the St. Jameses', I was never so glad to get out of a car in my entire life. Right then I decided Grandma was on her own until it was time to leave. I figured it would be the same exact situation at that time, only backward. If I was lucky, maybe Isabel and Ian would invite me to spend the night.

I don't know how many folks showed up at that party, but I'll tell you something: it was a good thing all those men had worked on that house, 'cause I think it might have exploded from all the people filling it. I tried to walk from one side of the room to the other, and it like to have taken me a year and a half to push through all those bodies. Not only had everybody brought food, they'd brought presents, too—doodads and wickyjiggers to set around and look pretty. Sandwiches and chips and cookies and pies filled all the counter space. The pile of presents—flower vases, baskets, candles, that kind of stuff—took up a spot underneath the front room window. That mound nearly reached the hem of the St. Jameses' short, white living room curtains.

Ole Isabel and Ian were speechless as two rocks for the longest time, just kinda standing there in the middle of that party and food and gifts and people and fun. I made my way across the crowd and edged in next to them.

"How do you like your party?" I asked. And I had to ask loud because there was an almighty amount of noise from everybody talking and laughing.

Isabel blinked a bunch of times, but Ian was the one who spoke up. "I can hardly believe everyone has been so generous and kind. The fact that they've given us so much when most of them hardly know us nearly renders me speechless."

Isabel nodded, and I'm pretty sure I saw a tear or two swimming in her dark eyes.

I looked out over that bunch of people, with their paper plates full of baloney sandwiches and potato chips and pickles and cookies. I knew it wasn't the kind of fancy food the St. Jameses were used to having at parties in their other life, but a look at their faces told me that, at least for that night, baloney sandwiches were just fine.

After a little while, Daddy and Mama got ready to go

home. I wanted to go with them, but you know what? Grandma caught me at the door and said, "April Grace Reilly, don't you dare desert your grandmother in her hour of need."

"That's right, honey. Stay and help clean up, please," Mama said. She looked around.

"Yes'm." And that's what I did.

Let me tell you something: I was none too happy about the whole business of that ride home, and I wanted to get it over with. When folks started getting their coats and leaving, I plowed through that house, picking up cups and plates and paper napkins, and I didn't stop until everyone was gone.

My sister wasn't much help cleaning that party mess, but Grandma made Myra Sue sweep the floor while she and Isabel put away food that people had left.

Ian and Ernie and Rob stood outside on the porch and talked. I reckon most men are allergic to housework 'cause it seems to me they always disappear when the brooms and dishrags come out. Daddy helps from time to time, but sometimes he ducks out, too.

"This was just lovely, Grace," Isabel said, wiping a dab of water off her nice new white countertop. "I don't know when I've had a nicer party."

Grandma smiled and folded her dish towel across the drying rack. "I hope you feel right at home now, honey. Having your own place will make it a lot easier on you."

"It will, but I can never express how grateful we've been for everything you and everyone else have done for us. It has been simply amazing."

I just stood there and watched and listened. I don't think

I'd ever seen Isabel look so content, and I know I'd never heard her speak so warmly. I was purely glad she was happy.

Ian came inside just then, and a chilly breeze chased through the open door before he closed it.

He looked around his house, and it was plain as day from the smile on his face that he was satisfied with what he saw there.

When he spotted Isabel wearing one of the floweredy aprons Auntie Freesia Maloney had sent in a box of kitchen linens and gadgets, his grin got bigger. She held a dish towel in one hand, and a lock of her short dark hair hung loose in a single curl on her forehead. The color of her cheeks and the sparkle in her eyes right then came from excitement and happiness, not makeup. She gave Ian a smile that lit up her whole face.

All of a sudden it felt like the rest of us weren't even in that room, like that moment belonged totally to them.

"Get your coats, girls," Grandma said in a real quiet voice, as if she thought that speaking out loud would change something.

Myra Sue and I went quietly into the small blue-and-white bedroom and got the coats from off the top of Ian and Isabel's bed. Their room was pretty cozy with neat white curtains and a braided blue rug on the floor. The dresser and the chest of drawers did not match, but they were clean and polished, and the light from a pair of round white lamps gave the room a soft, warm glow.

We went back into the living room and handed Grandma her coat. Isabel and Ian were kissing. I won't say a single, solitary word about it, except to remind you how I feel about kissing and all that slop.

Just as we opened the door, Ian said, “Wait a minute, ladies. Let me get my coat and keys, and I’ll run you home in the pickup.”

“You needn’t bother,” Grandma told him. “I’m sure Rob will take us home.”

Ian cleared his throat, and an odd look flickered across his face.

“Uh, Grace . . . uh, Rob and Ernie left,” he said.

Grandma’s eyes got big. “*They did?*”

He nodded. “I’ll get my keys.”

While we waited, Isabel gave each one of us a hug. “Thank you for everything,” she said, and smiled at each of us in turn.

“You’re so welcome, honey,” Grandma said, smiling back at her. But I’ll tell you something. Grandma did not say another word until she told Ian good-bye when he dropped us off at the house. She remained silent when we went inside, and then she went straight upstairs without saying boo to anyone. She did not even go knock on Mama and Daddy’s door to see how Mama was feeling.

Myra Sue and I looked at each other. All big-eyed, she bit her lower lip. “Uh-oh,” she said, real quiet.

I nodded ’cause I had a strong suspicion that instead of two boyfriends, Myra Grace Reilly now had none.

TWENTY-SEVEN

The Show Goes On

✫

Once the St. Jameses were a half mile down the road instead of just across the field from us, ole Myra Sue drooped around like a wet hound dog until I got sick of looking at her. At least working with Isabel on the Christmas program kept that goofy girl from drooping completely away. And we all had Thanksgiving to look forward to.

Around our table on Thanksgiving Day, besides us five and a half Reillys, there were the St. Jameses, the Freebirds, Melissa Kay Carlyle and her mother, and Mr. Brett because his family lives so far away. Our dining room held us all, believe it or not. That room was made for big dinners, 'cause my great-grandma used to feed a bunch of farm hands in there every day at noon.

I will not bother to tell you everything that was set before us, but besides the usual turkey and dressing, we had green beans, field peas, sweet baby peas, corn, pickled beets, bread-and-butter pickles, sweet little gherkins, dill pickles, deviled eggs, garden salad, cranberry salad, Jell-O salad, carrot salad, mashed potatoes, sweet potatoes, corn muffins, yeast rolls, biscuits, and I'll stop there without mentioning everything else and all those desserts still in the kitchen, because I'm making myself hungry.

I want you to know that when we finished our dinner, Melissa and I went into the bedroom and looked in the mirror at our tummies, which were actually Sticking Out from all that food. We'd have laughed ourselves silly at that if we hadn't been so all-fired full. And after a little nap that we seemed unable to control, we went back downstairs for a snack.

☆

By mid-December that play was coming along pretty good, and nearly everyone had learned their lines. All those kids who had auditioned and did not get a part had been asked to help find the rest of the props we'd need. Also, Daddy, Ian, and Forest had worked with the others in the church basement, making the sets Isabel insisted we have. Mr. Brett showed up a couple of times and helped with the carpentry part of it. Forest was an artist, and he painted rooms on the folding walls that Daddy and Mr. Brett made, and he'd done it so well, you would vow and declare that was a real fireplace and windows with curtains.

The only problem was Lottie Fuhrman, who made goo-goo eyes at ole J.H. instead of paying attention to when she was supposed to speak. I thought Isabel was gonna have a stroke a few times, she got so aggravated by that girl.

I knew ole Lottie's part as well as I knew my own and everybody else's, and I could've helped her if I'd wanted to. I wasn't so sure I wanted to. To make matters entirely worse between Lottie and me, she seemed to believe I was as crazy over that silly boy as she was, and she constantly shot me dagger looks and said all kinds of mean things. I do not know why she thought I liked J.H., because I told him to get lost, turn blue, and leave me alone about twenty times a day at school, and every bit as often during play practice.

I even told Lottie so, but you know what? She broke her Lottie rule about not talking to me and said, "You're just playing hard to get because you know that will make him like you even more!" Then she folded her arms and flounced away. She sat by herself because Aimee did not get a part in the play and she had flat-out refused to help with anything if she couldn't be one of the stars of the show.

Myra Sue's recent lessons on projection with Isabel had paid off. She spoke her part loud enough to be heard to the back of the sanctuary, and when Isabel praised her, she preened like a parrot and smiled until I thought her mouth would fall off. I hoped she'd be able to speak loudly when we had to put on the play in front of the whole world.

☆

Dress rehearsal, which crept up way faster than I'd wanted it to, was on the Friday night before we actually put on the play. Let me tell you, that rehearsal was *not* a barrel of laughs.

For one thing, ole Ethan Cole did not show up because he had a date with his girlfriend, Binkie Shumacher, who had threatened to break up with him if he did not take her to the basketball player/cheerleader Christmas banquet.

"Very well," Isabel said, miffed as all get-out. "I will read his part."

On top of that, wouldn't you know that every blessed one of us muffed our lines. For instance, Christy said, "We need children to buy milk," instead of "We need to buy milk for the children." And I completely forgot my mini-speech at the end. The more we messed up, the more Isabel thinned her lips. I was afraid she was gonna lose her temper and yell at us like she yelled at Pastor Ross that time.

"Isabel, we're messing up 'cause you make us nervous," I said.

She blinked a thousand times. "I fail to understand how."

"It's just 'cause you're the professional, and we're just kids."

Her face relaxed. "I see." She gathered us all around her on the stage. "Now listen to me, all of you. Forget that I'm reading this part. Banish from your mind that I am an adult, a female, and a professional. Replace that with the image of George Miller, a man who cares about his family and is desperate to help them. Can you do that?"

We all looked at each other and did not know what to say.

"I can," Myra Sue said after a moment.

"Me, too," Melissa piped up. But she had no lines, so why'd she even say that?

"I can, too," Christy Sanchez agreed.

I nodded, and in a minute all of us had promised to forget Isabel and pretend she was George. I don't know about anyone else, but it was easy once I put my mind to it. Maybe that was because ole Isabel was actually a good actress. When she read that part, it was like she *became* poor George Miller. It was like she believed what she (as George) said at the end about how God worked through all of us, from the most powerful to the most humble.

"Neither is more or less His child," she read. "We are all equally His children."

When she caught us gawking at her, she kinda shook herself and gave us a smile and a little shrug.

"When you allow yourself to be totally immersed in the character, you reach a depth that is almost mystical in nature," she said. We looked at her and at each other, and no one said a cotton-pickin' word because the way she'd read that part surprised us right into silence.

She clapped her hands. "Back to it, people! Nancy Burke, it's your line."

I closed my eyes, remembering where we were in the play, and jumped back into rehearsal mode.

We went through the play three times that night, and let me tell you, when I got home, I fell into bed and went smack-dab to sleep without knowing a thing about it until I woke up the next day. The day of the play.

That was Saturday, December 20, and the play started at seven o'clock that night. I was so nervous, I could not eat anything the whole livelong day.

With all the trouble and hard work we had put in, I surely hoped the weather would cooperate, even though it meant I'd have to be up there in front of the entire church and town and world and speak the words of that store owner's mean wife.

As it turned out, though, the day was sunny with a December kind of cold—not piercing and sharp the way it gets later on, but quiet and gentle. The kind of cold that closes around you softly, bit by bit, until you have to fasten your coat or go inside. In December in our part of Arkansas, you can walk through the woods and enjoy it more because the snakes are hibernating and the ticks and chiggers and mosquitoes are dead or asleep or whatever they do in the winter. The leaves are down and you can see the shapes of brown tree branches and the squirrels' nests up in them. In our neck of the woods, you'll find big green clumps of mistletoe hanging off the branches.

Let me tell you a little something: that year, I hoped no one got the bright idea to cut down fresh mistletoe and hang it in our house. My mama and daddy smooched every chance they got, it seemed to me—even more since that baby was on its way, if that was possible. In my own personal opinion, there had been enough kissin' in the Reilly household that year to last a century or two!

My mama begged the doctor to let her go to the Christmas program. I don't know what she told him, but he agreed. I wasn't convinced that her riding all the way to church and sitting on those pews for two hours was a good idea. But I've said it before, and I bet I'll say it a million more times: I'm just a kid, and no one listens to me.

We left way, way early that evening, and Daddy drove so slow, you would've thought he was 112 years old. Once we were on the highway, Mama said, "For goodness' sake, Mike, we won't get there until tomorrow if you don't speed up a little."

We got to the church earlier than most. Pastor Ross was there, of course, and a couple of the deacons and their families. Ian and Isabel were there, and had probably been there since noon, because ole Isabel had been nervous as a cat for the last two weeks.

One thing about it, though: she knew how to make the

place look the way she wanted. Inside our church, fat white candles burned in all the windows. A big ole candelabra stood on the piano, and it held about five million candles, all aglow. Big old runners of greenery were looped near the ceiling along every wall, and each pew had a pretty wreath of cedar and a red velvet bow.

"Understated elegance" is what Isabel called it. She did not want lots of lights and tinsel and colors, so we didn't have them. I have to admit, that church looked good and smelled nice, too.

The Tinker twins were dressed up and slicked up and looked right handsome for a couple of rotten, rowdy boys. It was a good thing they didn't get a part, or that Christmas play would have been a Total Disaster 'cause they woulda probably stood up there onstage, grinning like goons, waving at folks in the audience, elbowing each other, and snickering. They handed out the programs to people as they came in, and they acted like they had some sense because they were quiet and respectful.

The platform looked nice, like a real stage, even if the curtains had been made from two king-sized sheets strung on a wire.

"Just be glad Lottie's mother donated them," I whispered to Isabel shortly before the play started. "Otherwise, we would've had nothing."

"I suppose you're right." Her face was white and pinched as she walked around on that stage, moving things a fraction of an inch this way or a slight turn that way. All of us were standing around, waiting for her to tell us to take our places.

"Isabel," I said, grasping her thin arm. She was wearing a sleeveless black sheath dress that reached about halfway to her ankles.

Her skin beneath my fingers was so cold, I like to have got frostbite.

"Isabel," I said again, "everything is gonna be just fine. You've done a real good job, and all us kids are grateful for you teaching us what to do."

"You've been great, Mrs. St. J.," said Ethan. "Without you, we'd never have been able to pull it off."

"And the sets are awesome," added Christy Sanchez. "All this makes me wish Cedar Ridge had a real theater so we could have live plays more often."

And guess what? Nearly everyone agreed with that. Not me. I did not ever want to face this kind of terror again.

"Truly?" Isabel said, her face all soft and surprised.

"Yeah!"

"You bet!"

"Yes!" everyone chimed in.

"Radical," ole J.H. said.

Isabel looked at her wristwatch and beckoned all of us to gather around her like a flock of chicks.

"Thank you, young ladies and gentlemen, for your hard work. It hasn't always been smooth going because I know I'm not always the easiest person to get along with. But you've given your time and your talent, and you've worked hard. I'm very proud of each of you. I'm sure you'll do wonderfully tonight. Don't worry if you forget a line. I'll be right there on the front row with the script and I can prompt you, so be sure you're listening. Remember to enunciate, emote, project, and pause." She looked around. "Any questions?"

Myra Sue raised her hand somewhat timidly.

"Yes, darling, what is it?"

"Could someone say a prayer? Please?"

Ole Isabel blinked about ten times, but she nodded. "Very well. Shall I get the pastor?"

"I'll do it, Mrs. St. J.," Ethan said.

So we all bowed our heads and he prayed, "Thank You, Lord, for this opportunity to share this great play with our friends and family. We thank You most especially for Mrs. St. James, who has taught us so much. We ask that You bless her and hold her close to Your heart, and we pray that You will bless this play and all of us who will be in it so that the words we speak will have meaning for all who hear them. In Jesus' name, amen."

We echoed his "amen," even Isabel, who opened her teary eyes and gave ole Ethan a big smile.

"That was lovely, dear. Thank you so much." She glanced at her watch again. "And now, kids, it's showtime. And as they say, break a leg!"

She stepped quickly and carefully off the platform and sat down on the front pew. We took our places. The lights in the sanctuary went out, and the pulpit and platform lights were all that were left shining.

Two deacons pulled the curtains.

I thought for sure I was going to throw up from sheer terror, but I closed my eyes. Without forming words, I prayed for strength and smarts. I remembered that, right then, I was no longer April Grace Reilly, eleven going on twelve, but a selfish woman named Nancy Burke who wanted diamonds for Christmas, even if it meant someone else would go without a place to live or food to eat.

I opened my eyes, took a deep breath, and spoke my first line to my pretend husband: "I'm tired of hearing these sob stories every Christmas. If these people want to eat and stay warm, they should get jobs, not come into this store expecting handouts!"

From then on, it came natural as you please. I left the stage at the proper time and returned on the right cue. All us actors moved and spoke and did just what Isabel had taught us. Except for Lottie, who could not remember her lines *at all*. When I was close enough to where she stood, I murmured them to her as I brushed imaginary dust from my sleeve or adjusted my jewelry. But the rest of the time, Isabel had to prompt her from the audience. That caused some giggles from backstage at ole Lottie's expense, let me tell you.

Then it came time for ole Myra Sue and her theatrical debut. She walked out on that stage—no, that's not right. Instead of entering the scene with a dignified walk, she galumphed out on the stage as if big, heavy strides would give her courage. Instead of making a graceful gesture with her hand toward Holly Burnside, who played the blind woman, my sister threw her arms wide open like she was distributing candy from a float in the Christmas parade.

"Why does that blind woman just stand there?" she yelled, instead of projecting with a strong but refined voice.

Well, I tell you what. She had obviously forgotten every

blessed thing Isabel St. James had taught us about becoming and believing the part and not acting all over-the-top, but one thing about it: everybody in the church (and probably out in the parking lot and down the street) heard her.

Ole Myra Sue's face got red, and then it got redder. I was sure she'd bust out bawling and run off the stage, but she didn't. She walked stiffly to the place where she was supposed to stand during most of that scene, and she stood there. I don't think she blinked one time.

I felt sorry for her, but then, I didn't have much time to think about that because I had to be Nancy Burke, and it was nearly the end of the play, and Nancy Burke, who had learned something about being a good person, was about to say something important.

"How can a blind person see? How can the homeless give comfort? Where do the elderly find hope?" Step, step, step across the stage until I stood beneath the pulpit light. "From a heart that overflows with God's love."

When the deacons pulled the curtains closed, you never heard so much applause in the Cedar Ridge Community Church in your whole life. Isabel slipped back up onstage, smiling all over herself.

"You young people did beautifully!" she said. "I'm sure your parents are so very proud of each of you!"

TWENTY-EIGHT

Myra Sue in the Spotlight

After the play, I thought I might just pass out, I was so happy it was over. Even though I was so hungry that my stomach was gnawing on my backbone, I let everybody hug me or shake my hand or tousle my hair and say how much they enjoyed the play. Somewhere in or beyond all those people squishing me were my folks, but I couldn't see over the heads of everyone else. I knew I'd see them right soon in the fellowship hall, so I made a beeline to that big, long room where there sat more food than you've ever seen in one place in your entire life. I'm telling you, when it comes to a potluck or a party, Cedar Ridge Community Church knows how to put on the dog. In a good way. And just in case you don't know what "put on the dog" means, I'll tell you. It means going all out. If I'd eaten even a little bit of all the good stuff that was spread out there, like fudge and divinity and chocolate cake and red velvet cake and ham sandwiches and sausage balls and guacamole with chips . . . Well, you get the idea . . . But if I was to eat just a little of everything, I bet my whole stomach would explode and my body right along with it.

"April Grace, honey!" Mama said right behind me just after I crammed the biggest ole hunk of fudge you ever saw into my mouth.

I whirled around and tried to smile, but who can smile with a mouthful of black walnuts and creamy milk chocolate fudge?

"Globglob!" I said (which translates into "Mama!"). It's a good thing ole Melissa was with her own grandmother right then, or she'd have hollered at me for hollering at her previously for talking with her mouth full.

"Oh my," Mama said, laughing. "You do like your chocolate, don't you, sweetie?" Then she gathered me into her plump, soft arms and pressed me against her round body. "You did so good, sweetie! That was the best play I've ever seen."

I swallowed as much of that fudge as I could without choking to death or having it dribble out of my mouth. I looked up at her.

"Really?"

"Absolutely. You didn't look scared at all."

"I was awful scared at first, but then I just remembered what Isabel told us before the play, and I was okay."

All of a sudden, Mama gouged me right in the chest. Except it wasn't Mama who did the gouging.

"Ooh!" She laughed, pulling back a little. She rubbed her hand over her big, round tummy. "The baby is active tonight."

"Did it just kick me?" I asked.

"Sure 'nough!" Mama said, laughing. "Every time you spoke a line tonight, April Grace, this baby kicked and moved. I think he recognizes your voice, honey."

I jerked back and looked at her belly. "Really?"

"Seems like, yes."

I thought about that for a minute. It was kinda neat that the baby knew me already.

"Hey, baby," I said, leaning close to that big bump that used to be my mama's trim tummy. "This here is your sister, April Grace Reilly."

"Oh!" Mama gasped.

"I saw it!" I said, gawking at her belly. "I saw it moving around right there under your clothes. Wowee! Hey, kiddo, do it again."

And it did.

Right about then, I got pulled away from my little brother or sister and into some stinky arms and smothered with the biggest ole hug you can imagine.

"Tootsie Roll! I have never seen such a wonderful play. You were super!" And here came all kinds of kisses all over my face. Good grief.

"Thanks, Temple," I said, refraining admirably (if I do say so myself) from wiping my face. The Freebirds do not go to church, but it was sure nice of them to show up for that program.

"It was great," Forest agreed, grinning real big.

Those two looked all clean and combed for a change, and the odor wasn't too obnoxious—if you didn't get pulled into it like a giant vacuum cleaner the way I just did.

I tell you what: I got passed around and hugged by every grown-up I'd ever known, and while it was plenty nice to be praised and complimented, I was terrified there would not be any food left before I got to it because, believe me, that church was packed to the rafters and then some.

When people around me finally moved on to other people and other things or the food tables, I said to Mama and Daddy, "Where is Myra Sue? I bet she feels awful after she messed up that line of hers by hollering it out at the top of her lungs."

"I looked for her, but it's so crowded in here," Daddy said.

"Is she with Isabel?" I stood on my tiptoes, trying to see, but like Daddy said, there were so many people in that room, it was hard to see past them all.

"Isabel's over there, surrounded by her adoring public,"

Mama said, smiling. "I'm glad it all went so well for her. Why don't you see if Myra is with her, honey? I need to sit down."

I was mighty hungry, I tell you, but right then I sorta thought my sister was more important than my stomach. While Daddy led Mama to a chair, I went looking for Myra, and I'll tell you where I found her. I found her up on that platform, sitting beneath the pulpit light, with the sheet-curtains pulled where no one could see her.

All the lights were out except for that pulpit light, and it shone down like a beam right on top of her blond head. She sat there, knees drawn up to her chin and face buried in her arms. I did not hear a sob, a sigh, or a whimper. I wondered if she'd gone to sleep.

"Myra?" I said softly.

She kinda jerked, then real slow she raised her head and looked at me. There was something in her eyes I had never seen before, and it kinda scared me.

"Myra," I said again, coming to her. I knelt down, facing her on that almost-brand-new red carpet. "Don't you want something to eat? There's all kinds of good stuff. Carol Rhoades made divinity, and you know how you dearly love it."

She didn't change expressions. Instead she lowered her head on her arms again. "I can never show my face in this church again," she said, all muffled-like, coming as it did from beneath her arms.

"Oh, Myra Sue. Sure you can!"

She shook her head. "I was awful. I let down Isabel and Mama and everybody. I let down myself because I thought I had talent, but then I got up there and acted like the worst thing that's ever graced the American stage."

"You did fine, Myra. You were just a little nervous, probably, and overdid it a little. But it's just this one time. Next time you'll do way, way better."

She didn't say a thing. She just sat there, all bunched up.

"Myra? Let's go find Mama and Daddy."

She shook her head. "I just want to sit here and think about what an awful actor I am."

"Would you like me to sit with you?"

She lifted her head enough to glare at me. "Oh sure! Rub it in, April Grace, that you were so much better than me. That's all I need to hear, thank you very much." She put her head right back down.

I sighed.

"Just go away," she mumbled.

"Okay then," I said after a little pause. I got up and went back to the fellowship hall.

Isabel was standing near the door, talking with a couple of old ladies. I marched right up to her and waited until those women hushed because I have been taught it is the Ultimate Rudeness to interrupt people when they are talking.

"Isabel, Myra Sue needs you."

She lifted an eyebrow. "Oh? Where is the dear girl?" She looked around.

"Come with me."

As soon as we stepped into the sanctuary, I whispered to Isabel what Myra looked like and what she said.

"She needs you," I repeated.

"Well then, let's go talk to her."

"You go on. She don't want me there right now." I caught

her arm before she left me. "Isabel, I didn't mean to be better than her. Honest, I didn't."

She smiled at me and patted my hand on her arm. "I know, darling. I'll explain it to her. Thank you for telling me."

Once she trotted off down the aisle toward the spot of light behind the curtain, I went back to find Mama and Daddy.

"I found Myra Sue. She's sitting on the platform, and she's feeling bad about how she did tonight."

Mama started to get up, so I added real quick, "Isabel is with her now, so I'm pretty sure she'll be all right. You know how she loves and adores ole Isabel."

I glanced at Mama's cup, which held red punch. "Want some more punch, Mama? Daddy, you want me to get you a sandwich?"

"No, thanks," they said at the same time.

Mama stirred in her chair again. She looked awful tired.

"Mama, if you want to go home, I can hang around here until Myra is feeling better, then we can . . ." I gulped real deep and hard before I could finish. "We can ride home with Grandma."

"No, honey. I'm feeling a little better right now, so I'll go see to Myra Sue."

She grabbed Daddy's hand and heaved herself to her feet while Daddy balanced her by hanging on to her arm. Then she waddled off, the palms of both hands resting against her back like she was pushing herself.

"Daddy, is Mama really feeling better? She looks mighty miserable to me."

"Honey, I think she feels as good as possible, given her

condition. And the condition of her condition." He gave me a smile and gently flicked the tip of my nose with his pointy finger. "I want you to quit worrying so much, okay?"

We looked at each other for a minute, and I finally heaved a big sigh.

"I will try."

"Good!"

After a bit, I said, "I'm gonna go get some food 'cause my stomach has done took a bite out of my backbone."

He nodded and got up. "Okay, punkin. I'm going to go see about your sister."

I filled my plate with little tuna sandwiches, barbeque potato chips, mixed nuts, Oreos, chocolate chip cookies, pecan pralines, fudge-nut brownies, peanut clusters, butterscotch fudge, and pumpkin pie with whipped cream. Then I sat down and ate.

Just about the time I'd finished my second plateful, I spotted Mama, Daddy, Myra Sue, and Isabel coming out of the sanctuary. All of them were smiling, but Myra Sue's eyeballs were all red, and her lips and nose were puffy. I figured she'd been bawling pretty hard. Those four had not been in the fellowship hall two minutes before folks were going up to Myra Sue and shaking her hand, or hugging her, and telling her how proud they were of her, and bragging how brave she'd been to get up there in front of so many people. I tell you what: no one said a thing about how awful she'd done. I hoped that made her feel better.

It sure is nice to have folks around who love you even when you goof up Big-Time.

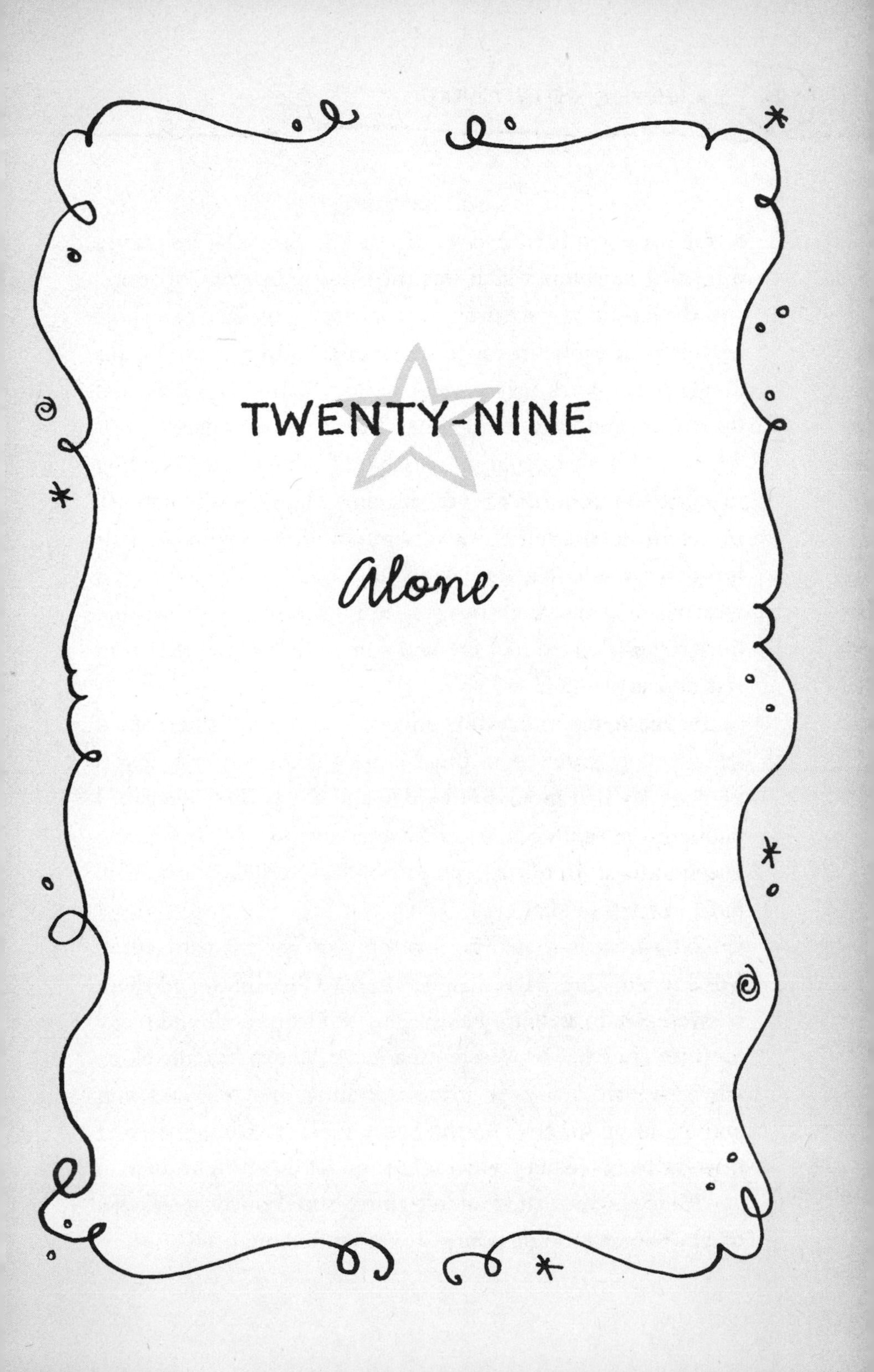

TWENTY-NINE

Alone

☆

The next morning, which was the Sunday before Christmas, was the little bitty kids' program that always took up the whole service with carol-singing and reciting Scripture and poems about Jesus's birth. My part of holiday acting was over and done with, and I was more grateful than you can imagine.

"Oh, I wish I could go with you!" Mama said, standing near the front door as we were leaving. Daddy was in his dark blue suit, and me and Myra were in new dresses with lace collars and shoulder pads and wide belts, and ole Myra was even wearing one-inch high heels. She looked pretty grown-up, but she still looked like she had some leftover sadness from last night's play.

Right then I wasn't too concerned about my sister. She'd start feeling better soon. But Mama did concern me. It was plain as day that going to the play and the potluck afterward had worn her out. She sort of leaned against the wall as she gazed at us all in our coats and holiday clothes. She smiled, but I saw tears in her eyes.

Now, that is something I rarely saw, my mama in tears. I got to thinking. Here it was, almost Christmas, and there we were, all dressed up, standing by the front door and ready to go to church. We were gonna leave Mama at home alone when she had always so loved watching the little kids sing and quote Bible verses on the Sunday before Christmas. She must've been feeling really lonely and let down right then.

And besides that, I didn't think she looked good, like maybe she was feeling poorly along with being tired.

"Mama," I said, taking off my coat. "I'm staying with you."

She looked at me. "No, honey. You go on to church and enjoy the music. Tell me all about it when you get home."

I turned to Daddy and said, "I'm staying home. I'm taking care of Mama this morning."

"April Grace," he began. Then he looked at Mama. Maybe he saw as well as I did that she was in no shape to be left alone that morning. "Lily, honey, are you okay?"

"I'm fine, Mike. I'm tired. As soon as y'all leave, I'm heading back to bed."

"I am staying, Mama." I slid off my new black shoes. They pinched my feet anyway. "You can ground me if you want to. You can make me scrub out the refrigerator; you can make me wash all the dishes in the cabinet. I don't care what you do, but I am staying with you this morning."

I reckoned I might get in trouble for being rebellious and stubborn, especially on a Sunday, especially this close to Christmas, but I didn't care. I marched right upstairs, carrying my coat over one arm and my shoes in the other hand. And you know what? Neither one of them argued with me. In fact, I think maybe my parents were a little relieved that, this once, Mama would not be home alone on Sunday morning.

I shucked off my new dark green, velvety dress, put on jeans, a dark blue sweatshirt with Santa's grinning face on it, and my good ole comfy sneakers; then I hurried back downstairs and went right into Mama and Daddy's bedroom. The door was open, and she was halfway propped up on the pillows, lying against them on her side. Her face seemed more flushed than usual.

"Honey, I wish you'd gone to see the little kids' program. It'll be so cute."

"I know, but I'd rather stay with you. It'll be fun, just you and me."

She smiled at that, kinda weakly.

"Would you like me to read to you?" I asked.

She shifted around in the bed, rearranged the covers a little, and settled her head against the pillow.

"Not right now, honey," she said. She closed her eyes.

I looked at that mound that was her tummy and vowed I'd never in my life have a baby. Ever. Especially one that seemed determined to wreck its mama's health.

"Mama?" I said softly.

"Hmm?" She didn't even flutter her eyelashes.

"Mama? Are you all right?"

"Mmm," she replied, and shifted in the bed again like she couldn't get comfortable. A small frown flickered across her forehead.

"Want me to fluff your pillows or straighten your blankets? Would you like a cup of tea or a glass of water?"

She sighed. "I'm just going to rest, honey," she mumbled, and that was all she said. She still had not looked at me.

I noticed the water pitcher next to the bed was only half full. I got it and whispered, "I'm gonna go fill this up with fresh water."

She didn't say a word, and I slipped out of her room. When I came back toting that pitcher full of ice water, she hadn't moved a muscle from the time I left and was just staring at the wall. I ran upstairs to my bedroom and got *The Clue in the Diary*, a Nancy Drew mystery, then ran back down to Mama's room and sat in the little antique wicker chair.

I bet I read one page at least 194 times, or more. I knew the book was good and I planned to read the whole entire series and had already read the first six, but that day I could not concentrate on Nancy or Ned or Bess or sleuthing or anything else. Finally I just set that book aside and watched Mama. She started stirring around again, and this time I noticed she was gripping the covers so tight, her hands were white.

"Mama?" I jumped up and ran to her side.

She groaned so loud, it was like she was trying to upchuck rocks.

"Mama, what's wrong? Are you all right?"

I looked at her round belly.

"Mama, are you having labor pains?"

But surely not. That baby wasn't due for another month and a half yet. Mama did not reply. Instead she moaned, and then she began to cry. She did not look at me at all.

I have to tell you right now, I was purely scared. Something was happening and there was not one person in that house to help me. Grandma, who was back living in her own house now, had gone to church. And Ian and Isabel and Forest and Temple had all planned to visit the church today to watch the little kids' program, so I knew that no one was home on Rough Creek Road, at least no one close by.

I started to shake like the last dry leaf in a cold November wind.

April Grace Reilly! I yelled at myself inside my head. Get ahold of yourself right this minute! You can't shake like a wet dog or cry like a little kid or pout like Myra Sue or get riled like Isabel! You have to do something, and you better do it now, or I'm gonna whomp you upside the head in about a minute!

I don't know how I could whomp my own personal head, but I didn't stand there and try to figure it out. Instead, I ran to the phone on the little table in the hallway. Zachary County did not have 9-1-1 like the rest of the world, so I dialed zero and called the operator.

"Ma'am," I said into the phone the second she answered, "something is wrong with my mama, and I need an ambulance at my house fast."

Then she asked me where I was calling from and told me to be calm, and then someone else was on the phone with me, and it turned out to be the sheriff's office. I don't know why I was talking to the sheriff's office, but I didn't care as long as they sent someone to help.

"There is something wrong with my mama, and I think maybe she might be having her baby, but it isn't due for a long time, and I'm here all by myself 'cause everyone has gone to church, and please, please, someone has to get out here and help!"

I wanted to bust into tears and go hide under the bed, but I didn't. Instead, I swallowed real hard and told that man on the telephone exactly who I was and where we lived and how old I was and what Mama was doing and how long she'd been doing it. Then he wanted to talk to Mama, and I pulled the phone as far as the cord would stretch, and it would not stretch far enough.

Boy, oh boy, I felt the sobs. They were right there in the front of my eyes, in the back of my throat, on the tip of my tongue, battling to spew right out and show off to everyone how scared I was and how much I didn't know what to do. But I wouldn't give in. No, sirree. I could cry later, but not right then, not when Mama needed me.

"The phone won't reach," I told the man on the other end of the line.

"Then can you talk to your mother for me?"

"Yes, sir."

"Ask her how she's feeling."

"Yes, sir. Mama, the sheriff wants to know how you're feeling."

"Bad," she moaned.

I gulped. "She says 'bad.'"

"Ask her if she's having contractions."

"Mama, are you having contractions?"

She groaned, then said, "Something's wrong."

"Mama!" I screamed before I could stop myself. I gulped again, swallowing my terror, and told the man on the phone, "She says something is wrong. When are you gonna stop talking to me and send an ambulance?" I hollered at him.

"Honey, an ambulance is on its way. It'll be there before you know it." And then he started asking me questions to ask Mama, and I did that until I heard the most beautiful sound I ever heard: the siren on that ambulance screaming its way down Rough Creek Road, nearer and nearer, bringing help to my mama.

I opened the front door and led those paramedics to her

room, and then I kinda stood back and watched as if I were someone else who didn't have a body or a mind or a mama or anything. I didn't even know a deputy was there until I sort of woke up to find myself in the front seat of his police car. We were whizzing down the road behind that ambulance with lights and sirens and everything.

I turned my head and looked at him. He was a big man with a big face and blond hair and eyebrows. He glanced at me.

"How you doin', little miss?" he asked me.

I stared at him for a good, long time, then I reached out and touched his arm, because I wasn't sure that this wasn't a dream. But he looked and sounded and felt solid, so I knew I was sure enough awake.

"Is my mama in that ambulance?"

"Yes. And we'll be at the hospital in no time. Your mama will be fine."

"They won't take her to Blue Reed General Hospital, will they?"

"It's the closest."

"People go there when they want to die," I declared.

He said nothing for a minute, then said, "It's what we have."

I gave that nice man a dirty look. "I want my daddy."

"He's been called."

"Will he be at that hospital?"

"I'm sure he will be. Don't you worry, little miss."

But how could I not? I stared out the window and didn't say anything else.

THIRTY

Waiting Rooms and the Waiting That We Do

☺

I don't know who called Daddy—maybe the sheriff's deputy—but I hadn't been in that waiting room five minutes before Daddy and Grandma and Myra and Ian and Isabel and Forest and Temple poured through those doors. I was so glad to see every one of them, especially my daddy and grandma, both of whom I ran to and hugged and who hugged me back real hard.

"You doing okay, honey?" Daddy asked.

Again, I swallowed back my urge to bawl my head off, and I nodded, 'cause Daddy did not need to add me to his list of things to worry about.

A nurse took them back into the official part of all the emergency room business. The rest of us had to hang around in that waiting room. Myra Sue looked as pale as I felt, and let me tell you, all four adults looked worried sick.

"It's far too early for that baby to be born," Isabel kept saying as she paced back and forth in her shiny high heels.

"I wish I'd brought my special tea blend. That would help stop Lily's contractions," Temple said.

Isabel halted. Her eyes bored a hole right through Temple, but Temple did not notice. Instead, that ole hippie woman just strolled over to the corner of the waiting room, settled down in a chair, rested her hands palms-up in her lap, and closed her eyes. She looked perfectly peaceful, so I knew she was probably meditating, which is something I wished I could do, but I couldn't. I was too wound up and scared.

I'm not sure how much time passed, but it felt like several years before Daddy came into the waiting room. His maroon-colored tie was loose, and the top button of his new white shirt hung open. He did not look too much like Daddy right then, and I reckon when you're scared and worried, you just don't look like yourself.

"They've put her on a drip that's supposed to stop the contractions." He shook his head. "I don't know. I just don't know."

"How's Mama?" I asked.

"She's in a lot of pain, honey," he told me. "And she's scared. It's too early for the baby to come."

"When can I see her? I need to see her."

"I know, honey, but right now, they aren't letting anyone be with her but Grandma and me."

I swallowed down that information, and it tasted bitter.

"Will Mama be all right?" My words came out all strangled and tight.

You could see his smile was forced. "This is hard on her, but yes, she'll be all right."

"What about the baby?" Ian asked.

Daddy glanced at him and shook his head again. "I don't know. There's still a strong heartbeat, but . . . it's too soon. It's just too soon." He raked his hands through his hair, then pulled me and Myra Sue into his arms and hugged us. He even gave both of us a kiss on the cheek. "You girls don't worry. The doctor is doing all he can to save the baby and to take care of your mama."

"But, Daddy, can't you take Mama to a hospital where people don't die?"

"Honey, they're taking real good care of your mama right here. We can't move her."

A cold shiver ran down my back, and I saw in my memory that gray-faced old man lying in his bed in the hallway while those dumb nurses ignored him.

"Don't let Mama die!" I said.

"Shhh," he said quietly, holding me close. He pulled back and looked at both of us. "You girls do me a favor?"

We nodded.

"You pray for your mama and your new brother or sister. Okay?"

We nodded again. I prayed harder than I'd ever prayed in my life for my mama. I prayed for that baby, who hadn't even been born yet and had already caused more trouble than most kids do in a lifetime. But I was sorta beginning to acknowledge that none of this was because that little baby had decided to cause trouble. Things like this are just the harder part of life.

All afternoon, while we waited for time to pass and Mama to get better, folks from up and down Rough Creek Road and from church dropped in to see how she was. Even Mrs. Fuhrman, whose name was not Mrs. Fuhrman anymore but Mrs. Ritter, came by and brought Lottie with her.

I was not happy to see that Lottie, I tell you. One thing I did not need was some smart-alecky, hateful comment about my mama being sick. I sort of had a feeling that slugging a snotty Lottie in the waiting room was probably against hospital rules, so I surely hoped I didn't have to do any such thing.

Guess what that girl did? She walked right up to where I was sitting, sat next to me, and said, just as nice as she used to be, "I'm real sorry your mama is sick, April Grace."

Well, I was so surprised she'd sit by a "hick" like me, I practically turned to jelly and slid out of my chair. But I said, all prim and proper, "Thank you."

"I like your mama. I hope she gets better soon."

"Thank you very much, Lottie."

There was what is called an Awkward Silence between us while the grown-ups talked to each other in low voices.

"Is she having the baby now?" asked Lottie.

I swallowed hard because I did not even want to think about that child, let alone talk about it, but I said, "They're trying to fix it so she won't have the baby, 'cause it's not supposed to be born until the end of January, or maybe first of February."

"Oh. I'm real sorry."

"Thanks, Lottie."

She sat beside me for a little while longer; then her mother called to her.

"Well," she said, standing up. "See you later, April Grace."

"Yeah, Lottie. Bye."

If I hadn't been so worried about Mama, I would have been purely bumfuzzled—to use a Grandma word—by Lottie Fuhrman. Other than hollering at me when she got pelted with peas from Micky and Ricky, and griping me out about ole J.H. Henry, that day was the first time she had spoken to me directly since school started.

Myra Sue had been looking out the window, but she walked over to where I sat and said, "You told me that Lottie had become a big fat snob."

"She has."

"She looked the same to me. And she didn't act any different from any other time I've been around her."

"I know," I said, shrugging. "Maybe she has the Christmas spirit."

"Or maybe you just make things up."

I refused to argue. I just gave my sister a dark look, then deliberately turned away. If she was in a bad mood, it wasn't my fault, and I didn't feel good enough my own personal self to cheer her up right then.

I kept watching those doors that Daddy had walked through earlier and wished he'd come and say everything was all right.

Pastor Ross walked in, and I was mighty glad to see him. He brought us a lot of comfort just by his presence. He read some nice scripture, Psalm 91. I liked it a lot, especially those last three verses that say, "Because he hath set his love upon me, therefore will I deliver him: I will set him on high, because he hath known my name. He shall call upon me, and I will answer him: I will be with him in trouble; I will deliver him, and honour him. With long life I will satisfy him, and shew him my salvation."

When he closed his Bible, he said a good prayer in his kind, deep voice.

He stayed with us for a long time, and before he left, he said, "My niece was six and a half weeks premature, and she's in third grade now, at the top of her class. There is great hope."

He had us gather around, then he prayed a real nice, comforting prayer. When he was through, he shook everyone's hand, including mine, and left.

"I hope his niece's mother is just fine, too," I muttered when he was gone.

"I'm sure she is," Ian told me. "April, please try not to worry."

"I'm tryin'," I told him, purely honest.

He smiled. "I wish you'd come sit beside me and tell me about school. I haven't gotten much of a chance to talk to you lately." He cut a glance toward Isabel, who was frowning at one of her fingernails. Ole Myra Sue was looking out the window.

Ian lowered his voice. "To tell you the truth, I'm a little lonely since we moved into our own place."

I shot a look at ole Isabel as I sat down in the chair next to him and asked softly, "Isn't your wife good company?"

We met each other's eyes, and he leaned toward me, whispering, "Not as much as you might think."

He grinned at me, and I had to laugh, because I knew—and I was pretty sure he knew that I knew—that Isabel was not a lot of good company for anyone other than Myra Sue.

Until right then I had never thought about Ian St. James ever being lonely, but I reckon anyone married to Isabel would get that way in a hurry.

"How come y'all don't have any kids?" I asked. "They'd be good company for you, I bet."

He got kind of a sad look as he nodded. "Yes. Kids would be company. When we were young, we were both so busy with our careers. And Isabel never was too keen on the idea, and now, oh, I don't know . . . At this point, I think we're too old for children."

"You're not any older than my folks."

"That's true." He seemed lost in thought for a while; then he nudged me slightly with his arm. "Tell me about school. How you doing in algebra?"

"I still hate math."

Then I caught him up on school and told him all about how that year had been so weird and how I'd been so worried about Mama and everything at home. I told him about the Lotties and what a pain they were.

"I wouldn't worry too much about them, April," he said. "Every school has a clique or two in it."

"You think so?"

"I *know* so. And I can tell you something about the people who are a part of cliques."

It sounded like he knew what he was talking about, and besides that, I liked and trusted ole Ian.

"Tell me," I said.

"I used to be in a clique."

That did not surprise me as much as he might have thought it would. Maybe he forgot how snobby he was when he first moved to Rough Creek Road. But I wasn't holding any grudges.

"I know something now that I did not know then," he said.

"What's that?"

"Kids in a clique don't feel good about themselves."

I gave him a look because I did not believe that for a minute.

"It's true. Take it from an old guy like me who has been around. People who make fun of other people are doing it because they want to make themselves feel better. These girls are probably as scared and insecure about being in junior high as you are, so to help them feel strong and brave, they act out. That way, the ones they pick on are so busy feeling bad, the girls won't notice how scared or vulnerable or confused they are inside. They feel second-best, but they sure don't want anyone else to know it."

Well, I tell you what. I just stared at that man for a good portion of time while I thought about how mean Lottie was to me, and how J.H. Henry was all flirty with me even though I could not stand him, and that seemed to make her meaner than ever.

"Are you telling me that ole Lottie Fuhrman feels insecure about a certain boy who likes me—who is a total creepazoid, by the way—and she feels like she's not as good as me because of *that*, and that's the reason she acts so rotten?"

"I'd almost guarantee that's part of it. You need to realize, too, that maybe Lottie and her friends have troubles at home that no one knows about. A bad home life can make people do rotten things."

"I see," I said slowly, as what Ian told me sank into my brain. Boy, oh boy, if he was right, that put a new light on everything. I reckoned I'd have to pay a little more attention to what was going on, and not be so quick to think mean thoughts about a girl who used to be one of my bestest friends. I mean, there must be some good friendship left in her, 'cause she'd been all nice to me just a little while ago.

I reckon next semester was going to be a little different than the one I'd just endured.

"You have given me something to think about," I told good ole Ian.

He smiled and gave my braid a gentle tug. "Good. It'll keep you from worrying so much about everything else."

It felt weird in that waiting room, strangers coming and going, and all of us getting so restless, we paced around those shiny tiled floors and looked at million-year-old magazines. Every time someone in those aqua-green scrubs came around, everyone in the waiting room looked up, and I'm sure every last one of us was hoping for good news. Most of the time those medical people just *shush-shushed* in their quiet shoes right on past us like none of us were even there, all worried and anxious.

Daddy kept coming in every little bit, telling us things like "She's doing fine, but her contractions haven't stopped yet," or "She's resting a bit."

I was beginning to think we'd be there all night long.

You won't believe this, but ole Temple and Isabel actually sat side by side and had the longest conversation you ever heard. It was all about vitamins and nutrition and food additives and all that kind of stuff. I have a feeling Mint Dreams did not make it onto their list of approved foods, but I was not invited to join that discussion anyway.

When the afternoon wore down and it started to turn evening-gray outside, Ian and Forest went to the farm to do the milking. Them dumb ole cows don't understand about being inconvenient, and they probably wouldn't care if they did understand. Cows don't think about anything but themselves.

Daddy came into the waiting room again.

"Her contractions have slowed considerably, and will probably stop completely soon." He rubbed his hands on his face like he was trying to rub away his tiredness. Then he dropped them and looked at Myra Sue and me. "It's getting late, and you girls need to go to bed."

"Oh, but, Daddy—" I said.

"No arguments. Grandma will take you home, and when there's any change, I'll call, and she can bring you back."

"But, Daddy—" I repeated.

Grandma laid her hand on my shoulder. "Hush, child. Let's not cause your daddy any more problems than he's already got. We'll go home, get us a bite of supper, and then get some rest."

I did not like this new development at all. I wanted to be Right There if Mama needed me, but there are times you just can't convince grown-ups of a blessed thing, and I knew as well as I knew my own name that this was one of those times.

I gave my daddy a big hard hug, made him promise to call us. Then I grabbed my coat and trudged out to the parking lot with Grandma and Myra.

THIRTY-ONE

Unto Us a Child Is Born

When I got into the car, I kept on praying that God would take care of my mama and that new baby. All the way home I prayed the same thing. When I took a shower, when I put on my pajamas, when I went to bed and I closed my eyes, that prayer just kept running through my mind like a long ribbon that was sewn together at the ends. In the morning, my prayer hung above my head and followed me from place to place.

"Are we gonna go see Mama today?" I said when I went downstairs for breakfast. Myra was sitting at the table, sleepy-eyed and silent. Grandma was scrambling eggs at the stove.

"You'll have to talk to your daddy," said Grandma.

"He's home?" Myra asked, as surprised as I was. "Why didn't he wake us up?"

"He came home only long enough to shower and get a change of clothes. He's heading right back to the hospital."

And right then he walked into the kitchen, buckling his belt. His hair was still wet, and he'd nicked himself shaving.

"Daddy!" I yelled and ran to him. He gave me a hug and kiss.

"How's Mama?" I asked.

"About the same."

"So she won't be home today?" I felt so disappointed I nearly cried.

"No, honey. I think they're going to have to keep her a long time."

"Oh, Daddy! Then I'll go get my coat and—"

"Me, too!" Myra Sue hollered.

"I'm going back right now, honey, and you girls haven't eaten your breakfast yet."

"I'm not hungry!" I started to dash out the door, but he stopped me.

"Me either!" Myra echoed.

"You can come later with Grandma. Right now I want you to eat a good meal. Grandma will make you whatever you want for breakfast."

He gave me and Myra Sue another quick kiss each, this time on top of our heads, and then he was gone. There wasn't much either of us could do about it.

Believe it or not, I was hungry. Sometimes when I get upset, like yesterday, I can't eat a single bite because food refuses to go down. Other times, like right then, I could eat the paint right off the walls. I turned to Grandma.

"Biscuits and gravy, please, with bacon and scrambled eggs and grits and hash browns."

And you know what? She made it all, every bit. And I ate it. Myra Sue, too.

About two o'clock that afternoon, Grandma called Ernie Beason and Rob Estes and filled them in on all that was going on, even though I figured they were all finished with that dating business.

"Grandma, are you and Ernie and Rob friends again?" I asked as soon as she hung up the phone. "You haven't gone riding around or to the movies or anything for a while."

She gave me a narrow look.

"Boy howdy," she said. "Nothing gets past you, does it, April?"

"Not much, if I can help it. So are you friends again?"

She blew out a breath. "We ain't never stopped being friends, child. But I reckon we all needed a break."

I frowned, trying to figure out my grandma's love life. She walked into the living room, and I trotted right along behind her. "So you gonna start dating that Methodist preacher, and if you do, you reckon he'd take me on a ride in his Mustang?"

"April Grace Reilly!" she said as she settled down into the recliner. "Number one: None of this is any of your business, and number two: Going out with someone just so's you can ride in his car would be a poor act of character. Now, leave me be. I want to take a nap."

I hushed up because I sensed if I probed much further into this subject, I might end up standing in the corner, which is what Grandma used to make me do when I was a little kid and she couldn't get me to hush.

Grandma adjusted the footrest and stretched out in that recliner.

I was reading my Nancy Drew book and my grandmother was snoring softly when the telephone rang. The sound startled her so bad, she like to have fallen right out of the chair.

"I'll get it!" I shouted, running toward the phone in the hallway. But wouldn't you know, that rotten ole Myra Sue reached it before I did.

"Hello? Hi, Daddy! Yes, Grandma's in the living room. Okay, hang on."

"Let me talk to him," I said, grabbing for the phone.

She jerked back, holding the phone to her chest with her back to me, and yelled, "Grandma! Daddy wants to talk to you."

"Ask him how Mama is! Myra Sue, ask Daddy how Mama is. Ask if he knows when they're coming home."

Grandma bustled into the hallway and took the phone from my sister. She frowned at us both like we were being brats. Which, I guess if you're gonna be technical about it, we were.

"Mike? How's Lily?"

I watched as her eyes got wide and the color drained from her face.

I reached out and grabbed Myra Sue. And she let me. In fact, she grabbed me back. We both stared at Grandma.

"Yes," she said into the mouthpiece. "Of course, Mike. We'll be there soon."

She swallowed hard and hung up the telephone.

"Grandma?" Myra Sue said, sounding as choked up as I felt.

"Girls," she said, gripping the edge of the telephone table, "your mama is in the delivery room."

We gawked at her until our eyeballs nearly popped out and rolled across the floor.

"Mama is having that baby *now*?" I hollered.

She nodded.

"But . . . I thought it was too early," Myra Sue said. "Daddy said they were going to stop her pains so it wouldn't get born so soon."

Grandma took a deep breath, let go of the table, and stood straight.

"Sometimes modern medicine doesn't do what it's supposed to." She took another deep breath. "Well, it's in God's hands now."

"Grandma?" I asked.

"Woo?" Her *woo* came out all soft and not like her usual *woo* at all.

"Will Mama die having that baby so early?"

She shook her head. "I don't think so, honey. Babies come early all the time."

"But . . ." Myra's voice came out all watery. "But that baby might die being born too soon, mightn't it?"

Grandma didn't answer, but I could tell just by looking at her face that the answer was yes.

"No!" I yelled. "No, no, no! I don't want our baby born before it's ready."

"I know," Grandma said softly. "I don't either, but all we can do is pray for the best and place our trust in the good Lord."

I did not have anything to say to that.

"Go get cleaned up right quick, girls. We're going to the hospital soon as you're ready."

I don't know why we couldn't just go the way we were, but we hurried upstairs, washed our faces, brushed our teeth, and brushed our hair.

"I need a shower," Myra Sue whined, and I like to have come undone.

"You had a shower just this morning," I told that goofy girl. "No one is gonna look at you anyway. Don't you care about *Mama*?"

She glared at me as she tied her sneakers. I just let my laces flap until I had time to tie them.

"All right then," she snarled. "I won't take a shower, even though we're going to a hospital that is full of *sick* people."

I looked at that dumb girl. "Myra Sue, you are a dipstick."

When we got downstairs, Grandma was on the telephone with someone. I figured out real quick she was talking to Ian because she said, "Mike says to get Forest to help you with the milking tonight and in the morning, since Brett is gone to see someone in Fort Smith." There was a pause as she listened, then she said, "I surely will, honey. I'll call just as soon as I know anything. And you two say a prayer, you hear?"

Although it takes more than an hour to get to Blue Reed, I did not even notice Grandma's awful and terrifying driving skills on that trip. I was too busy feeling sick about everything else.

We rode the elevator up to the fourth floor of that hospital and stepped out into the maternity ward. Grandma paused at the nurses' desk.

"We're here for Lily Reilly."

The nurse smiled and said, "Room 403. Right over there." She pointed with the tip of her pen to a room two doors down. She did not even ask my age or gripe about me being there. Boy, ole Nurse Frizzy ought to come to that part of the hospital and take lessons from Nurse Very Nice.

Grandma gave her a funny look. "I thought she was in the delivery room."

"She was. And now she's in there."

"Oh my."

We scurried along behind Grandma as she trotted to room 403. The door was about half open, and she rapped on it. A moment later, Daddy opened it. He was wearing some of the hospital scrub things that all the doctors and nurses wore, and he sure looked funny in them. Not funny ha-ha, either. Funny weird.

"Mike?" she whispered.

"Daddy!" I said. "How's Mama? Is she okay?"

"Hush, child," Grandma scolded. "This ain't the circus. Mike, where's Lily? She ain't had that baby yet, has she?"

"Come in," Daddy said. "Girls, come in. Mama's here. She's had the baby, and she's just fine."

We all tippy-toed past him, and I saw my mama. She looked white and tired and her red hair was all matted and tangled, but she smiled weakly at us and held out one hand.

I ran to her and grabbed her hand. It was cold.

"Mama. Mama, are you okay? Are you going to be all right after all this mess?"

"April Grace," Grandma said softly.

"It's okay, Mama Grace," my mama said. "She's been worried, and these last months *have* been a mess. Haven't they, sweetie?" She smiled at me. "And I'm going to be just fine, and so is your brand-new baby brother."

I think my brain jerked a little inside my skull. Surely I did not hear her correctly.

"My brother?" I echoed.

A boy. For cryin' out loud.

THIRTY-TWO

Shake Hands with Michael Eli Reilly

☆

"Where is he?" Myra Sue said, looking around that small room like she was playing in a game of Hide the Thimble and someone hid the baby behind the window curtain or under the bed.

"He's down the hall in a special place for babies who are born early. You may go down and see him."

"Why, we can't really go see him, can we?" Grandma asked. "Don't he have to stay away from everyone and everything?"

"He weighs three pounds and six ounces. And he's as healthy as he can be for such an early arrival," Mama said. "You can see him and even hold him. So, please, go see him."

I felt a little swimmy-headed from all that excitement, and to tell the honest truth, I wasn't sure I ever wanted to leave my mama's side again.

But Daddy said, "Come on, girls and Grandma. I'll take you down to meet Michael Eli Reilly."

"We'll call him Eli," Mama added.

"Oh, I like that name," Grandma said, grinning real big. "I'm glad you decided to name him after you, Mike."

"And it's about time we had another man in the family," Daddy added. All the adults laughed at that.

He met Mama's eyes, and they smiled all dopey and gooey at each other, which I felt was Totally Inappropriate since Mama had been so sick. The Blue Reed hospital was no place for being all lovey-dovey romantic, believe me.

Daddy led us out the door and down that long hallway with the shiny gray floor and fluorescent ceiling lights. We paused by a big window where a row of babies was laid out like it was a J. C. Penney store display made up of little people in pink and blue blankets.

"Which one is ours?" I asked, eyeballing all those kids. They were kinda cute and kinda funny-looking all at the same time, bundled up tight with squished-up red faces.

"None of them," Daddy said, but he cast a brief, admiring gaze across the babies. "Ours is down the hall, just a little farther."

"But ain't they all just as cute as bugs' ears?" Grandma said, grinning at that row of new kids.

We followed Daddy to another, smaller baby-keeping room. The lights weren't so bright in that room, and no babies lay in a row for anyone to see.

A nurse came to the door.

"Hi, girls," she said, smiling real friendly. "I bet you're all excited to see your new brother, aren't you?"

We just looked at her and very meekly said, "Yes, ma'am," because I'm pretty sure you aren't supposed to yell out, "Let me see our baby!" to a nurse.

"Because he's so tiny and new, you need to be all clean and scrubbed before you can be around him."

"We washed up before we left the house," I told that woman.

The three adults laughed like they thought I was joking.

"You have to do it a special way here, honey," Daddy said.

"Lead on," Grandma said to the nurse. "I want to meet my new grandson."

So the nurse led us to a room with a sink, then told us

how to wash our hands all the way up to our elbows with a special soap. When we were finished with that, we had to put on some goofy-looking gown-things that tied in the back and some awful-looking masks that covered our mouths and noses in case we had germs.

After all that, she took us into the nursery and to a bed she called an incubator—which did not look a thing like the incubators we use for keeping our chickens when they first hatch. Inside that bed lay our new brother.

I'll tell you something right now: when I saw that baby, I was so stunned I stopped in my tracks and stared. He did not look real. I mean, I have never in my whole entire life seen a human being that tiny, and I wasn't sure I was looking at one right then. How could he be that small and still be a person?

Daddy took that tiny little baby right out of his bed. He was so weensy, he fit perfectly in Daddy's two big hands.

"Girls?" Daddy said, smiling at the baby, then looking at us.

Myra Sue stood where she was, like she was glued there, but I wanted to get a closer look. I stepped right up, and Daddy held the baby where I could see him real well.

I don't know what I expected, exactly, but it wasn't that teeny-tiny little scrap. I reckon I thought he'd come out half grown and ugly, looking like Myra Sue and pitching a fit to get his own way. But he didn't. He looked all little and helpless and breakable.

I reached out, then paused.

"Will it hurt if I touch him?"

"Of course not, honey. I know he's awfully small, but don't be afraid."

I touched a hand so tiny that I didn't see how it would ever be big enough to hold anything. His skin was warm and smooth. I ran one finger up his arm, and he squirmed a little. That tiny face was perfect, not squished or red or goofy-looking at all. He had the teensiest little nose you ever saw, a tiny, rosy mouth, and the itty-bittiest chin ever. He wore a little blue cap, too.

"Does he have hair?" I whispered.

Daddy nodded. "A little bit. Red, like yours."

I raised my eyes from the baby and met Daddy's gaze. "Red?"

"Yep."

I looked at that baby again. He was in for some teasing 'cause redheads always get teased. I reckoned he'd need me to make sure he learned how to put up with it.

"Can I hold him?" I asked. I figured I better get used to him, and he might as well get used to me, 'cause we were gonna be stuck with each other for a long time.

"Sure, honey."

"Be real careful," Grandma cautioned. "Myra Susie, don't you want to hold him, too?"

Ole Myra Sue just stayed right where she was, but she watched real close. I looked at her over my shoulder.

"C'mon, sis," I said. "Come and look at him."

You could hear her swallow clear across the room, but she crept up in tiny little steps.

"He won't bite you," I told her.

Like me, she reached out one finger and touched his arm. Then she touched his face. She smiled.

"Can I hold him when April's through?" she asked.

"You bet," Daddy said, grinning at us both. Daddy put that kid in my arms, and when I felt him and looked at his face up close that way, I have to tell you, something happened. I don't know what it was, but a warm, squooshy feeling from the middle of my chest filled my whole entire body. I could hardly breathe.

"Oh, Daddy, look at him," I whispered.

"I know, honey."

Eli moved like he was cuddling, like he knew who was holding him and had forgiven me for being so mean about him being a part of us. I held him closer and felt a tear slip out of my left eye. It fell right on the blue baby blanket.

THIRTY-THREE

Homecoming

Christmas was a little peculiar, but at least Mama had come home from the hospital the day before. Eli was still there, though, in that special little bed.

On Christmas morning, we opened presents. I got a whole set of the Little House on the Prairie books, a brand-new dictionary, two pairs of jeans, some warm, fluffy, dark green pajamas, a gloves and scarf and hat set, and a cute little ceramic cardinal that looked real enough to fly away on its own. As soon as we finished our biscuits-and-gravy breakfast, we went to see Eli again. That whole day, we looked at him and held him and talked to him and sang to him and wished and wished and wished he could come home with us. But he was still too tiny, and it was better for him if he stayed right where he was until he and all his parts were strong enough to live at home.

We were quiet going back to the house that evening. Who would've thought you could miss someone who hadn't even been home yet?

But we didn't have to wait long. Michael Eli Reilly was such a good boy that he gained weight fast. He was breathing good and growing just fine.

So, on the morning of New Year's Eve, he got to come home. Boy, oh boy, you never saw such a homecoming, either. Grandma made a big celebration lunch and invited Ian and Isabel and Forest and Temple.

He got passed around from person to person like a sack of candy so much, I felt sorry for the kid. But he just slept and made funny faces and grunted sometimes.

Mama showed us how to hold him so his head was supported and so his new little muscles wouldn't get sore. She also demonstrated changing his diaper, including how to clean the poopy messes, which would not be fun, let me tell you.

That day, Ian and Isabel stood in Mama and Daddy's bedroom by the little blue bassinet and stared at Eli for what seemed like hours. It made me wonder if either of them had ever seen a baby before. They held him forever and stroked his skin and hair and smiled all goofy while they were at it. I figured that kid was gonna get spoiled big-time by the St. Jameses.

Temple brought some kind of goop she said was good for a baby's delicate skin and encouraged Mama to feed him only healthy things, as if she thought Mama was gonna take Eli to the nearest McDonald's and order him some french fries tomorrow.

But Mama just nodded and smiled all nice and sweet and said, "Thanks for your concern, Temple. I'll be sure he eats well."

After a while, everyone left the bedroom except me and Mama and Eli because it was time for him to nurse. I sat at the foot of the bed and watched as Mama rocked him and sang to him, sometimes looking up and smiling at me, sometimes looking down and smiling at him.

As soon as she was finished, I said, "Can I hold him now, Mama?"

"Sure, honey," she said, and handed him over to me just like she trusted me with the greatest treasure in the whole entire world.

I looked down at that little face and the fuzzy red hair. Then I gave him a tiny, gentle kiss right on his soft cheek.

I bet you're thinking, "April Grace Reilly, what happened to you? All this time you've been a rotten girl, thinking rotten ole thoughts about that tiny little baby who can't help being a tiny little baby, and you kept wishing, in the secret part of yourself, that he didn't exist. How come you felt that way?"

I have to tell you: I had been afraid. Afraid Mama would no longer want me, afraid our family would fall apart and I'd lose Mama and Daddy to that baby as well as Grandma. I guess being afraid makes you think things that make no sense. You see, deep down I knew Mama would always be my mama. Daddy, Grandma, and even ole Myra Sue would still be my family. That would never change just because someone new joined us. I mean, if Ian and Isabel hadn't torn us apart, how in the world could little Michael Eli Reilly do it?

Sure, our home life would never be the same. Mama would be tired and frazzled, and ole Myra Sue and me would have to do way more chores than we do now, and Grandma would probably spend way more time rocking that baby than was necessary—but I'll bet she rocked me just as much.

Eli hadn't taken away anything. I still had my home, and my friends, and lots of love from lots of people.

What else could I have possibly needed? Well, there was one thing.

I needed to be a big sister. I needed to teach Eli some things.

Number one: Not to put bugs in his mouth (because kids, especially boys, do that). Number two: How to deal with the red-hair-and-freckles-teasing business. Number three: How to be polite to Temple and Forest in spite of how they smell, and number four: How to put up with Isabel St. James when she acts like a knothead. But maybe I wouldn't need to teach him that because, really, she's pretty cool once you get to know her.

I'd probably have to teach him a few things about dealing with Myra Sue, but maybe she'd not be such a pain when it came to Eli.

There's something else. I had been worrying for the longest time about becoming all snooty and prissy because I thought maybe being that way just naturally came with big sister territory. But here's what I realized: I, April Grace Reilly, am not a snooty, prissy person, not even down in the far depths of my own personal heart. I doubted I'd ever be in a clique or anything that even looks like a clique. In fact, I'd rather be a hick than belong to a clique, because hicks tend to be a lot nicer to other people.

So, looking at my little baby brother, who was gonna need me a lot as he grew up, I realized what a big sister is and what a big sister is *not*. I figured I stood a good chance of being a pretty good one. At least I was sure gonna try.

ACKNOWLEDGMENTS

Many thanks go to my husband, Brett, and daughter, Holly, for their understanding about meals on their own, a less than neat house, and my taking over the entire dining table with my laptop, notes, stacks of papers, a variety of pens, the dictionary, the thesaurus, the Bible, sandwich plates, and never-empty glasses of cold tea during the writing of this story. (Honey, I really must have my own office someday soon.)

Much appreciation to Mary Bishop and Jamie Taylor from our community theater for telling me how a nit-picky professional performing arts person like Isabel St. James might try to stage a downhome church play.

As always, thank you, Jeanie Pantelakis from Sullivan Maxx Literary Agency. You are a terrific hand-holding, back-patting, shoulder-to-cry-on, rah-rah-rahhing cheerleader!

Thank you, editors MacKenzie Howard and Kristin Ostby, for your tireless work and boundless patience while we labored over this book to find the perfect balance of story, scene, and character.

Get ready for more adventures with your favorite redheaded spitfire, April Grace Reilly!

First April discovers there are a few surprises to having Isabel St. James as her new P.E. instructor:

Isabel is taking her job as teacher seriously. Very seriously. If there's one thing I've never seen in a P.E. class before, it's a teacher in spiky killer-heels handing out *notes*. At least we weren't getting out there on the gym floor doing twirly toes and pirouettes in front of each other and looking like complete goofs. Yet.

Then there's the sudden appearance of a long-lost relative:

Her face was as wrinkled and crispy as wadded-up sandpaper, and her hair was a color I had never seen before on a real human person. Now, I believe if you're a million years old, you should not wear mini-skirts. So when she announced who she was, I prayed for someone, anyone, to please, *please* tell me this "Mimi" woman was not my other grandma.

And now even her silly sister Myra Sue is up to something—and it looks mighty suspicious!

What do you think I saw outside that window? I saw my sister acting weird, that's what. I watched her sneak over to the mailbox and look around like she was a bank robber casing the joint. And if you know me at all, you know my curiosity itches me worse than poison ivy and mosquito bites put together. I just had to find out what that girl was up to!

Find out what all the fuss is about in the hilarious third installment of the Confessions of April Grace, coming soon!

www.kdmccrite.com
www.facebook.com/AprilGraceReilly